PRAISE FOR DAVE CREEK'S WORK:

No matter how far one of (Creek's) stories travels across the universe or through time, his focus remains on the characters and their reactions to the world around them.

-- Jason Sanford, two-time Nebula Award finalist

"One of the best ways to get a fix of otherness is with expertly-conceived and well-depicted aliens...That's why it's such a joy to find an author who can do it well.

"Dave Creek is one of those authors."

-- Donald Sakers, ANALOG SCIENCE FICTION AND FACT

To:
H.G. Wells
Orson Welles
George Pal

ALL HUMAN THINGS

DAVE CREEK

Chapter 1

As he squeezed his way through the hole blasted into the crippled Jenregar starcraft, Mike Christopher thought, *All right, so this is the last place I want to be — but a Human's apparently a captive in here, so it's worth the risk.* A quick glance behind him — the Earth Unity light cruiser *Admiral Susan Kojima* was boosting away from the Jenregar craft, a shadow in motion against a spray of stars.

Mike lowered himself carefully through the jagged tear in the Jenregar ship's skin, being especially careful of the small propulsion unit on his back.

The first thing Mike saw in the narrow corridor was the body of a Jenregar individual. It was missing an arm, and bodily fluid leaked from the hard carapace of its body. Its small eyes, which for the Jenregar were secondary sensory organs, stared, unseeing. The slender antennae extending from its forehead, which were smell receptors, hung limply. *If the energy bolt from the* Kojima *didn't kill it*, Mike thought, *the sudden vacuum would have.*

With the height of an average Jenregar being a bit less than a meter, Mike couldn't quite stand upright in the corridor. He glimpsed movement down the hallway and pulled his disruptor. Two Jenregar, each of them wearing lifesuits, came around a corner, each carrying a different piece of equipment. They ignored Mike as they passed him and began working on the hole in the side of the ship. One instrument, it seemed, created a mesh over the hole. The other emitted a beam that caused the hole itself to smooth over at its rough edges and begin filling itself in.

Can't allow that, Mike thought, and aimed his disruptor at the Jenregar. A couple of pops from it, and they fell to the floor.

A voice over his datalink was loud enough to make him wince. "Mike — we read disruptor fire from over there. Are you all right?"

That was the voice of Kelda Lee, the captain of the *Kojima*, which had punched the hole in the Jenregar ship. She'd "borrowed" him from the exploratory craft *Asaph Hall* just for this mission.

"Don't worry, Captain," Mike said. "Just making sure my escape route wasn't about to be blocked."

Mike could hear the relief in Captain Lee's voice. "Thanks, Mike. Find out what you can, but be careful."

I will, Mike thought as he checked his wrist sensor. The Human on board was located somewhere toward the front of the ship. Mike headed in that direction. The Jenregar craft was a small one, barely twenty-five meters long, with a crew of only 27. It was part of a swarm of such craft that had been detected out past the orbit of Neptune, headed directly for Earth.

Mike knew the Unity was probably correct in its assessment that the Jenregar was about to attack the Earth ("Was," because the Jenregar possessed only a single hive mind, with individuals acting only by hard-wired programming and coded chemical messages).

The corridor took a turn, and Mike found himself before an energy field, presumably one that had closed off most of the ship from the part now open to space. *I wonder, does the shield also recognize pheromonal cues?* He reached out a finger toward the field, and sure enough, it passed through easily. *Damn*, he thought, *I'll take being lucky over being good any day.* But as he stepped through the energy field, his first thought was, *Maybe not so lucky after all.*

A dozen Jenregar stood within a small room, several of them operating ship's systems, others just standing around. *Looks like the bridge, or at least some sort of command center,* Mike thought. *But pretty crowded. I'd guess some of these Jenregar were evacuated from the damaged parts of the ship.*

The Jenregar recognized one another and imparted information to one another by smell, so Mike's lifesuit had been infused with what he hoped were the appropriate scents that would allow him to pass as a member of the Jenregar crew. *I would* have to be one of the few Humans to have made contact with the Jenregar, *he thought. Unfortunately, I'm probably the best person qualified for this mission. The alternative was shooting our way in with some Unity Marines and likely getting this Human killed.*

Too bad all of my effort is for an ungrateful Earth.

So far none of the Jenregar took notice of him — in the

same manner, Humans didn't normally recognize one another by scent. Another glance at his wrist sensor, and Mike realized he was quite close to the other Human on board, who was probably just down a short corridor to his right. Mike headed that way —

— And found himself nearly face-to-face with that other Human.

The man sat at the end of the short corridor, his head in his hands as if in despair. *I can't blame him*, Mike thought. *Captured who-knows-where, brought aboard this Jenregar ship, which then comes under attack, with no hope of rescue as far as he knows.*

The man seemed to sense Mike's presence and looked up. He was in his thirties, with pale skin, curly hair, and a wide-eyed expression. Mike knew that in return, the man saw his unusual features that reflected all of Humanity's origins — light brown skin, tightly curled, nearly nappy hair, bright blue eyes.

But Mike's next thought was, *Did the Jenregar torture this man*? He had a series of cuts all around his eyes, and his left eye in particular was swollen, as if he'd been beaten. His clothing seemed to sag around him, as if he'd started out as a much bigger man.

"Thank God," the man said. "Are you here to bring me out?"

"That's my intention," Mike said.

"Don't get me wrong, I'm glad you're here — but why am I so important?"

"We need to to find out what the hell the Jenregar are up to."

"That's what I was going to ask you!"

Mike took another step forward, but the other man

stood, almost bumping his head on the ceiling, and motioned for him to stop.

"Don't get any closer. If I try to take more than about four steps from this corner, I guess some kind of alarm goes off. The Jenregar come after me."

"I don't see anything," Mike said. "But I'd guess there's some kind of pheromonal barrier on the floor or the walls." He looked at the other man. "What's your name?"

"Jeremy Sheffield — have you heard anything about my wife?"

"I'm Mike Christopher — no, we didn't know anything about *you* until a few hours ago. There aren't any other Humans on this ship other than the two of us."

"Oh, God — *Julia*! We were on holiday — it was supposed to be a time we reconnected." Then Jeremy looked up at Mike. "Your name sounds familiar."

Mike couldn't be concerned about that right now. Over his datalink, he said, "Captain Lee, I've made contact. I'm about to get him out of here."

"Heard and understood," Captain Lee said. "Make it fast as you can. It looks like they've got automatic systems repairing their stardrive. You don't want to take a trip with them."

"Shit," Mike muttered. "You've got that right."

Jeremy asked, "Who were you talking to? What's wrong?"

"Unity warcraft — the *Susan Kojima*. They're the ones punched the hole in this ship and disabled it."

"Warcraft? Oh, dear Lord, has it come to that?"

"That's part of what we're trying to find out. Listen, Jeremy — we've got to get you out of here. Do you still have your lifesuit tech?"

"Yes, thank goodness."

"I'm going to risk reaching my arm past that barrier." Mike pulled a small tube from a wrist pocket. "I'm going to want you to activate your suit, then take this tube and smash it over the top of it."

"I think I get it — Jenregar pheromones?"

"It'll be as if you transformed into a Jenregar right in front of them. Ready?"

"Ready," Jeremy said, and pressed his left middle finger into his palm. His lifesuit formed itself around him, Mike handed him the tube, and Jeremy smashed it over the top of his helmet.

"Com'on," Mike said. "We've got to get ourselves into the Jenregar population where they won't notice us."

Mike watched as Jeremy took a deep breath, then took that step. Mike put his hand on his disruptor, looked all around. The Jenregar took no notice of either of them. He told Jeremy, "Let's get you back to Humanity," and he led the way back down the short corridor.

"I'm ready for that," Jeremy said. "You won't believe how long I've been in there, how many times they've knocked me unconscious." He shook his head. "This is like being inside a virt, only not as much fun."

Great, Mike thought. *A virt enthusiast. Well, maybe a dose of reality will do him good.* They reached the command center. But as Mike started to hurry through the crowded room, he sensed Jeremy wasn't right behind him. A look back, and he saw the man standing stock still in the middle of the room. *Goddam it*, he thought, and made his way over to Jeremy as quickly as he could, trying not to run right into any of the Jenregar.

He grabbed Jeremy's arm. "*Com'on*," he said. "This is no time to lose your nerve."

Jeremy's features behind his helmet faceplate were a study in fear. "This is *exactly* the time," He said.

Mike eased his way past a couple of Jenregar, got behind Jeremy, and pushed, *hard*. "*Go*," Mike said.

Jeremy went.

As they approached the energy field that led back to the damaged part of the Jenregar craft, Captain Lee spoke up again. "You've *got* to hurry, Mike — our sensors show their stardrive spinning up."

"We're getting there as quickly as we can."

"You may not have a chance to — "

A tearing, rending sound broke off Captain Lee's words — *Is this what a stardrive jump for a Jenregar ship normally sounds like?* Mike wondered.

Mike didn't even have a chance to get through the energy shield before every nerve in his body felt as if it had caught fire and he screamed in agony as he slumped to the floor.

And fear not them which kill the body, but are not able to kill the soul....

— Matthew 10:28

RAMIRA ESPINOZA, ALREADY NEARLY BREATHLESS, A STITCH forming in her side, tried to run even faster, as much in a desperate attempt to distance herself from her "boyfriend" and his brother as from the Jenregar horde behind her.

Goddam this city, she thought — with so many of the lights out in this part of Santarem, she had no idea where she was, or where she was headed.

In the next moment, however, she crossed herself at the blasphemy, a habit that said as much about a childhood habit as any remaining piety.

Ramira looked behind her — Diego Fernandez, her boyfriend-who-was-really-her-pimp, was just a few steps behind her, his brother Julian right behind.

And behind *them* — the sight that spurred Ramira to put on another burst of speed, no matter how much her heart already pounded, how much sweat already poured into her eyes, how much the wood, metal, and glass debris on the sidewalk tore at the soles of her bare feet.

Dozens of Jenregar poured down the street as if part of a single mass — although shorter than Humans, they elicited a vital fear within Ramira with their bodies like crab carapaces, their tentacle-like arms and legs, and insectile bodies and antennae extending from their foreheads.

"Ramira, slow down," Diego shouted. "We'll never make it back to the hotel like this. We have to take shelter somewhere." Another glance behind, and she saw Diego waving his old-fashioned pistol, an actual slug-thrower, illegal as all hell. *I won't even waste my breath telling him he won't shoot me*, Ramira thought. *I'm his meal ticket.* The Jenregar were only the latest horror she'd had inflicted upon her since Diego's promises of riches and an easy life had brought her here to Santarem, the capital of the Amazon Confederation, from her home in Columbia.

Ramira recalled, *Diego told my older brother Matias, "All things are possible in a market economy where you're allowed to make money. With all respect, that's the problem — unless you're part of the government or big business, you're never allowed to make money." We imagined a life where we never had to live on the dole again like we did in our little village, or where we could leave the country entirely and live in a more modern replicator economy like Brazil where people had freedom as well as food, clothing, and shelter.*

It was a tempting vision for an 17-year-old orphan girl.

She recalled Matias telling her, "I know you'll do as the Lord wishes, Ramira. "You'll make me proud."

"Ramira!" Diego shouted again. "Into this building!"

Diego and Julian stood at the entrance to a storefront that was a little less damaged than most in this neighborhood; its door was still solidly on its hinges and none of its windows was broken.

I could just keep running, Ramira thought, *running away from everything, from the Jenregar, from Diego, from a life where I'm sexing with a dozen men a day just to keep living, just to keep from being beaten — doing things I thought I'd only do with my eventual husband.*

Images tore through her memory — men huffing and puffing over her, spending themselves and tossing money on the bedstand, or forcing her to lean over them for other kinds of pleasure.

Now, Ramira wondered, *who would have me for a wife*?

But the sight of the onrushing hoard of Jenregar made Ramira stop — she knew she'd collapse from exhaustion within moments, while these aliens seemed tireless.

Diego held the door open for her as she pushed past him and Julian. The two brothers followed her inside to what appeared to have been a jewelry shop, its showcases now shattered, its merchandise long gone. *I wonder what the odds are that the owners were the ones who got to take everything*, she thought.

Some parts of the city off toward the horizon had

retained power, and therefore lights, but the dim glow from that distance didn't reveal much else here in the store. It did, however, reveal another horror — against the outline of some of Santarem's taller buildings, she could see the curve of the Jenregar mound in the center of the city.

One of the few things Ramira knew about the Jenregar was that they were leveling the interiors of Human cities and raising their own mounds that provided them a place to live, a base of operations, and, it was rumored, a site in which to perform terrible, horrifying, medical procedures upon Human captives.

I'll kill myself first, Ramira thought. *I won't become one of their guinea pigs.*

Diego said, "We've got to find a place to hide — somewhere they can't break into. I'll look around — maybe there's a vault or an attic or something."

"I'll guard the door," Julian said.

Diego gave his brother his gun. "You know how to use that?"

"I'll give the bastards what's coming to them."

"You'll come back here with us the instant we find a place to hide." Diego grabbed Ramira's arm and pulled her along with him — pain from previous bruises and cuts shot up from her wrist to her shoulder. *He doesn't have the gun,* she thought. *Maybe I can get away.*

And then what? Go back out in the street and have the Jenregar tear me apart? Although — would that really be so much worse?

Despair washed over her, and Ramira let herself be dragged along a short hallway to the rear of the building. They came upon steep stairs that led upward to a closed trap door. "I told you we'd find something — we can go up to that attic and close if off against these goddam aliens — Julian!"

"You found something?" came Julian's response.

"Get back here — we've found — "

The door to the jewelry shop burst open, and half a dozen Jenregar came through it. Julian fired the pistol repeatedly, and the impacts seemed to make a couple of the Jenregar take a step backwards, but they quickly recovered and continued toward him.

Diego started toward the front of the store. "I've got to help him," he said, and Ramira found herself about to grab his arm to stop him from heading toward the danger instead of away from it —

— and stopped. Another glance toward the top of the stairs, and Ramira began climbing. She paused just beneath the trap door, looking down as the Jenregar revealed stingers on the thumbs of their three-fingered hands and fell upon Julian, who screamed as Diego hesitated a mere three meters away from him.

Even over Julian's cries, Ramira heard a hissing sound that she realized was coming from the man's skin as it melted away. *The Jenregar sting is full of acid*, Ramira realized.

She pulled down desperately on the trap door, fearful it was stuck even as Diego, however reluctantly, turned from his dying brother and headed back toward the stairs. "Get that open!" he commanded her.

That's the last command you'll ever give me, Ramira vowed. *And the first one I'll disobey and get away with*. She turned a handle on the bottom of the door and realized the door opened upward, not down, and nearly leaped up the final steps into the darkened attic.

Now's no time to hesitate, Ramira thought. *Not if I want to live*. She slammed the door down even as Diego shouted,

"Keep that open, you bitch!" She heard the dull pounding of his footsteps as well as a chittering noise, apparently from the Jenregar right behind him.

There wasn't a lock on this side of the door — Ramira looked all around in the dim light of the attic, spotted an unused display case to one side, and with all her strength in the few moments she had left, she pushed it onto the attic door just as Diego began pounding on it. "Let me in! Goddam it, let me in! They'll kill me!"

The chittering grew louder, and so did Diego's shouting and, seconds later, his screaming. Ramira laid her body across the display case, adding her own weight to it, as the pounding from the other side of the door subsided. She thought of the dozens, hundreds, of men who'd been allowed to abuse her for these many months until her only reaction had been a quiet acceptance of what she thought she could never change.

Soon all was quiet on the other side of the doorway, but Ramira kept her body across the display case for a long time afterwards, just as a precaution, and so she could revel in the beginnings of the smile that lifted at the corners of her mouth, ever so slightly.

"I saw the Winged Victory fall from the Metropolis Building today," Carrie Molina told Damian Rivera and Luisa Torres. "I couldn't help but think about all the times my Papa took me there, just to look up at that statue. I always thought Winged Victory was looking down at me, protecting me and the rest of Madrid. Then the rest of the building collapsed around it."

Dirty and exhausted, the three were hiding in a dark,

damp wooded area in the Parque del Oeste overlooking a dark and devastated Madrid, Carrie's hometown. Damian and Luisa had just dried off and slipped into dry clothing Carrie had provided them. She'd helped them escape from one of the Jenregar mounds in the middle of the city by providing them with breathers (something Carrie didn't need), and bringing them out through a water pipeline. The Madrid mounds were among hundreds the Jenregar had established in various places — Zhengzhou, China, Santiago, Chile, and Tijuana, Mexico, among others.

In her youth, this park's well-tended gardens, Egyptian temple, and quiet pathways had been places of peace and reflection. Even now, the late-summer breezes caressing her hair and stirring the leaves around her provided Carrie some comfort.

She thought, *My Papa would bring me and my sister Adriana here when I was a child. Back when Adriana — and Mama — were still alive. Afterwards, that's when we'd take the tram down to the Metropolis Building and just stare up at it.*

But no longer. Now, my father's almost certainly still within the Jenregar mound, possibly being experimented on and tortured, perhaps even dead.

"So how much of Madrid has been overrun?" Damian asked. He was clearly struggling to form his words; his mouth been made smaller surgically, just one of the atrocities the Jenregar had committed against him. Despite all they'd been through, Carrie was hard pressed not to show her disgust at the alien biotech that had been implanted into her companions' bodies, or the surgical procedures that had mutilated them.

Carrie indicated the center of the city, lying mostly beneath darkness — the Jenregar's doing soon after they'd landed upon the Earth. "Most of the Gran Via has been leveled." That was the historical preservation area depicting the shops, restaurants, and malls that dated from the time, just decades earlier, when Spain was still a market economy. "Most of the governmental buildings are gone."

Damian said, "It looks...looks..." Damian's mouth fought to form his words, and Carrie suspected that not only had his mouth been reconstructed, but that his brain had been altered in an attempt to reduce his sense of individuality.

In other words, to make him more like a Jenregar, Carrie thought. "Take your time," she told him.

Damian took a deep breath and said, "It looks like the suburbs haven't been touched yet."

"Give them time. So far hundreds, maybe thousands have died in the city. People panicked, tried to get the hell out of town. A lot of them didn't make it."

Luisa spoke up. The Jenregar had replaced her left arm with a "biological hydrostat," a limb that maintained its shape by the pressure of internal fluids, similar to an elephant's trunk or — Carrie tried, unsuccessfully, not to think of the usual example — the Human penis. "Why are the Jenregar doing this, anyway?"

"The Jenregar's actually an 'it,' a hive mind. The individual ones you've seen only know hard-wired programming and coded chemical messages."

"And they're trying to take over the Earth?"

"Trying," Carrie said. "But a lot of us are working to make sure they don't." *What I can't bring myself to tell them,* Carrie thought, *is the rumors that if the mounds end up taking over most of the city, the Earth Unity feels it may have to nuke it to save it.*

Damian asked, "When are we being picked up?"

Carrie touched behind her left ear to activate her datalink. "Carrie Molina to *Dorothy*. What's your ETA?"

"This is shuttle *Dorothy*. ETA two minutes."

"Copy. Carrie out." She told Luisa and Damian, "The shuttle should be here in just a couple minutes. But I won't be going with you."

Luisa touched Carrie's webbed hand. "You're going back, aren't you? After your father."

"Yes. I have to."

"But you're not armed. You don't have a disruptor, or even a knife."

"The Jenregar have learned to recognize them — I'd never be allowed into that mound."

Luisa embraced Carrie and told her, "Be safe, my child. Get Gilberto out of there, and let him know I'm waiting for him."

Before Carrie could respond, the Earth Unity shuttle *Dorothy* swooped low over the Parque del Oeste, then landed about fifty meters away. "*Go*," Carrie said. Damian didn't hesitate — he ran immediately toward the shuttle. But Luisa held back a moment, holding onto her altered arm and looking back toward Carrie, appearing as if she was going to say something. But Luisa turned toward the shuttle without speaking, followed Damian aboard, and *Dorothy* lifted and she was gone.

I'll bring you back to her, Papa, Carrie told herself. *I promise.*

Mites fight bloody battles for nests on a mosquito's eyelash;

    Tiny kingdoms are at war over lands on a snail's horn.

> If we looked down across our own world from highest heaven,
> We would see heroes fighting to the death for a speck of dust.
> — "On Birds and Bugs," by Bai Juyi.

ONLY AS THOMAS JIANG TOPPED THE FINAL RISE AND TOOK HIS first weary steps onto his father's land did he finally feel safe. *It seems as if the world, so recently turned upside down, has finally righted itself*, he thought.

He halted at the top of that rise, rolled his shoulders to rearrange the heavy backpack that carried all his Earthly belongings, and found himself surprised at how his heart soared as he looked out at the landscape below him, green, rich, pristine, unsullied by the foreign — no, not just foreign, extraterrestrial! — threat that perhaps approached only a few tens of kilometers behind him.

To view his father's land meant to view a history of Chinese agriculture, in this village devoted to preserving traditions from earlier years, decades, centuries. From the opposite side of the broad field before him, Thomas realized that he found comfort in the sound of distant lumbering harvesters, as well as the sight of men and oxen plowing a portion of a field closer to him.

The village grew everything from rice and peanuts to watermelon, but immediately before him, he made out the fresh, sweet smell of newly scythed wheat.

His father, Jiang Shun, wielded that scythe, and in its eternal rhythms Thomas understood the connection to his family, the land, and his now-endangered nation. *I can feel the pull of such traditions, and understand why my father and other men choose to live this way.*

At the same time, Thomas forced down a familiar frustration, watching what he thought of as his father's needless exertions: *He could do so much, achieve so many things — yet here he stands, muscles straining, shirt soaked with sweat, eyes deadened beneath his straw hat. It seems as if we live in the Second Century, not the Twenty-Second. But he, like most everyone in our village, has his ways.*

Jiang Shun paused and looked up toward his son. Thomas knew his father saw a man standing on shaky legs, drawing shallow exhausted breaths, dirty, unshaven. *I didn't know which would offend him more*, Thomas thought. *Showing up like this without warning, or calling him over the datalink he uses only grudgingly, and never for mere "family matters." And after all the trouble I went to in obtaining that link for him. He doesn't realize how tightly the government controls such things.*

Thomas descended the small rise as his father watched him without emotion. Thomas made a fist with his right hand, cupped it in his left. He bowed deeply. "It...fills my heart with joy to see you, Father."

"I feared you may not escape this...alien incursion...safely."

"A grueling journey, Father. But I've come home."

Jiang Shun, still grasping his scythe, folded his arms. "I heard the maglev link from Zhengzhou went down."

"Yes, Father. I left it behind and waited a long time for a bus. So many people crowded aboard, and I saw many women and children desperate to board them."

"You let them go ahead of you."

"Of course, Father."

"It looks as if you've walked a long distance."

"Many kilometers, for the better part of a day."

"You should come to the house, get cleaned up, and have something to eat." Jiang Shun started toward the house, his scythe tucked under one arm. Thomas, all his muscles and newly-acquired bruises aching anew with each step, followed close behind.

Chapter 2

For Mike Christopher, in the instant of the Jenregar ship's stardrive transition, it was as if the universe disappeared...

— As a five-year-old, he rushes toward his prospective foster parents, only to run right through their images.

— At age sixteen, he stands his ground with three bullies and holds his own against them thanks to the special abilities of his artificially-conceived body.

— Just months after turning twenty-one, he watches the image of the receding Earth on a viewscreen, wondering if he'll ever want to return to his homeworld again.

...and the universe returned, faster than thought.

Mike shook off those unpleasant memories. He knew he was lying on the floor, but he didn't know where and couldn't remember what made him pass out. When he tried to rub his head, his hand clunked against his bubble helmet.

He opened his eyes. *Damn*, he thought. *The Jenregar ship. Hell of a place to wake up.*

And what the hell knocked me out like that?

He looked over at Jeremy, who was still unconscious. *The stardrive jump*, Mike realized. *We could be anywhere — for all I know, the Jenregar homeworld. There's no amount of pheromones can hide us much longer.*

Mike got to his feet and found himself standing right next to one of the Jenregar. Instinctively, he froze, expecting this particular Jenregar to walk right past him as if he were nothing unusual.

But this Jenregar individual looked right at him!

Mike was so startled it took a moment for him to concentrate and take a good look right back. *This Jenregar's eyes are bigger than what's normal for them*, Mike thought. *They're comparable to a Human's eyes.*

Mike's attention flashed back for an instant to his first sight of Jeremy, of the cuts and bruising all around his eyes, and Mike had to wonder — *Have the Jenregar been performing experiments on him?*

The Jenregar individual tried to grab Mike, but it only came up to his waist, and its tentacle-like arms didn't have the strength to hold onto him. Mike pulled himself free, pulled his disruptor, and shot the Jenregar, who crumpled to the floor.

Now the other Jenregar in the command center took notice, but only of the Jenregar Mike had just shot. *Gotta be grateful for small favors*, Mike thought, as he pulled Jeremy up to a sitting position. "Wake up, dammit," he said, wishing he could slap the side of the man's face. Resigning himself to the inevitable, he pulled Jeremy up, laid him over one shoulder, grateful for the little bit of added strength a "normal" Human didn't have, and headed back down the corridor toward the damaged part of the ship.

They passed easily through the energy field as Mike

activated his datalink: "This is Mike Christopher to Captain Lee. *Kojima*, do you read?"

No response.

As Mike reached the hole the *Kojima* had made in the side of the Jenregar ship, Mike found himself with a dilemma. *I still have no idea where we jumped to*, he thought. *We might be in the middle of nowhere, waiting for a repair crew. Or in the midst of a Jenregar fleet.*

Mike reached up and pulled himself just high enough out of the jagged hole in the ship to catch a glance all around. What he saw made him gasp.

Earth! Mike could barely believe he was seeing the sun-drenched outlines of Europe and Africa, plainly visible even amidst the cloud cover, the strings of light on the world's nightside that were the cities of Asia.

It looks like we're just beyond synchronous orbit, Mike thought. *And if it's not my imagination running ahead of me, it looks like the planet's getting closer by the moment.*

Mike lowered himself back through the hole, his mind racing. Did he dare stay aboard this Jenregar ship? *I've no idea where it's headed, whether into orbit or some kind of landing. If it's part of an invasion fleet, what are my chances of survival?*

Mike saw several Jenregar starting down the corridor toward him and Jeremy. *That settles that*, he thought. *Whether through that Jenregar who looked right at me or some other way, they've started to perceive us.*

Time to go.

He grabbed the still-unconscious Jeremy, and lifted him up. *We're better off taking our chances on our own*, he thought. *I can only hope my lifesuit's propulsion can get us a reasonable distance from this ship.* Mike was careful not to let Jeremy's lifesuit catch on the hole's jagged edges as he pushed him through. He managed to hold onto one of Jeremy's legs as he pulled himself up.

Earth *was* getting closer. *I can't make out any Human ships, or even other Jenregar ones*, he thought, *but what would the chances be that either would be within visual range?*

Mike grabbed Jeremy in a close embrace, which at least was easier here in zero-G conditions on the skin of the Jenregar ship. He flexed his knees and jumped away from the Jenregar ship. Fortunately, Jeremy was slender enough that Mike could reach with his right hand around Jeremy's back to punch controls on his own lifesuit's left wrist. The small propulsion unit on his back pushed him and Jeremy away from the Jenregar craft at an angle perpendicular to its trajectory.

Soon the Jenregar ship receded from view. Over his datalink, Mike said, "This is Mike Christopher of the Unity exploration craft *Asaph Hall*. I'm on an unknown trajectory out of a Jenregar ship apparently approaching Earth. Does anyone copy?"

No one answered. He turned off the propulsion unit now that he and Jeremy were on somewhat of a different course than the Jenregar ship. *Fuel's pretty limited*, he thought. *No telling when we might need to make a course correction.* He set his lifesuit to send a constant distress call and activated a proximity alarm that would let him know if any craft approached, then took a closer look at Jeremy's face behind the bubble helmet. To his relief, he saw the man's eyelids flutter, saw him licking his lips. *Com'on, dammit*, he thought. *Wake up!*

Jeremy's eyes opened and Mike saw the instantaneous flash of fear in his features. Jeremy started to push away from him, but Mike held on tight. "No you don't," he said. "You've got to stick right here with me."

"What happened?" Jeremy asked. "How'd we get out here?"

"The Jenregar took a stardrive jump — when we woke up, they'd started noticing us. That's when I got us out of there."

"So that jump — that's when we lost consciousness, just like I told you had happened several times. That's what caused it?"

"Jenregar stardrives aren't calibrated for Human physiology. The same thing happened during the early days of Human stardrive flight."

"And would people have — some kind of dreams, or flashbacks?"

"They would," Mike said, not wanting to recall those he'd just experienced. "People would have to medicate themselves before a jump."

Jeremy looked all around. "Wait a minute — is that Earth?"

"It is."

"Then we're saved!"

"Not yet — I've got a beacon going, and I've tried to contact someone — anyone — on my datalink. But I haven't gotten a response yet."

"But we're headed toward Earth — that has to be good."

"Let's hope so — but even though I've gotten us out of sight of the Jenregar ship, we still have most of its momentum. We'd be running parallel to it, and I think we're headed right for the planet. Our lifesuits wouldn't survive re-entry. And this propulsion unit isn't powerful enough to put us into orbit."

Jeremy said, "So we could still die."

"If we'd stayed on that Jenregar ship, we'd already be dead — or worse."

"I think I know what worse would amount to."

"I saw a Jenregar that had larger eyes than normal — similar to a Human's."

"They poked and prodded at my own eyes enough. I thought they were going to carve one out of me."

"How did they — " Mike was interrupted by his lifesuit's proximity alarm. "Oh, I hope that's good news."

"What is it?" Jeremy asked.

"Something's within a couple thousand kilometers."

"Thank God. Rescue!"

"We don't know that. Could be another Jenregar ship."

"I'll pray that it's a Human craft instead. Will you join me?"

"Sorry. I don't care if you do. But I know a god didn't create me. I'm — "

"Mike Christopher! I *knew* I recognized that name. You're the artificial Human!" Jeremy squirmed in Mike's grasp. "Let me go! You're an ungodly being — I don't want to have anything to do with you!"

Mike's anger helped him hold on that much tighter. "Now, listen — I'm your lifeline! I have the propulsion unit — I have the spacer experience. Whatever happens, I'm your best chance at staying alive."

"I may be better off with the Jenregar."

As Mike saw some sort of spacecraft silhouetted against the stars, he told Jeremy, "If we come out of this alive, you're welcome to go visit them again."

It was hours later before Ramira Espinosa got up the nerve to come down from the attic and leave the building. A part of her didn't want to look at what was left of Diego and

Julian, but another part of her couldn't keep her eyes off the battered and acid-burned remains.

The inside of the jewelry shop was even more trashed than before, as if a tornado had somehow struck only the interior of the building; Ramira had to be careful not to cut herself on shards of glass as she worked her way toward the door.

Now her dilemma was: where to go? *I want to get back home,* she thought, *back to Matias — he's my only family. "You'll make me proud!" he told me.*

But after all I've done, all the men I've been with — how could he ever be proud of me?

Still, I've got to get out of the city.

But how? And I can't start out tonight — I don't have any money, I can't start a trip right away. I need a place to stay.

Unbidden, the thought came to her — she could head back to the Hotel Augustina, where Diego had kept her.

No! came the immediate response within herself. *Too many memories there, all of them bad, of all those men and all the things I had to do.*

But I don't have anywhere else to go.

The front door of the shop stood open. She peeked outside, looking in either direction. The Jenregar were gone, at least for now. *But for all I know, they could come back at any moment.*

A couple of steps down the street, and Ramira realized that, without thought, she was headed toward the hotel after all.

She allowed herself to continue in that direction, waiting for something to divert her, to show her a better alternative.

None came. And by the time she walked up the broad stone steps of the Hotel Augustina, Ramira had decided she would enter it with her head high and proud, her own woman this time, not a virtual slave to Diego or anyone.

CARRIE MOLINA MADE HER WAY OUT OF THE PARQUE DEL Oeste and at the edge of a line of trees approached the Jenregar mound standing in the center of Madrid, not far from the wreckage of the Metropolis Building. It was nearly a quarter-kilometer across, and still growing. Carrie watched as Jenregar individuals hurried about their assigned tasks.

Some of the workers she saw were expanding the mound; they were called builders, and the backs of their otherwise red carapaces were a bright yellow. Others, whose backs were blue or the same red as the rest of their bodies, entered or left the mound through the ubiquitous tunnels that appeared to be made of the same material as the Jenregar's own carapaces. The blue ones, she knew, were called protectors, and were responsible for the security of the mound's queen. The all-red ones were scouts, responsible for establishing a perimeter around the mound and occasionally venturing out to identify threats to it. No one had been able to explain to Carrie why, if the Jenregar depended so little on sight, that they were color-coded.

Carrie steeled herself to go back into the Jenregar mound. *Loyalty to my mission, my homeworld, led me to take Damian and Luisa away from here*, she thought. *But now the only loyalty I have is to Papa.*

Carrie was an Earth Unity "fixer," a bio-engineered woman who could exist underwater for long periods of time, which was why she'd been tapped for this mission — the water pipeline was the most direct way into the mound, and she could enter it without depending upon Human tech the Jenregar might notice.

She couldn't think of those abilities without also thinking of her father, of all the times he'd shook his round face and balding head, folded his arms, and said in his deep, familiar voice, "You do this...this *thing* to your body, Carriden. I don't understand how you can mutilate yourself, give yourself gills."

"I don't have gills, Papa. I still breathe air." In a smaller voice, she'd add, "And people call me Carrie nowadays."

Inevitably her father would say, "I refuse to call you by that monstrously informal name."

Carrie's mission had been to sneak into the Jenregar's Madrid mound and learn as much as she could about the Jenregar/Human hybrids being created there — if possible, to rescue a couple of them. She'd accomplished that the moment Damian and Luisa got onboard the shuttle.

Now it's time for a more personal mission, Carrie thought. *I'm heartsick to think that my Papa may be in the process of becoming a hybrid — this man who held me for hours when I was sick, who read Shakespeare to a little girl who didn't understand half of what she heard at the time, but found comfort enough in her Papa's voice.*

Even if he is a hybrid, at least he would still be alive — which means I have a chance of getting him out.

THOMAS DIDN'T WANT TO SIT AT THE KITCHEN TABLE WHILE his father prepared the meal. "I would not bring you disrespect, Father — I should help you."

"I say you should obey your father! Sit!"

Reluctantly, Thomas eased his backpack off and sat.

Despite his discomfort, he reveled in the familiar sounds of spatula against wok and the sizzling rice, along with the rich aroma of the soup's broth. *None of this replicated stuff for my father*, Thomas thought. *Right from the field into the home.*

Within minutes Jiang Shun placed the rice and soup in the center of the table and set two bottles of a local beer on the table. Thomas folded his hands before him and refused even to pick up his chopsticks before his father sat, served himself, and began eating. Once Jiang Shun had taken his first bite, Thomas allowed himself to partake.

With his own first bite, Thomas felt himself transported back to his childhood; his father cooked with the same sure touch his wife, Thomas's mother Jiang Linqin, had always shown before her death ten years ago — his father had gotten the datalink implant a year before that when she'd first fallen sick, so he could call for medical help if needed, a tacit admission that modern tech had its uses. *But the wallpaper remains the same, all the cooking smells remain the same. Though I've made my life in the city, devoted it to biological research, to anything new, how good it feels to have something constant to return to.*

Jiang Shun asked, "Tell me of these Jenregar — these aliens."

Thomas said, "The scientists refer to the Jenregar as 'it.' The Jenregar acts as if it exists as one being rather than many."

"And it has decided to destroy Zhengzhou?"

A shot rang out in the distance and Thomas, startled, rose from his chair. Jiang Shun touched his arm. "You know how the old woman Han Ling likes to hunt pheasant."

Thomas sat again, managed a small smile. "You've asked her time and again not to shoot so close to our fields."

Jiang Shun said, "She doesn't like to hunt where the others do."

Impulsively, Thomas stood again, made a quick bow to his father, and went into the living room. He couldn't help but feel confined in the traditional small spaces here — two hardwood chairs, a small couch, and a table stood crowded together. *I've become too accustomed to city life — more room, replicators, virt games, night life, the company of new people.*

Thomas stood in the center of the room as his father entered. "I know you've had a house comp installed, Father. How do I access it?"

"Who tells you such things?"

"After shooting pheasants, Han Ling's next favorite pastime remains gossip."

Jiang Shun touched behind his left ear to access his datalink. "Activate comp," he said.

A cube image appeared against one wall, displaying a series of menu items. "Father, I see you've embraced some of the modern world after all — such a wonderful job monitoring the correct levels of fertilizer, anticipating weather conditions, looking at the best ways of protecting against crop diseases!"

Jiang Shun said, "I still work hard. A full stomach becomes its own reward."

Thomas turned toward his father, but, respectfully, lowered his gaze. "I would never suggest anything otherwise, Father." He turned back toward the display. "Can my voice activate the newsfeeds?"

"It can — a precaution, in case you must take over the farm someday. The codeword — well, I picked, 'newsfeed.'"

Thomas said, "Comp — *newsfeed* — display latest information regarding the Jenregar."

The holographic image changed, and Thomas examined

the summaries of the various feeds. "Show 'Evacuation of Zhengzhou.'"

Thomas saw foreshortened images of a skyline obscured by smoke, of wrecked maglev trains, of refugees dirty and desperate, trudging along the cracked pavement of roads often blocked by broken-down buses. An obviously frightened announcer said, "…decimated by the Jenregar forces. A full retreat by most of our soldiers in Zhengzhou to the army base forty kilometers south of the city has begun, even as reinforcements advance from there. The latest reports say two hundred seventeen people died in the…"

The feed wavered; the sound failed, and the images defaulted to 2-D intermittently, even to black-and-white at times.

Jiang Shun asked, "Why can we not see these Jenregar?."

"Father, any camera close enough to the Jenregar would find itself destroyed in an instant, along with whoever operated it. Comp — turn off newsfeed."

"How do they kill? What sort of weapons do they use?"

"They have pulse rifles just as our soldiers do. But mostly their bodies contain their weapons — an individual Jenregar stands only just short of a meter tall. Their legs look as if they bend backwards. Some, their soldiers, can kill with a stinger on their thumbs. Others come behind them and excrete substances that kill native plant life and prepare Earth's soil to accept their own planet's vegetation." Thomas asked his father, "Have you truly not viewed any of this?"

"Watching a cube broadcast does not harvest the wheat."

"Father, you may soon not have any wheat — you may not have a farm or a village!"

"What of the Earth Unity Starforce? What of the army?"

Thomas said, "Many Starforce units have fought well,

but so have the Jenregar. As for the army — I passed a unit in which several soldiers confided they may have to retreat from the city soon."

"I will speak to the other men in our village. We will fight."

"Father, I fear you will die! The Jenregar — "

"The soldiers will stand next to us. When I served as a Senior NCO, I saw the bravery of those who served with me. Their superiors may make them abandon the cities. But without the replicators in those cities, who will feed those refugees we saw in the cube broadcast? Who will shelter them? We must do so here in the villages — the backbone of our country!"

Chapter 3

Mike sat in the commons aboard the Earth Unity light
cruiser *Admiral Susan Kojima* and wondered how long
Jeremy was going to sit across the table from him and
ignore him.

*Though, given the alternatives, ignoring me might be the best
thing that can happen*, Mike thought. *Jeremy represents my
worst fear of the reception I might receive back on Earth.*

Mike had left his homeworld 25 years earlier, having
grown tired of the irrational reactions so many people had
to his status as an artificial Human — someone created
"from scratch" in a lab rather than through "natural" means.

Many organized religions didn't consider him to have a
soul, and death threats were common. Artificial Humans
were banned from coming into many governmental
jurisdictions; never mind that the fear of them far exceeded
their number; Mike, for instance, had never met another
artificial Human.

But Mike himself had never known the details of his
own background that had only recently come to light — his
genesis had been possible only after what he thought of as a

"catalog of horror." The project that originated him, the Genome Advancement Project, had been successful only after countless failed attempts at creating artificial life. Mike had seen the holos of preserved specimens of newborns that had developed without a brain, or with vestigial limbs, or with a single eye in the center of their face.

All that had happened before Mike's birth. *But to someone like Jeremy,* he thought, *none of that matters. It's as if I'd created and killed those children myself to make sure I'd be born with a "normal" body. Not just normal in fact, but advanced — a little stronger than average, more resistant to disease. Even those slight advantages brought more resentment back on Earth than I could deal with, though the mere fact of being artificial, "soulless," led to me being denounced within churches, synagogues, and mosques around the world, and the target of constant death threats.*

And now my homeworld expects me to risk my life to help save it.

Mike wished Captain Lee would show up to give them their initial debriefing. *Thank goodness they caught up to us,* Mike thought. *But Jeremy hasn't cast one eye my way since we entered the cargo bay and got checked out in the infirmary.*

Mike blew on the hot chocolate which was the only thing he felt he could stomach right now. *Later will come a more substantial meal, and a change of clothes, and maybe even a real-water shower,* he thought. *But right now I'd be satisfied to get a polite word out of Jeremy.*

Staring at the man didn't work. Neither did a discrete cough. Jeremy only sat there with a glass of water he hadn't sipped yet, by all accounts trying to ignore Mike's presence. *OK, fine,* Mike thought. *The direct approach.* "Listen, Jeremy — "

"I don't want to talk to you."

Mike was grateful that's when Captain Lee walked in. She was a tall woman in her sixties, with silver hair that showed she'd never had youth-extension treatments. *She's waiting kind of late to take care of that,* Mike thought. *If she wants to. None of my business, I suppose.*

Mike rose and shook Captain Lee's hand. "Thanks for rescuing us."

Jeremy managed to set aside his sulk long enough to rise and accept a handshake, as well. "I appreciate what you've done for us, Captain."

Captain Lee regarded Jeremy, then Mike, as they sat. "I was told the two of you don't seem to get along. Anything I should know about?"

Jeremy spoke up before Mike could get a word in: "I don't belong to an organized religion, Captain, but I do have a sense of God's word. And this — " He indicated Mike with a tilt of his head. " — *person* was a mistake. He isn't of God."

Captain Lee looked questioningly toward Mike, who replied, "I'm the first to acknowledge that. Humans made me, not some sort of deity."

Captain Lee said, "Since this has nothing to do with the issue at hand, I'd like to set this conflict aside. Jeremy, what can you tell us about the Jenregar?"

"We were leaving Costaguana." That was a Human-colonized world whose inhabitants were largely devoted to literary scholarship and scientific research. "They attacked our ship, came on board, killed several people, grabbed others — like me — like my wife Julia. Captain, have you heard anything from Costaguana? Anything about Julia?"

"I'm afraid we haven't. The first thing we knew about this Jenregar incursion is when some of their ships arrived in the outer system. The ship you and your wife were on probably isn't even overdue yet."

Jeremy put his head in his hands and sobbed.

Mike thought, *I shouldn't feel so unkindly toward him. What he thinks about me isn't as important as the fact that he's concerned about his wife.*

Jeremy cleared his throat, swallowed, and wiped his eyes. "I'm sorry."

Captain Lee said, "Nothing to be sorry about. What happened once you were on the Jenregar ship?"

"Julia and I were separated. I don't know what happened to her."

Mike said, "We couldn't detect any other Human lifesigns on that Jenregar ship."

"I think we may have docked with another ship at some point. I heard a lot of activity from the Jenregar, and the whole ship shook a couple of times — I heard a couple large 'clunking' sounds. It all seemed like some standard thing, the Jenregar weren't all excited or anything."

Captain Lee said, "You have to hold on to that little bit of hope about your wife."

"This whole trip was Julia's idea. I resisted, but she convinced me to go along — I wish I'd put my foot down and refused. She wanted us to do something 'real,' as she put it. Instead of, you know, virts all the time. But I have to ask, Captain, do you have a virt center here on your ship?"

"You're a virthead!" Mike blurted out.

Captain Lee shot Mike a *not-now* glance, and Jeremy said, "I consider that term insulting — as if I'd called you a 'synth,' which I know is a hateful term for your kind of people."

Mike couldn't help rolling his eyes. He knew many Earth natives had gone beyond using virtual reality as mere entertainment, or for informational purposes — they'd become addicted to the artificial realities created by total-immersion virtualities — some people spent significant portions of each day in such dreamworlds, slaying fantasy monsters, having sex with entertainment figures, even exploring hyper-realistic versions of real alien worlds.

Mike said, "You've just been saved from torture or death, or both, by the Jenregar, rescued from deep space, your wife is still missing, your home planet may be in danger, and you ask about a virt center. Wouldn't that definition apply?"

Jeremy started to reply, but Captain Lee said, "Gentlemen — we have more important matters before us. I'm supposed to make sure the two of you get down to Brussels as soon as possible for a more extensive debrief." The headquarters of the Earth Unity was located in Brussels. Captain Lee told Mike, "You were right about one thing, Mike. Earth is in danger."

Mike was surprised at his own emotional reaction — concern, even fear, for a world whose inhabitants had often treated him so poorly. "What's the Jenregar doing?"

"Attacking cities, trying to establish their own hives. Santiago, Chile, Tijuana, Mexico, Zhengzhou, China. We think North America's next."

"I don't understand," Jeremy said.

Mike told him, "The Jenregar live in these great mounds of earth — their hives. That's where they reproduce, bring all their food, establish living quarters."

Captain Lee activated a holo of a view looking down onto a city from orbit. Several large fires burned in scattered sites all through the city. In the middle of downtown, Mike saw what he recognized as a Jenregar mound. "This is Zhengzhou. The Jenregar has established its mound, and it's sending troops out to create a perimeter to protect it. It's even sending squads out into rural areas. And they're purposely doing this in the middle of cities," Captain Lee said, "because they know that limits our response. We can't just start shooting or bombing indiscriminately, or we kill our own people. I'll leave the rest to the folks down at Brussels. I'd hope they could — "

"Battle alert!" came the warning over the ship's P.A. "Incoming Jenregar ships — Captain to the bridge!"

Captain Lee stood and told Mike and Jeremy, "Mike, access your datalink and the ship's computer will get both of you to your proper stations." Then she was gone.

Jeremy just sat there at the table. "You heard her," Mike told him. "Let's go."

"With you? No, thanks!"

Mike grabbed Jeremy's arm and pulled him up from his seat. "How the hell did I get saddled with you? Do you want to live?"

"Of course I do," came the reluctant response.

"Then you're coming with me."

As they went out into the corridor, Mike said, "Computer — action stations for Mike Christopher and Jeremy Sheffield."

The answer came over Mike's datalink: "Lifepod two, deck four, corridor seven." A map of the route appeared on the inside of Mike's wrist.

"Lifepod?" Jeremy asked. "Don't tell me we're about to end up out in the middle of space again!"

"It's just a precaution," Mike said as he led the way down the corridor.

The ship shuddered under an impact, and Jeremy said, "Precaution, huh? Why would they send us there if we're weren't going to have to use that pod?"

"We don't have a combat role, so they put us into position just in case, so there's less last-minute scrambling around."

They found themselves at a grav tube leading down to deck four, and Mike stepped aside to let Jeremy go first. Jeremy looked at the tube, looked at Mike, and said, "I'm not gonna just step out into thin air."

Mike tried to keep the disgust out of his voice. "You *can't* tell me you've never used a grav tube before."

"Not aboard a spaceship under attack — or that might be about to go into stardrive!"

Mike tried to grab Jeremy again, but the man stepped back. "Oh, no — you're going to quit pushing me around. I can do what I want!"

"What you want," Mike told him, "is to live — now get the hell down there!"

Jeremy said, "I'm posting an official complaint about you when this emergency is over."

Fine, Mike thought as the ship shuddered again. *That could be months or years away.* He watched as Jeremy stepped into the grav tube and landed on the deck below. Mike followed, and he and Jeremy were standing before a row of lifepods of various sizes. "Here we go," Mike said, indicating a small two-person pod. "This is ours."

"It's awfully damn small," Jeremy said.

"It's just for the two of us. And being smaller means it's less likely to be picked up by Jenregar sensors if we have to use it."

Jeremy began a verbal tirade of such vehemence and so many words that Mike could barely make out what the man was saying. In the midst of that, he heard over his datalink, "Mike and Jeremy, this is Captain Lee. If you're not in that lifepod yet, get in there and get ready to eject!"

"Oh, crap!" Mike said, and opened the pod's hatch. Its internal systems powered up automatically. It contained two recessed seats side by side, but facing in opposite directions.

Now it was Jeremy who grabbed Mike's arm. "Did she really say that? We really *do* have to blow ourselves out into space again?"

"I thought that was your big prediction — now get in!"

Jeremy stepped down into the pod. Mike followed and closed the hatch. "Strap in," he told Jeremy. "This thing's too small to have inertial compensators."

Jeremy sat in one of the two recessed positions in the lifepod. Mike moved in next to him in the cramped space and started checking out the pod's systems.

Captain Lee's voice came over his datalink as the ship rocked again: "I read you as inside the pod — is that correct?"

"We're here and strapped in."

"Stand by for launch."

Mike told Jeremy, "Hold on — we're about to launch."

"Wait a minute," Jeremy said. "Why can't we — "

It was as if the bottom dropped out of the small pod. Jeremy yelped in surprise and Mike didn't blame him. *I've never liked thrill rides*, he thought. *Give me some good old inertial dampeners any day.*

Something slammed into the lifepod, and Mike's head struck the wall, *hard. I'd always believed "seeing stars" was just a phrase*, he thought. *All told, I'd rather look at them through a viewscreen.*

Another impact, and the pod began to spin, a movement Mike hated even worse than the falling feeling. He hoped his own expression didn't mirror Jeremy's — the man was grasping the sides of his seat and had his mouth open to scream, but nothing was coming out.

Then the pod slowly stopped spinning.

"Thank goodness," Jeremy said. "Did that stop on purpose?"

"The gyros kicked in," Mike told him. He reached to one side to call up a readout on their trajectory.

"Should we activate our lifesuits?" Jeremy asked.

"They'll come on automatically if we lose air. But that's not what I'm worried about." Mike kept checking the readout, but to no effect. "The readout on our trajectory doesn't want to come up right."

"What the hell does that mean?" Jeremy demanded.

"It means I think we're coming down in the northern hemisphere, but I can't tell you exactly where."

"That covers a lot of ground, you know!"

"As long as we come down on the ground," Mike said.

"What does that mean?"

"It means the Earth's surface is covered by a lot more water than land. What if we we land in the middle of the Pacific Ocean? We have to be ready for that."

"Dear Lord, this thing will sink like a stone!"

"It won't," Mike said. "And as long as its beacon is working, someone will find us."

Jeremy looked all around the interior of the pod, as if it were closing in on him. "What if they don't know to look for us? We don't even know if the *Kojima* survived, if they got to tell anyone about us."

"Brussels knows about us, Jeremy. They'll find us." *I hope*, Mike thought.

Jeremy clapped a hand over his eyes. "We don't even know what the Jenregar are doing — they may have taken over the Earth by now."

Mike put his hand on Jeremy's shoulder. "I've dealt with the Jenregar before. Being a hive mind makes them tough and efficient, but it's also their weakness. We have the advantage here on our homeworld. We'll beat them."

Jeremy lowered his hand. His eyes revealed a

determination and inner strength Mike hadn't glimpsed in him before. Jeremy told Mike, "Take your hand off my shoulder."

Mike did. "I only meant — "

"I don't want you to touch me."

Mike made a show of examining the sensors again. "People like you are why I haven't been back on Earth in a quarter-century."

Jeremy said, "You feel you've been wronged."

"If you consider the other students beating me up in school. Death threats. Being spit upon. Yeah. You might say that."

Jeremy shook his head. "The whole thing was wrong."

Mike said, "How I was treated, you mean?"

"I mean the project that led to your conception. I've seen the pictures of those monstrosities — those babies. They died so you could exist."

"I never even knew they existed until a few weeks ago."

"But their short and terrible lives define you, Mike, whether you like it or not — what's that sound?"

A roaring that sounded at first as if it was coming from a great distance grew louder and louder, and a great buffeting rocked the pod. Mike said, "We're re-entering Earth's atmosphere."

Jeremy glared at Mike. "And you don't know where we're landing?"

"Like I said, a water landing is most likely. But we could end up in the arctic, or the middle of a Siberian forest, or —
"

"Enough!" Jeremy said. "I don't want to hear all the different ways we might die!"

"Then just hang on, and hope for the best."

Mike gave up trying to get the sensors to reveal anything,

but that meant his imagination ran free as he considered the force of the atmosphere trying to break the pod apart, its heat trying to turn it into slag. He imagined what Jeremy didn't want to — the ocean splashdown, or being deposited within that thick Russian forest, the hopeful wait to be rescued. *That's assuming anyone even knows to look for us,* Mike thought. *Unfortunately, Jeremy was right the first time. We don't even know what happened to the* Kojima. *It might've been destroyed before it had a chance to confirm to Brussels that we're on our way.*

The roaring of the atmosphere beyond the skin of the lifepod began to fade, replaced by a low rumbling. "What's those sounds mean?" Jeremy asked, as he clearly fought to keep his voice from cracking.

"It just means we're slowing down," Mike said. "Which is a good thing."

"What's slowing us down?"

"Pretty old-fashioned stuff — retro-rockets — "

The lifepod shook violently for several seconds, then became still again.

" — then parachutes."

"What is this, the Dark Ages?"

"This pod's too small for gravitics — just that simple."

Their small craft shuddered again a couple of times, then came to rest. Then began to rock back and forth, smoothly, rhythmically.

"Well, I didn't want to be right," Mike said. "But I was. Water landing."

"How do we find out where we've landed?" Jeremy asked.

"Well — the most practical way I know will be just to open the hatch and take a look outside."

Jeremy said, "And let whatever's outside come it — it

could be water, like you said, or if you're wrong it could be a mountain lion or some sort of diseased plant life!"

Mike held up a hand and Jeremy wound down. "Gimme an alternative to just opening the hatch."

Jeremy seemed to deflate. "I guess we don't have one."

Mike stood up, made sure his disruptor was handy at his side, and opened the hatch. A strong breeze brought in plenty of fresh, damp air. *Funny thing*, Mike thought as he started to pull himself up out of the hatch. *The air doesn't smell salty like it would in the ocean.*

But before he could stick his head outside the hatch, Jeremy pulled him back down, saying, "The hell with it — I'm not afraid to face what's out there!"

Mike could only watch as Jeremy stuck his head out of the hatch. "You were right!" he said. "Just water as far as I can see!"

Mike squeezed next to Jeremy and, looking over the other man's shoulder, indeed saw only water, beneath a beaming sun that told him it was mid-morning. Then he looked in the opposite direction. What he saw made him tap Jeremy on the shoulder. "Look this way," he said.

In that direction stood the familiar sight of the Sears Tower (which at one time was called something else, but Mike couldn't remember that any more than he knew who Sears was), the Shedd Aquarium, and the rest of the familiar skyline of Chicago.

"So I was only a little right," Mike told Jeremy. A water landing's much better if it's in Lake Michigan!"

<hr>

Carrie decided the best way to infiltrate the Jenregar mound this second time was the same way she'd done it the first — dive right into the small pond that accepted the drainage from the mound and swim against the slight current until she reached the interior.

Her idea was to avoid the type of Jenregar Humans referred to as protectors. They were especially alert around the perimeter of the Jenregar mound, and many of them had augmented eyesight — an ability the Jenregar was developing in the research it was conducting inside the mound. Even without that ability, although the Jenregar individuals might not be able to perceive whether Carrie was a real threat, they certainly wouldn't allow her to go inside without a specific pheromonic "password" — thus, entry through the pipeline.

Fortunately for Carrie, the drainage was relatively pure water and not sewage — the Jenregar apparently used it for drinking water and, it was believed, to cool some of its equipment.

Carrie stepped to the edge of the stream and stripped down to her skinsuit. *I'd consider going nude, but I'm not sure Papa's heart could take the shock*, she thought. She took several deep breaths and stepped into the stream.

Her heart rate quickened, the better to keep her body warm, and her lungs expanded to half again their usual size, visibly expanding her chest and shoulders. Her skin had micro-dermal ridges that trapped water molecules in a thin layer against her skin, giving her less resistance in the stream.

Those with her bio-adaptation were sometimes referred to as "fish," but that was a misnomer — she breathed air, not water, but could stay down for extended periods, much as a dolphin could.

Her adaptation also provided the strength in her arms and legs that propelled her against the pipe's current — that was important, as she had nearly a kilometer to swim to get to her destination.

About fifteen minutes later, Carrie broke the surface in a reservoir of water about a hundred meters wide at one end of a long corridor in the Jenregar mound.

Carrie pulled herself out of the water, grateful for the relative warmth of the mound. She marched with a confidence she didn't feel down the corridor and farther into the Jenregar mound, even as her heart rate slowed and her lungs shrank, and her chest and shoulders along with them.

She passed a couple Jenregar scouts who were headed in the opposite direction — they didn't have the sight augments, and didn't appear to notice her, anymore than the two builders or even the protector who came in immediately behind her from an intersecting corridor did. *Maybe the sight augmentation is only for protectors standing guard outside,* Carrie thought. *And thank goodness for my own augments.*

Before embarking on this mission, Carrie's body had been implanted with nanotech giving her the ability to "deploy" scents designed to fool the Jenregar's sense of smell. For the Jenregar, sight was purely a secondary sense, thus their small eyes; once she was past the increased security at the mound's entrance, an individual Jenregar was unlikely to perceive Carrie as a threat as long as she smelled right, just as the average Human wouldn't perceive a threat in someone who looked and sounded Human but smelled a little "off."

It was the Jenregar's greatest weakness, but it recognized that weakness and the experiments going on inside the Madrid mound were designed to graft Jenregar qualities onto Humans and vice-versa to see if it could overcome those limitations.

Carrie followed the same path she'd taken into the dim interior of the mound the first time, heading toward the research lab where she'd discovered Luisa and Damian. As she proceeded, her body's adaptations to the water began to reverse themselves — her heart rate slowed and her lungs contracted.

As the corridor slowly widened, Carrie began to hear sounds all too familiar to her — the scrape of metal against bone, a dull thud punctuated by a low groan, a terrified scream followed by an abrupt silence.

Perhaps the worst part, Carrie thought, *is that the Jenregar isn't consciously torturing anyone. Its only goal is knowledge, and the idea that it's sending people through agony never even occurs to it.*

She entered the research lab, instinctively keeping close to one wall as a couple Jenregar scouts passed. *It's still spooky*, she thought, *to be here in plain sight and still go unnoticed. I have to hope I don't run across any Jenregar with augmented sight.*

Carrie looked down a line of what she thought of as examination tables. Rather than lying flat, though, each one tilted upward at an acute angle. The ones closest to her were occupied by dead Human bodies strapped in place, those the Jenregar had used up and discarded. Others held people who still lived, but perhaps wished for the release death would bring.

As much as I wish I could help them, I can tell many of them are too far gone — too mutilated, with too many Jenregar augmentations — barely even Human anymore. I can only hope to catch a glimpse of my father. I have to know whether he's well...or whether these beasts have mutilated him...

Or killed him.

She made herself look at how these people had been

experimented on, most of them while still alive — eyes gouged out, ears cut off, arms or legs removed and replaced with Jenregar limbs, as had happened to Luisa.

And what is Luisa to my father? Carrie wondered. *He's never mentioned her.*

Of course, why should he? It's none of my business. The Monaco Virus took Mother 22 years ago. My sister Adriana died of her abuser's injuries just last year. He's endured enough grief in his life. Of course he should reach out to someone.

Carrie moved down the line of tables — each person she saw was held to their table by a single wide strap around the middle of their bodies that also bound their arms to their sides. She saw a man with some kind of shunt inserted into the side of his head, a woman whose face had been torn off. *All this goes into my report*, Carrie thought. *A document of horrors.*

In the distance, she could hear a chittering sound that she associated with Jenregar individuals experiencing extreme pain. *Try as I might*, she thought, *it's hard to work up much sympathy for them.* She knew, though, that eventually more Jenregar than Humans would undergo such procedures — the whole point was to create Jenregar who had keener eyesight, the better to detect the presence of Humans such as herself, and the Jenregar felt no sympathy or responsibility for its individuals, only for its broader inhuman goals.

Carrie passed two empty tables, the ones where she'd found Damian and Luisa. This was as far as she'd gotten earlier before deciding she had to get *someone* out as soon as possible to complete her mission. *They were still alive*, Carrie thought, *and they were among the least mutilated. I can only hope their bodies can be restored to their original conditions.*

But now movement out of the corner of her eye caught

Carrie's attention, and in the next instant, she realized a blue-backed Jenregar protector had paused about ten meters away from her — and was *staring* at her!

A closer look, and Carrie realized the protector had much larger eyes than the typical Jenregar. *About the same size as a Human's*, she thought.

The protector advanced toward her. Carrie started to back away, but the protector, in a sudden burst of speed, caught up to her and grasped both her arms. *It knows I don't belong here*, she thought.

The top of the protector's head only came up to Carrie's shoulders, but it was stronger than she was, and she couldn't break its hold upon her.

Even as Carrie struggled, she managed a closer look at the Jenregar's eyes, and could tell they were modeled upon a Human's, wider, with more distinct pupils, and darting around as if to take in every detail around it.

In an instant of horror, Carrie realized the protector's eyes looked familiar — as if they were her father's eyes!

Carrie's mind recoiled from that image, and in a sudden burst of strength she tore her arms away from the protector. She ran out of the research lab, but when she looked back, she saw the protector wasn't following her.

It only wanted me out of the research lab, Carrie thought. And realization came: *The protector knew I shouldn't be there because I didn't look right, but my scent was still that of another Jenregar.*

But if I keep trying to get back in the research lab, it's just going to keep pushing me out. And I've got to find Papa and get him out of here.

What would make it accept my presence?

If won't accept me as a Jenregar, I have only one other choice.

Carrie's heart was pounding. She was breathing so

rapidly she had to consciously force herself to take a single deep breath and let it out slowly. *This will be the most difficult thing I've done in my life*, she thought.

But leaving Papa behind would be harder.

Knowing she had to hedge her bets, Carrie ran back to the reservoir where she'd entered the mound and dove in. Her body began its familiar transformation, including the expansion of her chest.

When it was complete, she returned to the entrance to the research lab and touched behind her left ear to activate her datalink. "End pheromone protocols," she said. "And maintain open link."

Carrie stepped back across the threshold of the research facility and waited, arms at her sides but head held high, as the protector advanced toward her again, no doubt finally perceiving her in all her Humanity.

EARLY THE NEXT MORNING, EVEN BEFORE JIANG SHUN AROSE for the day, Thomas awoke with a start at a loud banging on the front door and shouted commands to "Wake up!"

Thomas had barely eased himself out of bed before he heard his father padding to the door and opening it. He made it to his bedroom's doorway just as four soldiers, three men and a woman, pushed past his father and crowded into the room, pulse rifles at the ready.

The lead soldier, a Junior NCO, looked frantically around the room as if he expected an attack from any quarter; he ignored both Thomas and Jiang Shun as he peered briefly into the kitchen, then into Thomas's bedroom.

This man had clearly not had a bath or shaved for

several days. Of the other three, the woman had a bloody bandage wrapped around her head, one of the men sported a nasty scar on his face, and the other man had one eye that had swollen shut.

The Junior NCO looked around the room and said, "This should serve our purposes nicely."

Thomas looked closely at his father, saw a flash of anger cross his features, then watched as Jiang Shun took a breath, composed himself, and approached the soldiers. He bowed before them and asked, "How may this humble servant help our brave soldiers?"

The Junior NCO said, "We require shelter. We require food. The villagers refer to you as the most respected man living here."

An honor my father might wish to forgo today, Thomas thought.

Jiang Shun lowered his eyes. "I cannot say. But I once served as a Senior NCO myself, and wish to serve again."

The Junior NCO turned his back on Jiang Shun. "Your home will serve. You will provide us with food. In return, we will protect your village against the Jenregar." The Junior NCO pointed at the other three soldiers, all Privates, and indicated they should fan out through the rest of the home, including the small courtyard.

Jiang Shun said, "And, esteemed Junior NCO, certainly the rest of your force has deployed nearby?"

The soldier turned back toward Thomas's father. "Your see what remains of our force."

Jiang Shun's eyes widened and he looked at the Junior NCO in disbelief, then averted his eyes again. He cupped his right fist with his left hand and bowed, almost imperceptibly, to the soldier. Thomas took the lesson of his father's reaction to heart, and fought his own rising anger. *I must not speak a hasty word*, he thought, *anything unworthy of my father's teachings.*

Jiang Shun said, "No doubt your fellow soldiers fought bravely. The Jenregar will soon retreat."

"No doubt," the Junior NCO said. As the female Private — Thomas thought of her as "Bandage" — came back into the room, the Junior NCO bellowed, "Report!"

Bandage said, "The house seems defensible. We can leave our equipment in the courtyard. And the village as a whole has a good supply of food."

Jiang Shun asked, "Do you intend to house yourselves in my home?"

The Junior NCO shifted his rifle in his hands. "Do you object?"

Jiang Shun stood tall. "Not at all! I appreciate the honor! During my own service, I excelled in — "

The Junior NCO held up one hand and Jiang Shun fell silent. "Old man, your previous service holds no bearing on the fight against the Jenregar. We will respect you as leader of this village, but I suggest you become accustomed to standing aside and allowing us to perform our duties."

Jiang Shun responded with another bow. The Junior NCO grunted to catch Bandage's attention, then said, "Gather the others. We'll examine the rest of the village, then make our preparations for food and shelter." The soldier left. The Junior NCO aimed a slight head tilt rather than a full bow at Jiang Shun. Then he looked at Thomas, saying, "I don't see you as one of these primitive peasants."

Thomas could barely keep his voice from quivering: "You should not speak of my father that way."

"You act as if you've come from from the city — *have you?*"

Thomas saw no point in trying to lie: "I live in Zhengzhou. I work as a biologist."

The Junior NCO looked at Thomas with disdain. "Oh, a smart boy."

Bandage returned with the other soldiers — Thomas thought of them as "Scar" and "Wounded Eye." The Junior NCO pointed to Thomas and told them, "This one probably has a datalink. Carve it from him."

Thomas tried to step backwards, but Bandage and Wounded Eye grabbed him by the arms. Scar reached down, lifted his right pants leg, and pulled a mean-looking serrated knife from a sheath. He wrapped one arm around Thomas's neck, held him tight.

Thomas, fear coursing through him, strained against the soldiers' hold, but to no effect. He gasped as the tip of Scar's knife pressed against the side of his neck.

Then the knife pierced Thomas's skin -- he screamed, and strained that much harder against the three soldiers. He heard Jiang Shun speaking forcefully to the soldiers, but the intensity of the pain kept him from making out any of his father's words.

The soldiers released him. Scar raised a bloody hand in front of Thomas's face and showed him the small black rectangle of his datalink. The soldier dropped it to the floor and stamped on it with his booted foot. Thomas grimaced, held his hand to the side of his bleeding neck, and eased himself into a chair.

The Junior NCO said, "I can't imagine anyone else in this backwater village has a link." Thomas had to fight to keep his gaze from darting toward his father. "If they do," the Junior NCO continued, "turn them in, or we will not give them the same respect we have given you."

Thomas knew only he could perceive the barely

contained fury behind the tiny narrowing of his father's eyes, the thin line of his mouth.

"One more thing," the Junior NCO said. "You can activate the newsfeeds from here?"

"Yes," Jiang Shun said, and Thomas saw the effort it took for his father to keep his voice steady.

"Say your codeword."

Jiang Shun took a deep breath, and Thomas feared what would happen if his father refused. But after a moment, he said, "*Newsfeed.*"

The Junior NCO smiled. "Very clever. Tell it to note my voice and follow my next instruction."

Jiang Shun hesitated again, but then said, "Comp — follow the order of the next voice you hear."

The Junior NCO said, "Deactivate newsfeed service until this voice tells you to re-activate."

The comp's soft female voice replied, "Confirmed."

"I cannot take the chance of this village hearing false and misleading information," the Junior NCO said. "Anything you need to know, *I* will tell you." He led the way through the front doorway, the other soldiers following.

When the front door closed behind them, Thomas said, "What do you think of your precious soldiers now?"

Jiang Shun went into the kitchen and ran water across a towel. "If I had ever acted as their Senior NCO, I would have them severely reprimanded — thrown out of the army if possible." He came to Thomas and wiped his son's neck gently as Thomas gritted his teeth against the pain. "You cannot know how much shame I feel, my son."

"You have no reason to feel such shame, Father."

"Please -- I wish you would call me 'Baba,' as other Chinese sons do."

Thomas bowed his head toward his father. "I promise to do better...Baba."

"Notice that we see only these enlisted men — no officers."

"Perhaps the Jenregar killed their officers."

"In which case, they should have reported to the army base we heard about in those news reports — the one forty kilometers from the city — but only fifteen from here! But they did not."

"I don't understand," Thomas said.

"They have undertaken their own mission. One in which they concern themselves only with saving their own skins."

"Then the greatest threat facing us today, Baba — "

"Comes from our fellow Humans, not the Jenregar."

"So what shall we do, Fath — Baba?"

"We'll prepare to feed them, of course. Start making preparations. I'll join you shortly."

Chapter 4

Within minutes, a hydrofoil boat just over twenty meters long headed toward Mike and Jeremy. Once it got within a couple hundred meters of their pod, though, it began to circle, as if taking their measure.

"Wave," Mike said. "Look friendly. Try not to look like a Jenregar."

"Not funny," Jeremy said. But he waved, as did Mike.

The hydrofoil drew closer, and Mike saw the logo CHICAGO POLICE MARINE OPERATIONS on its side. Four uniformed men and women left the boat's pilot house and lined up along a railing at its bow. *All of them armed,* Mike thought. Mike waved again. No one waved back. *I can't blame them. They probably have no idea who we are or why we're here — just that we dropped out of the sky in the waters next to a likely Jenregar target.*

The hydrofoil drew within shouting distance. One of the women at the railing, her hand on her disruptor, said, "Identify yourselves, please!"

Mike said, "We're from the Unity warship *Admiral Susan Kojima*. I'm Mike Christopher and this is Jeremy Sheffield."

The woman checked her wrist comm. "It seems we received a bulletin on you, Mr. Christopher — Mr. Sheffield. Along with about every other law enforcement and military unit in the world."

"What about the *Kojima*?"

"Seems it took some hard hits, but got away. Let's get both of you aboard, and we'll get you on your way to Brussels as soon as we can."

Moments later, Mike and Jeremy were standing on the bow of the hydrofoil as it rushed back to shore. The officer who'd greeted them, Lt. Sharon Nyquist, told Mike, "Welcome back to Earth. "I understand it's been quite a while since you've been here."

"Not exactly the way I intended to make it back, either."

"I understand that. Look off in the distance, there, to the northwest. See that?"

"Some kind of plume of smoke — the Jenregar?"

Lt. Nyquist nodded. "They're making one of those mounds in Arlington Heights."

"Damn. How serious is it, overall?"

"Serious enough. It's going to be tough getting you and Jeremy to Brussels — and we do want to get you there in person — comm channels are spotty. No orbital or suborbital craft are up. Except, rumor has it, some pretty dark intelligence missions. Wouldn't know about those."

"So we have to go on the surface?"

"Looks like it. Most of the main underground maglev routes are still running, at least within continents. Getting across the Atlantic or Pacific is the tough part — plenty of power disruptions, that kind of thing. Imagine being stranded in a tube as much as five or six klicks underground, and beneath the ocean, to boot."

"No thanks."

"I'm glad you came back, Mike. I...know what your circumstances were when you left. And I know of your previous experiences with the Jenregar. I think they could be valuable here."

Mike had been present on Korolev Habitat, a Human colony cylinder orbiting a distant star, seven years earlier when the Jenregar tried to take it over. He'd been the one to discover how to disguise himself against them using their own pheromones. He'd also figured out how to create another pheromone that fooled half all the Jenregar within the habitat into thinking the other half had died. They'd fallen over themselves trying to dispose of one another.

"I hope you're right," Mike said.

Lt. Nyquist said, "I guess you could say I also know what your circumstances were with other Humans, too. I believe you might find things are better for you now."

Though he had his doubts, Mike said, "I hope that's true. I have to admit, I'm struck by how *right* it feels to be back here — to be on a planet rather than on my ship and feel a single grav pulling on my body. To smell the air — I never realized how distinct a particular planet's atmosphere might be until just now. Even the way the clouds are formed, and how the waves around us rise and fall, seem to tell me I'm on Earth — and that it's home."

Jeremy rolled his eyes, told Mike, "Spare me," and headed toward the stern of the hydrofoil.

Lt. Nyquist raised her eyebrows in a silent question. Mike said, "He's a religionist. Doesn't think I have a soul, all that. He wouldn't wish any harm on me — at least, I don't think he would — but he considers me a 'mistake,' as he put it."

Lt. Nyquist clapped a hand onto Mike's shoulder. "Don't

worry about him, Mike. You'll find enough people who support you these days."

"I hope that's true — I've got enough to worry about with the Jenregar to keep an eye over my shoulder for threats from Humans."

The hydrofoil soon settled into the waters of Lake Michigan as it approached the 31st Street Harbor, which was crowded with people watching. Lt. Nyquist told Mike and Jeremy, "The Unity's trying to route you the best way it can to get to Brussels. We've got a capsule to get you to the nearest maglev station, but then you're on your own."

"I appreciate your help," Mike said, then indicated the line of people along the dock. "What's with our reception committee?"

"You're still an object of fascination, Mike. Once people realized who'd just landed in Lake Michigan, it was all over the social and news nets."

Jeremy said, "I can see a bunch of news flitters, too." He pointed to a section of sky to their right that seemed to contain a cloud of buzzing insects.

"Don't worry about them. Flight laws only allow them to get so close, even if they aren't any bigger than a bug."

Jeremy said, "But their cameras can make it look like they're up in our faces."

"I'm not worried about any of that," Mike said. "I just want to get to Brussels."

Crewmembers jumped onto the dock and started tying the hydrofoil down. Lt. Nyquist joined the other uniformed officers and asked the crowd to move back. Mike smiled at the thought that just minutes earlier the same officers had been glaring at him and Jeremy with their hands on their disruptors.

Most of those gathered at the dock moved back willingly — but several began shouting comments:

"We love you, Mike Christopher!"

"Go back to your filthy spacer friends!"

"Please, save us!"

"Leave the Earth alone — now!"

So, mixed reviews, Mike thought. He stepped down from the boat, marveling at this response, marveling as well at the latest clothing fashions, with their strange lapels and bright swatches of color, far from the utilitarian modes of clothing, unattached to pop culture trends, that spacers tended to wear. They even seemed strange in the ways they walked and gestured, their fluttering hands and wide eyes revealing an excitement Mike couldn't begin to associate with his own presence among them. He muttered, "How the hell do they even know who I am?"

Jeremy indicated the flurry of news flitters. "I'm sure this went worldwide the moment anyone spotted our pod. And once we stuck our heads out, facial recognition tech took over."

"Yeah. I'd forgotten how much people are devoted to their ideas of news."

"You're no doubt the latest fascination, Mike — though why anyone would want to glorify you I have no idea."

"I'm not looking to be glorified, Jeremy — I'm just trying to do the best I can for the Earth. It *is* my homeworld — despite all the people here who hate me and want to kill me."

The officers were having to be a bit more stern with the crowd, as many of the individuals within it didn't want to move back. Some were starting to push back against the officers, who pushed that much harder. The shouts were no longer about Mike:

"Police thugs!"

"We just want to see Mike!"

"Let us at him — we'll make him go home!"

Mike saw Lt. Nyquist was growing more impatient by the moment. Finally, she pulled out her stunner and shot a blast into the air that echoed across the docks. The crowd stopped cold and became quiet.

"That's the only warning you're getting," Nyquist said. The next person who pushes against one of my officers will be stunned and taken into custody. Is that clear?"

No one in the crowd spoke. Each individual settled into place, and they even formed a pathway toward the sleek black two-seater capsule that was at the curb awaiting Mike and Jeremy.

Lt. Nyquist holstered her stunner. "That's better," she muttered. She extended an arm toward the capsule, beckoning Mike and Jeremy toward it. "Gentlemen," she said. "Your steed."

"Thanks, Lieutenant," Mike said. "You couldn't have been more helpful."

Mike and Jeremy piled into the automated capsule, its nearly silent electric motor began to hum, and it pulled away from the dock. "Destination — Union Station," the capsule's voice said. "ETA twelve minutes."

Mike looked behind the capsule, and saw several people break away from Lt. Nyquist's officers and try to run alongside them, but the capsule quickly outpaced them and began racing along Lakeshore Drive. They were the only vehicle in sight on the broad streets, but plenty of people were taking in the sights along Lake Michigan. In the opposite direction stood the city's eternal skyscrapers, most either devoted to housing or standing as museums dedicated to the former market economy.

"That was disgusting back there," Jeremy said. "The people who took your side, that is."

"You might not believe this," Mike said, "but I agree with you. I'm not here to be the subject of adulation. And the ones who disapprove of me are exactly why I haven't been back here in so long."

"You simulate Human emotions very well."

"Listen," Mike said, "I'm as real and Human as you are — and I'm getting goddam tired of you trying to imply I'm not."

"You're right, Mike. I should probably just feel sorry for you."

Mike seethed silently as their capsule turned right onto South Canal Street, and soon was pulling up before Union Station's tall columns. They entered the building, the news flitters still hovering above.

<hr>

THE JENREGAR PROTECTOR DIDN'T WASTE ANY TIME. IT grabbed Carrie by one arm and led her back into the research lab. It walked her toward two other Jenregar of a type she'd never seen before — both their backs were green. *I'm seeing a type of Jenregar no one else has,* Carrie realized. *This could be important, if I can only find Papa and get the hell out of here.*

The protector stopped before the other two Jenregar and handed Carrie over to them. She didn't resist, though she could tell these Jenregar weren't as strong as the protector. *And these green-backed Jenregar also don't have the protector's augmented eyes, thank goodness.*

Carrie allowed herself to be led along by the two

Jenregar even as she kept an eye out constantly for any sign of her father.

There's another sensory disadvantage the Jenregar have, she thought, *and now's the time to use it.* "Papa!" she shouted, knowing the Jenregar seldom reacted to sounds. "Gilberto Molina! Are you here?"

Carrie strained to hear even the slightest sound she might recognize as her father's voice, but heard nothing.

"Gilberto Molina — it's Carrie! Can you hear me?"

Still no response.

The two Jenregar were guiding her toward one of the exam tables. *Good thing I planned on this*, Carrie thought. *In fact, the sooner the better.* She allowed herself to be placed against the table. One of the green-backed Jenregar brought the wide strap across her chest, which also pinned her arms down. But within moments, she knew, her body's adaptation to water would begin to fade and her upper body would reduce in size just enough, she hoped, to be able to squirm out from under that strap.

Not ashamed to admit I'm a little panicky here, Carrie thought, as the two Jenregar walked away from her. She craned her neck to try to see where they were going, but quickly lost sight of them. *For the next few moments I'll be helpless if the Jenregar decide I'm ripe to start experimenting on*, she thought.

Got to stay focused on Papa. This is the only way I could get back in here.

The two Jenregar were coming back. One of them held a small box in one hand. *What the hell's in there?* Carrie wondered. She felt her heart rate slowing, felt her lungs beginning to contract. *But is it happening quickly enough?*

The two Jenregar stopped in front of her and the one holding the box opened it and pulled out a small metal device. It leaned forward as Carrie flinched and pressed herself back against the table, the strap still binding her as her body slowly contracted. *Just one other chance*, Carrie thought, and muttered, grateful she'd thought to keep her datalink open, "Activate pheromone protocols."

The Jenregar froze, its hand holding the device still extended toward Carrie. The other Jenregar simply stared, immobile. *It's as if I transformed into a Jenregar right in front of them*, Carrie thought. *And they don't have enough individual intelligence or initiative to adapt to a new circumstance.*

Carrie felt the strap loosen around her, but try as she might, she couldn't quite wriggle free.

The Jenregar, as if awakening from a dream, finished extending its arm and pushed the small device against the left side of her head.

It was as if a lightning bolt struck Carrie in the forehead — she screamed, and struggled that much harder against the strap, but couldn't budge.

The pain began to fade, and Carrie could focus more on what was happening around her. Both Jenregar were staring at her, but she couldn't interpret the meaning, if any, of their expressions. *They don't even glance at each other*, Carrie thought. *They communicate only with the hive mind, or at least the portion of it that's down here on Earth.*

At least Carrie could move more easily behind the strap now, and she wriggled her body down until she could duck under it and was free. The Jenregar continued staring at the table, as if they hadn't even noticed she'd moved.

Carrie reached up gingerly and touched the side of her head. The device the Jenregar had placed against her had dug into her flesh. She gently grasped it with two fingers and, tentatively, pulled.

Another flash of pain. *So it stays, at least for now*, she

thought.

Carrie took that first step away from the two Jenregar and —

Stopped cold. Blinked. Looked all around.

I had a strange feeling just now — an awareness of something that wasn't there before — what was it? Carrie knew she didn't dare linger, though, and took a couple of steps farther into the research lab.

And stopped again. She turned back toward the Jenregar, who were just beginning to stir again, as if they were wind-up toys that that had been newly-wound.

It's them, Carrie thought. *Somehow I'm aware of those two Jenregar. I can feel their presence, and something else...a connection to something.*

Her next thought sent a cold wave of fear through her consciousness. *Is that connection to the hive mind? Is this just a type of empathy, or is it accessing my consciousness, attempting to take over my mind?*

The two Jenregar, without even glancing at Carrie, walked away, headed deeper into the research lab. With each step they took, she felt their consciousness? — presence? — fade.

But not quite completely, Carrie thought. *And I can feel the presence of other Jenregar, as well — dozens, hundreds of them. Scouts, protectors, builders — and a great many like the two that just left, I guess we'll call them researchers.*

And even more, of types I don't recognize. I know they have everything from hunters to gardeners, but I can't quite figure out —

Awareness of another consciousness arrived. *The queen,* Carrie realized. *If I can find her and...kill her —*

Then she remembered from her briefing: *That won't work. The Jenregar is too efficient. The instant a queen dies, another Jenregar individual alters its form and takes the queen's place.*

Carrie forged ahead, following the same general path the two Jenregar had taken. Again, she shouted: "Papa! It's Carrie! Are you here?"

More silence, and she began again: "Gilberto Molina! Papa!"

Strain as she might, Carrie heard nothing, to her despair. *But underneath my usual Human perceptions of sight, sound, and all the rest* she thought, *I can perceive something else — a consciousness, a sense of...belonging, an unspoken certainty that I'm at the pinnacle of creation, and that all other beings are lesser intelligences, existing only for me to use.*

It's an odd manner of expression — not intellectual, not emotional. It simply — is — just as a planet or a star, or a rabbit, or an apple simply exists. It requires no explanation, no rationalization.

Then, though Carrie still heard nothing, came the perception of a different kind of being mixed in with her perceptions of the many Jenregar in the mound — a being without any sense of connection to the Jenregar hive, but whose presence and emotions flowed easily toward her.

Carrie gasped. "Papa?"

She moved down the line of exam tables, finding Humans, some dead, some alive, lying upon them. None of them was the source of the feelings being transmitted toward her.

But those feelings were growing ever stronger. Was she drawing closer to her father?

"Papa!"

There — just ahead — was it? Had she heard him? Certainly her sense of his presence was stronger than ever, and with it came waves of pain, both physical and emotional. She fought to steady her voice: "Papa — is it you?"

"Ca...Carriden...."

No one else called her Carriden — it *was* him! She reached the exam table holding her father and gasped at the sight of him — she'd almost gone right past him without recognizing him. His right eye had been gouged out, his left leg was gone, and some sort of device was attached to the side of his head. *Something similar to what the Jenregar gave me?* she wondered. *Is that why I was able to perceive him?*

"Oh, Papa," she said.

Tears ran from her father's remaining eye. He had several deep slashes across his face. Dried blood was caked on either side of his mouth. But as he looked up at her, he managed a smile, and in that instant, Carrie felt more waves of emotion — this time a sense of unrestrained love and deep affection. *Is this how Papa feels when he sees me?* Carrie wondered.

Gilberto Molina's voice was strained, soft. "It's been too long since we've spoken."

Carrie ran her fingers down his face, as gently as she could. *The slightest touch could be excruciating for him*, she thought. "I got to you as quickly as I...yes, you're right. It's been too long. And this is *not* the time to have this conversation. I've got to get you out of here!"

Her father could barely manage to shake his head. "No, Carriden, I am past saving."

Carrie felt tears running down her cheeks. She grabbed at the straps binding her father to the table. "Don't say that!"

"Carriden, they've done...terrible things to me."

Carrie kept pulling at the straps, wishing she could've brought a knife or even the simplest tool with her. "I'll get you out of here, Papa — I've *got* to."

"It's *you* who must leave, Carriden. Tell the world the evil things they're doing in here."

Carrie let go of the straps and cupped her father's face in her hands. "Oh, Papa, you're so handsome — the most handsome man in the world. I could never let such a man go."

"And my Carriden — still beautiful despite making yourself into some sort of half-fish."

The same perception that had transmitted her father's love for her now broadcast his frustration and beneath that, anger. Carrie clasped her hands over her ears and told her father, "Even now, we have this argument. Just once I'd like you to catch a glimpse of me and watch your mouth widen into a fantastic grin."

"I do that constantly when I'm with you, Carriden!"

"I wish you could just take me into your arms and tell me you love me and not feel you have to make a comment against me."

Carrie's father said, "This is why we haven't spoken in so long. Anything I tell you, Carriden, I say out of love."

"I'm sorry, Papa, this isn't the time or the place — it *isn't!*" Carrie leaned forward and kissed her father's ravaged face. "And I know how much you love me — I've always known it, but this thing you see on my head lets me feel everything you do."

"And I, as well!" Gilberto Molina said. "I didn't realize —

"

"Oh, Papa, then you know — you *know* — how much I love you."

"I *do* know," he said. "I knew already. You're all I have left. Your mother's been gone for so many years...And Adriana just last year...you're all *I* have left, too."

"Are you sure, Papa? I promised a woman named Luisa I'd bring her back to you."

"Oh, Carriden — I didn't want you to know. I was afraid you'd think I wasn't respecting your mother."

"Never, Papa — I'm happy for you."

"When you see her — give her a kiss for me."

"You can give it to her yourself — you're coming with me!"

"Carriden, no. You don't understand."

"What's to understand? I'll find a way — "

"These straps — no, don't look! They're all that's keeping me together. Free me, and I'll...spill out, and bleed out, in minutes."

"Oh, Papa, what'll I do? I can't stand to see you like this."

"And you shouldn't. Stand up straight. Give yourself the dignity you deserve."

Carrie stood straight, saying, "Yes, sir."

"I know we never say the words we should, Carriden. We never express our love and concern as we should. We let them hide beneath the nagging and the bitching."

Carrie couldn't help chuckling. "That's us, all right. Especially with Mother not here to stand between us."

"Yes," Gilberto Molina said. "Especially. Oh, Carrie, my life's nearly over."

"Oh, Papa, I — I can't bear to leave you."

Her father looked at her with an intensity she'd never seen, and which the Jenregar tech embedded within her only made even stronger. "You *must*, Carriden." He tilted his head toward three distant Jenregar scouts who were headed toward them. "I think they have their new eyes. They'll see you for what you are!"

"Oh, Papa, one had its own version of *your* eyes, I was sure of it!"

"*Not* the legacy I want. You have important information that I pray will help you destroy these Jenregar bastards once and for all!"

Carrie cupped her father's face in her hands again, even as he said, "Carriden, please go — if you don't, I'll become angry with you. Please don't let that be the last emotion you feel from me! Tell me you love me, and I'll tell you I love you. Those will be the last words between us, the only words with meaning."

Her voice cracked as Carrie said, "I love you, Papa."

Gilberto Molina's mouth trembled, and tears still ran down his face as he said, "Carriden — I love you." Then he stared at her with a determined expression that let Carrie know she was to leave *this instant*.

She tore her gaze away from her father as she rushed out of the Jenregar research lab, back to the reservoir, and dove in. As Carrie waited for her body to adapt before heading into the main pipeline to the outside, she thought, *If I could just get outside in time, convince the Unity to send a force into this mound, maybe my father could —*

No. He couldn't survive. Carrie let herself dip beneath the reservoir's waters and headed toward the pipeline. *He may be dead already, or he may linger a few more hours. The Unity could never get its shit together that quickly.*

Carrie made herself concentrate on her swimming, the rhythmic movement of her arms and legs a comfort to her. Eventually the water gushing through the pipeline spilled out into the small pond about a kilometer from the Jenregar mound. Carrie splashed into the pond, then broke the surface of the water and swam until she could wade onto dry land.

She was barely aware of the water sluicing off her body, of finding her clothing and getting dressed again. Carrie reached her hand toward the Jenregar device on the side of her head, and found touching it wasn't as painful as before, but it still wouldn't budge. She had no awareness at the moment of the presence of any Jenregar. *It must be pretty limited in distance, then. That could be important.*

She headed back toward the center of Madrid without conscious thought. With her pheromonic protocols activated, with most sight-enhanced Jenregar clustered back at the mound, and without the necessity of sneaking Damian and Luisa through the city, Carrie knew she could travel through the city with little chance of being disturbed.

She found herself returning to the rubble of the Metropolis Building. *Not a sign of the Winged Victory*, she thought, *or anything else looking down upon me, providing the comfort it did when I was a child.*

As Carrie began walking back toward the Parque del Oeste, she touched behind her left ear to activate her datalink. "*Dorothy*," she said. "I'm ready for pickup."

"Copy that," the word came back from the shuttle. "Mission accomplished?"

Carrie thought about that for a long moment. She said, "I have a lot of information I hope will let us — " Her father's phrase returned to her: " — destroy these Jenregar bastards once and for all." *And do it without having to nuke my hometown in the process*, she hoped.

"Copy that, and approve the sentiment, Carrie. We'll be there in just a few minutes."

Carrie stood in the park overlooking Madrid, as she had been just hours earlier. From that vantage point, she could see the entirety of the Jenregar mound where she'd abandoned her father. *No*, she thought, *never abandoned. He lives on in my heart.*

As the shuttle *Dorothy* descended toward her, Carrie

realized, *And the best way to honor him is to find a way to defeat the Jenregar.*

JIANG SHUN DISAPPEARED INTO HIS ROOM, AND MOMENTS later, Thomas thought he could hear his father's voice, a low mumble. *The poor man,* Thomas thought. *In there talking to himself.*

Moments later, when Jiang Shun returned, he didn't say anything to Thomas about his brief absence as they prepared a meal of rice, beef with vegetables, and plenty of soup. *I appreciate him letting me help out with the meal this time,* Thomas thought. *But I can't help but wonder what he intends to do. He distrusts these soldiers just as I do. I can't imagine he'll allow them to take over our village.*

But what can he do? We remain helpless against those pulse rifles. One good blast and your component atoms blow away in the wind.

After a little more than an hour, Thomas heard the soldiers' voices in the distance, growing louder by the moment, with odd inflections he hadn't sensed before. Jiang Shun told Thomas, "Place the food on the table, quickly." As Thomas did so, his father said, "Whatever they do, however they act — treat them with the courtesy and respect you would give to any soldier."

As the soldier's voices became louder, Thomas realized why they sounded different than they had earlier: "Baba, they appear drunk."

Jiang Shun waggled a finger at Thomas. "As you would *any soldier.*"

Thomas placed the last item, the large bowl of soup, on

the table. "Yes, Baba," he said, and stood by the stove and waited.

The front door burst open, and the Junior NCO entered, with Bandage, Scar, and Wounded Eye right behind. The Junior NCO had his pulse rifle in one hand and a beer bottle in the other. "We discovered your village's fine hospitality!" he said.

A hospitality enforced at gunpoint, Thomas thought, but didn't dare say. *I don't know what restrains me more, what these soldiers might do to me or what my father might say to me.*

Jiang Shun spread his arms wide, indicating the food spread all along the table. "That hospitality continues, my friends. If you finish this, I have more we can prepare."

Scar, his speech slurred, asked, "Do you have beer?"

Jiang Shun told Thomas, "Get these gentlemen a beer."

The Junior NCO said, "Get all of us *several* beers."

Thomas hesitated, and his father said, "You heard the man. Beers for all!"

Thomas fetched the beers, placed several in the middle of the table among the food, and stood aside. His father caught his eye and nodded almost imperceptibly toward Thomas's bedroom. Thomas moved away from the table, and as he approached his bedroom, he heard his father telling the soldiers, "Anything we have belongs to you. Just let us know what you desire!"

Thomas heard the soldiers' only response as a series of grunts, chewing sounds, and clanking of bottles. He stood quietly in his room as his father joined him, pulled the door shut behind him, then appeared to reconsider and opened it just a crack.

Jiang Shun took Thomas's arm and guided him to the far side of the room. Thomas asked, "With all respect, Baba, I must ask — "

"Anytime a son begins a sentence by saying, 'with all respect,' the next sentence emerges shorn of any respect whatsoever."

Thomas stood straight and bowed. "Then I shall stand here, silently."

Jiang Shun stepped close to Thomas, who could tell his father fought to keep his voice low: "Now you *do* disrespect me, boy! I don't require silence — only that you say things straight out, without qualifying!"

Thomas asked, "Why must you cooperate with these soldiers? You said yourself they do not have our best interests at heart."

"You see their rifles. They command my respect whether they earn it or not."

"Can we not contact the authorities? They cannot approve of these soldiers' actions."

"I *have* tried to contact the authorities," Jiang Shun said.

Over his datalink, in those moments I thought he spent muttering to himself before fixing the meal, Thomas thought. "Their response?"

"I've received none," Jiang Shun said.

Thomas could see the despair revealed in his father's face despite his best attempts to maintain his usual stolid features. He said, "Certainly fighting against these...alien beings...must take all their time."

Jiang Shun's mouth quivered, and Thomas feared his father would cry — but instead, his face broke out into a wide smile that quickly spread to his eyes. "You make it sound as if they have many chores — perhaps mopping the floor or watering some plants."

Thomas couldn't suppress his own grin. "It gladdens my heart to see you smile, Baba."

"Yet those soldiers still sit there eating our food, drinking our beer, and occupying our home."

"When they drink some more, then sleep, Baba — perhaps we can get the drop on them."

"All depends upon the Junior NCO — I fear he may reveal more craftiness than we expect. But I cannot fault your reasoning. Perhaps we will learn more as they sleep than we have while they remain awake."

"How do you intend to do that, Baba?"

"Once a soldier, always a soldier," Jiang Shun said. "We have our ways."

THE NEXT DAY, RAMIRA ESPINOSA WOKE UP IN HER ROOM IN the Hotel Augustina, as well-rested as she'd been in months.

Without opening her eyes, she reached out her hand, unthinking, to the other side of the bed. She found only cold, rumpled sheets, which led her to remember the events of the day before. The Jenregar. Diego dead, torn apart in the jewelry shop alongside his brother Julian.

Those events comforted her more than the lingering ghosts of all the vile acts she'd been forced to perform in this very bed haunted her.

Ramira opened her eyes. She squinted against the glare of sunlight through the room's thin curtains. She rose, parted the curtains, and saw smoke rising near the waterfront. A cargo barge was chugging down the Tapajos River, whose blue waters ran parallel to the silty waters of the Amazon here, but the usual pleasure boats were nowhere to be seen.

Closer to the hotel, Ramira saw no movement on the streets around the shopping malls or tourist attractions. *Now's my chance to get the hell out of here*, she thought. *Find*

Matias, get to the border, get the hell out of this godforsaken country to someplace civilized.

And then what? What should I do with my life after that? I've never had a real job — but of course, in a proper replicator economy I wouldn't need one.

What do people do in such societies?

How can I ever make Matias proud of me — that is, of the person I've become? A whore.

And I can't forget that, no matter how evil Diego was, it couldn't have been good that I smiled when he died.

The room's comm buzzed. *Who the hell could that be?* Ramira wondered, as she felt a sudden chill.

Stop worrying, she told herself. *Diego's dead. And anyone with bad intentions isn't going to ring me up.* She punched the audio-only button. "Hello?"

"Miss Espinosa?"

"Yes?"

"This is Mr. Keyes at the front desk. There seems to be a problem with your bill."

"My bill?"

"Yes — could you come to the front lobby, please, so we may discuss it?"

We're in the middle of an attack by aliens, Ramira thought, *and this guy's worried about the bill?*

Oh, well. I'll go down and tell him whatever he wants to hear, and get the hell out of here.

A community is like a ship; everyone ought to be prepared to take the helm.

   —Henrik Ibsen, *An Enemy of the People*

"I can't believe you won't even consider giving people the option of leaving here for their own safety," Nathan Carlsson said. He ran a hand through his shoulder-length blond hair, then tried to rub some of the tension out of his neck muscles.

Nathan and Supervisor Adam Garrick stood at the boundary line between the "ag" and "tech" sides of Newton Habitat, which was a cylinder four kilometers long and two across. It rotated once a minute, creating a standard one gravity.

Behind Adam, workers kept busy among the neat rows of grapevines that were the basis for some of the finest wine in the system, weeding, hoeing, and building new trellises. Dozens of farmhouses were scattered among the fields, many of which also produced corn or soybeans or other crops that supplemented the more usual replicated fare among the habitat's residents.

Nathan, who was the habitat's Assistant Supervisor, stood before the solid rows of research buildings where scientists and state-of-the-art tech performed much of the system's finest scientific research. Beyond them were the neat rows of homes, some sleek and ultra-modern, made of artificial building materials and filled with tech, others constructed of actual wood from trees force-grown here on the habitat and evoking a simpler time that perhaps had never existed.

The two halves of the habitat curved around until they met again two K overhead.

Adam shook his head as he scratched at one side of his

graying beard, saying, "Anyone can leave anytime they want — you know that."

"This is different," Nathan told him, frustrated at being the assistant who had to explain the obvious to his supposed "superior." "This is a clear threat to the habitat — any of the orbital habitats. We're obvious targets."

"And we've all been left alone so far. The Jenregar has concentrated on establishing as many mounds as it can on Earth's surface."

Nathan said, "But if it changes tactics — and we come under attack — it'll be too late to organize an evacuation. And we have to coordinate with the Unity — it'll have to provide the ships to take us out of here — getting ten thousand people out of harm's way takes time, and planning."

"We have the standard ways to protect ourselves — the meteor deflectors and shields — "

"Adam — a meteor is something we can detect and plan for days or weeks out. If a Jenregar ship wants to attack, it's not going to announce it's on the way."

"I just don't want to create a panic."

"Having an evac plan doesn't create panic. Trying to suck in that last breath of air — while watching your wife or child doing the same thing — *that's* what causes panic."

Adam scratched the other side of his beard. "I'd guess that's what this is all about, isn't it?"

"What do you mean?"

"Tana and Randi."

"And the loved ones of everyone else in this world."

"Very well," Adam said. "Make your plans. But do it quietly." He turned and walked toward the vineyards.

Nathan let out a deep breath. *I'm glad I convinced him*, he thought. *Especially since I was going to do it anyway.*

Chapter 5

Mike and Jeremy got out of the capsule and entered Union Station's Great Hall. Mike made his way down the marble steps that had felt the tread of so many feet through countless decades that smooth grooves had been worn into them. He found his eyes drawn to the five-story atrium ceiling, marveling that he had more of a sense of wide-open spaces here than he had out in the open air.

Mike spotted a large screen off to one side that indicated upcoming departures. He went there, Jeremy right behind him, and scanned the listings.

Next to most of the departures for anywhere in Europe was the indication: POSTPONED. Others went right for CANCELLED.

"Dammit," Mike said.

"What do we do now?" Jeremy asked. "This is ridiculous that we can't get to Brussels."

"It's just like Lt. Nyquist was saying. The Jenregar has disrupted a lot of routes. Let's look at something non-direct. See — if we head west instead of east, we can get to California, up through Alaska and Siberia, and go that way."

"The long way around?"

"We do what we gotta do," Mike said.

What's too hard for a man must be worth looking
into.

— Kenyan proverb

IN ALL OF MY 92 YEARS, KAMAU KIMATHI THOUGHT AS HE
watched a Jenregar mound taking shape in the middle of
the city he adored, *I've never felt so helpless.*

His gaze flicked from one image to another on the giant
holoscreen in the city of Nairobi's command center as the
mound spread rapidly across the Uhuru Gardens.

He watched in fury as the mound moved inexorably
across the public park, knocking down trees and tearing
down monuments to Kenyan freedom that featured soaring
towers, clasping hands, and a dove of peace. *My training in
biological systems*, he thought, *tells me it could be using the very
materials of the trees and structures it's enveloping to provide the
material to grow larger. And it's incredibly efficient — spreading
out at nearly the rate a Human could walk.*

Dozens of city managers surrounded Kamau, each of
them gathering information over their datalinks or at
computer consoles, each tackling a different aspect of the
emergency. *But this emergency is much more than city
managers or a county governor such as myself can tackle. We
need help from the nation, even from the Earth Unity itself.*

Which is why he touched behind his left ear again, saying over his datalink, "This is Nairobi County Governor Kamau Kimathi to Earth Unity Headquarters." *They* have *to answer this time*, he thought. *The city may not survive otherwise.*

Over his link, he heard, "This is Neriah Fulton. How can I help you?"

"Ms. Fulton, we have a Jenregar mound forming in the middle of Nairobi. The Kenyan military is mobilizing, but it could be too late — what can the Unity — "

"Governor Kimathi, we have mounds forming over Santiago, Tijuana, Zhengzhou, China, and many other places. The Unity's concentrating on trying to intercept their ships as they approach."

"So we are on our own down here, that's what you're telling us?"

"We want to try to help with evacuations, but we just don't have the ships to spare right now."

"How can such a thing happen?" Kamau demanded. "Such an attack — "

"Governor Kimathi, I don't want to be rude. But I've got three more mayors, five city managers, and about a dozen other city or national leaders trying to contact me. I'll let you know more when I can."

"Ms. Fulton — " Kimathi began, but she was gone. A glance at the various screens before him, and he saw the mound was still spreading outward as well as growing upward. *It's like watching a tsunami come ashore*, Kamau thought, *except it's spreading out in all directions from that central point. It'll be only a matter of minutes before it reaches office buildings and homes.*

So how does *a city governor waiting on military resources and without help from the heavens manage to repel an alien invasion?*

And is there any possibility of somehow negotiating with these beings?

NATHAN CARLSSON FELT THE TENSION FLOW FROM HIS BODY AS he finished replicating supper — fermented herring with boiled potatoes and salad — placed all the dishes on the table, and sat with his 15-year-old daughter Randi. Beyond the curtained windows on one side of the dining room, the arbitrary "daylight" was beginning to fade; late suppers were often the rule rather than the exception in their household.

Nathan's wife Tana came into the dining room with the drinks, took one look at Nathan, placed the drinks on the table, and began rubbing his shoulders.

Nathan felt like purring. "This is why I married you," he told Tana. He wagged a finger at Randi. "You can quit rolling your eyes, young lady."

"I'll quit rolling my eyes when my parents stop acting like...like..."

Tana said, "Like what? Two people who love one another?" She gave Nathan's shoulders a final pat and sat across from him.

More eye rolling from Randi, but applying herself to her meal quickly silenced her. *It's like she has a mental button marked "ignore,"* Nathan thought. He told Tana, "I hope things were less hectic at the hospital than they were in my office today." Tana was an emergency physician at the Newton Habitat Hospital.

Tana paused with a forkful of herring halfway to her mouth. "Probably not — thanks to you."

"To *me*? What'd I do?"

"Set that evac plan into motion. Do you realize how complex an undertaking it would be to get a couple hundred patients, many of them non-ambulatory, in position to leave this habitat at a moment's notice?"

"I can't imagine there wasn't such a plan in place to begin with."

Tana said, "There is — but it assumes a meteor or asteroid chunk's on the way and it's too big to stop."

"In other words, there's time to react."

"Exactly."

"It's the same lack of planning I've seen everywhere on this habitat."

Tana stirred potatoes around, not looking at Nathan. "I knew you should've run for supervisor last year."

"Then I'd be hearing how I was never home for you or Randi."

At the sound of her name, Randi looked up for an instant. Her eyes searched the room. Then she returned to her meal. Nathan couldn't help grinning. *Teenagers*, he thought. He told Tana, "Listen, honey, I'm going to be working long enough hours as it is. I know you will, too. All we can do is hope that we don't ever need these evac plans."

Randi said, "*Adults*. You do all this work for something that may never happen."

"Better that," Nathan said, "than the other way around."

Later that night, in the darkness of their bedroom, as Nathan was undressing, Tana, naked, came up from behind him, wrapped her arms around him, and said, "Don't get out the P.Js just yet. Right into bed with you."

"Well...aren't you tired?"

Tana's grip on his loosened. "Are you?"

Nathan turned within her embrace. "Not *that* tired."

"You're sure?"

Nathan swept his wife up into his arms and, despite himself, emitted a quick groan before placing her on the bed. Tana struck his shoulder playfully. "I saw that!" she said. "And it isn't so dark in here that I couldn't see how wide your eyes got when you picked me up!"

"I don't think you're any heavier — "

"Liar!"

" — I'm just older." He placed a hand on his lower back and tried not to let Tana see him limp as he went around to the other side of the bed.

As he slipped beneath the covers, Tana said in a mischievous voice, "You *are* kinda old."

"I'll show you old," Nathan said, reaching for her. Another twinge in his back. "Oh — maybe not." He settled onto the bed.

"Oh, fine," Tana said, straddling him. "I'll just have to navigate."

RAMIRA ESPINOSA COULD BARELY KEEP HERSELF FROM stamping her feet in frustration as she stood in the lobby of the Hotel Augustina. "What do you mean, I can't leave the city until I've paid my bill?"

The desk clerk was a man in his fifties. His name tag identified him as Tremayne Keyes. Beneath his receding hair, and behind his mustache, his expression told Ramira he'd dealt with too many people just like her. "We're a market economy in this city, and in this country."

"My uh...friend was paying the bills," Ramira said, as she

twisted her features into what she hoped was a reasonable facsimile of grief. "The Jenregar killed him."

"So very unfortunate," Keyes said. "And as we suspected. At the moment he died, our AI was informed, and when we examined your financial situation -- well, it wasn't promising."

"My financial situation is that I grew up in a small village, which is only a semi-market economy. I've never had to deal with any of this. I want to go to Brazil."

"Of course," Mr. Keyes said. "Very colorful there, replicators making your food and your homes and your dogs -- "

"They can't create animals."

"Perhaps a job brought you here to the Confederation?"

"My friend brought me here."

"But you do have a job?"

Ramira said, "I don't...any more."

"Let's not be ashamed of our words, Ms. Espinosa. I know your...friend...brought you down here to be a sex worker."

"A whore, you mean."

"Oh, goodness, Ms. Espinosa, moderation in all things, including our words. All the same, will you use your skills to obtain some money to pay your bill?"

"*My* bill? Diego brought me here."

Mr. Keyes squinted at the comp display before him. "Yes, Mr. Diego Fernandez. Nice man."

"Nice men don't enslave women to become prostitutes."

Mr. Keyes's eyebrows narrowed sympathetically. "Neither do they become deceased without making plans ahead of time to pay their bill. Still, it must be paid. Your name is on the register, alongside Mr. Fernandez's. You share the responsibility."

"You can't keep me here."

"Actually, we can. Even in such an emergency as we now face, it's a simple task for the AI or Human at any border crossing to learn you haven't taken care of your responsibilities. Most likely anyone trying to cross the border will need the assistance of local authorities. Who do you think will receive such help? Why, it is those who pay."

"Pay bribes, most likely," Ramira said.

"Now, now. More bad thoughts, which lead us nowhere."

"This is all so new to me. I've never actually lived in a pure market economy before."

"Many people have not. But those who do pay their bills."

"Certainly other people have found themselves in this position. What have they done?"

"Found jobs and paid their bills."

"And gotten the hell out of here as quickly as they could?"

"No doubt, Ms. Espinosa."

"So how do I find a job?"

Mr. Keyes leaned forward. "I'm sure you've handled far more difficult assignments on behalf of Mr. Fernandez," he said.

Ramira drew herself up to her full height, cursing the couple of centimeters she fell short compared to Mr. Keyes. "I'll be in my room, then, trying to make contacts." She started across the lobby to the lift.

"The meter's ticking," Mr. Keyes said.

But she didn't make it to the lift. Another woman, dark-skinned, with round cheekbones and a too-perfect smile, approached her. "I'm here to help you," she said.

Ramira stared at her skeptically. "Just like that?"

"Just like that. I was notified of your situation the same

moment the hotel was." She reached out to shake Ramira's hand. "I'm Miyanda Mukela. Why don't we head to the bar instead of your room?"

Ramira grinned. "I suppose you're paying?"

Miyanda shrugged. "I "guess I'll have to."

Chapter 6

The call over Nathan Carlsson's datalink came in the middle of the night, from a voice so harried that he sat straight up in bed. It was Reiko Nylund, a technician on duty in the habitat's main control room. "Several Unity and Jenregar ships are fighting it out in orbit — about ten thousand K from our position."

"Could they be heading our way?" Nathan asked as Tana roused herself next to him.

"Quite likely," Reiko said.

"I'll be right there. Make sure to wake Supervisor Garrick."

"He was the first call." Reiko broke the link.

"What's wrong?" Tana asked.

"A battle between the Jenregar and our own ships," Nathan said as he got out of bed and began dressing.

"Heading this way, of course."

"Maybe."

Tana eased herself out of bed. "I'm heading in to the hospital."

"My first instinct is to tell you not to worry — that all this was just a precaution."

"And your second thought — "

"That it's a good idea you're going in. I'll let Randi know — "

Their daughter's voice came from the hallway. "Let Randi know what?"

Nathan opened the door and their daughter was standing there, eyes barely open, hair mussed, arms wrapped around her pillow — a habit from childhood. "You guys aren't very quiet, you know."

Nathan pulled the pillow aside and embraced his daughter. He told her why he and Tana were leaving, and said, "We'll be back soon, I hope."

Randi held Nathan tighter than anytime in recent memory. "I hope so too, Daddy."

Moments later, Nathan boarded a tram for the control facility. He sat quietly, forced his breathing to calm, and made a conscious effort to set familial concerns aside. He thought, *I'll have enough to deal with just thinking about the Jenregar, my responsibilities toward everyone in the habitat, and whether Adam Garrick can take this seriously now.*

THE SHUTTLE *DOROTHY* ARCED NORTHWARD THE 1300 kilometers between Madrid and Brussels, which held the headquarters of the Earth Unity. Carrie marveled at the skills of the pilot, who barely kept the shuttle 150 meters off the deck the entire time — the better not to become the target of Jenregar interceptors.

To Carrie's surprise, *Dorothy* sat down in a grassy area of Luxembourg Square, next to the stately old European

Parliament Building that was now Unity HQ. As she stepped down from the shuttle, to the stares of people walking among the many buildings of the complex, a woman stepped up to Carrie and shook her hand. "I'm Neriah Fulton," the woman said. "I'll be debriefing you."

"I'm ready," Carrie said. "Anything we can do against these bastards, I want to help."

As they advanced toward Unity HQ, Neriah said, "It sounds personal for you."

"I had to abandon my father in a Jenregar mound. He was being tortured when I left him."

Neriah took Carrie's arm. "Oh, you poor dear! Let's get you inside — do you need some time alone before the debrief?"

"No! I'm here to work against the Jenregar — to help with anything I can do to kill as many of them as possible."

"I'll see if we can arrange that," Neriah said, and took Carrie to quarters that had already been set up for her in the basement of Unity HQ. They were basic, just a bed, couch, and a couple of chairs in the main room, along with a small kitchen and bath. "We've kept the surface features of the building the same for historical reasons," Neriah explained. "But it extends a lot farther underground than you may think."

When Neriah started to show Carrie how to activate the wall holo, thought, Carrie said, "I know what you're doing."

Neriah stopped in mid-demonstration. "And what might that be?"

"You're purposely letting me know about mundane things for a these few moments — before we start talking about the Jenregar. About my father's death. About how to kill as many Jenregar as we can."

Neriah extended a hand toward one of the chairs.

When Carrie sat, Neriah sat across from her. "I see you're even tougher than I thought. Well, a lot of us are finding strength we never knew we had. I just spoke to the county governor in Nairobi, for instance. He was looking for help, and I couldn't give it to him. But even over the datalink, I could tell how determined he was. I think he'll do well. But enough of that — tell me all you know about the Jenregar."

Carrie explained how she'd infiltrated the Jenregar mound in Madrid and rescued Damian Rivera and Luisa Torres. Neriah said, "They got here ahead of you. I've been debriefing them, as well."

"I'm glad to hear that. With enough information, maybe we can find out enough about the Jenregar to find a weakness we can exploit." Carrie described how she'd returned to the mound, allowed herself to be taken by the Jenregar, and how she'd had a device implanted within her head that allowed her to perceive the Jenregar collective consciousness.

"They have a sense of self-worth that is indestructible," Carrie said. "The Jenregar cannot be reasoned with because they do not reason. They simply *are*."

"So, any attempts at negotiation would be fruitless."

"The Jenregar are closer to a force of nature than what we consider to be sentient beings. You don't negotiate with a hurricane. You get out of its way or you try to deflect it."

Neriah said, softly, "But we want to do more than that with the Jenregar."

"We *have* to do more. Or Humanity may not survive. At least not on Earth."

"What can we do?"

"They can be made to back off from a goal — Mike Christopher learned that on Korolev Habitat."

"He's on his way here, you know. With a man he rescued from a Jenregar ship — fellow named Jeremy Sheffield."

"Were they torturing that man?"

"About to experiment on him, it seems. Mike got him away just in time." Neriah indicated the Jenregar implant still embedded on the left side of Carrie's forehead. "I see they got to you, too. Immediately after we finish here, I've got people who can start to work on getting that thing off of you."

"It's given me some unusual abilities. But I'd just as soon do without them."

"We have to hope it'll give us some insight into how they interact."

Carrie said, "We have to disrupt their society — something more than just killing a queen in a particular hive. Do that, and another Jenregar individual becomes the queen. They have a very efficient line of succession that means they're never without leadership."

"I understand they're trying to develop their sense of sight — make it more like Human perception."

"Which really means they're rewiring their minds — whether those of individuals or the group mind. Their problem isn't just how well they see — it's how well they interpret what they see."

"Which means," Neriah said, "it's still a weakness we can exploit."

"I hope so. And by exploit, I mean kill them. Kill them all."

"Or at least force them off the planet."

"*No*," Carrie said. "I mean kill every single goddam one of them. All of them on this planet, then we find their homeworld and kill all of them there, too."

"That...may be overreaching. Not to mention..."

"Immoral?" Carrie looked directly at Neriah, to make her intentions plain. "I can live with that."

Neriah said, "We have someone for you to work with. He's probably one of the best in the world when it comes to figuring things about about biological systems. I suspect he could use your help — your insight into the Jenregar"

"Send me to him!"

"I will — I just spoke of him, in fact. But given what I found when I looked into his background, you may find he has different goals from you."

As Carrie listened to Neriah's description of the Nairobi County Governor Kamau Kimathi, she wondered if she'd be able to hold her anger in check enough to work with this man.

Kamau Kimathi, still monitoring the situation in Nairobi's command center, turned to Masika Bilali, one of his city managers, just as she ended a datalink call in obvious frustration. She looked up at Kamau and said, "I've not had any more luck with the Unity than you did. I had some backchannel resources — "

"Never mind about them now," Kamau told her. "Commandeer every public vehicle you can. Get them programmed to head toward the area of the mound. Get a warning out over every datalink channel, and to all the instant news media — everyone should leave the city as quickly as possible, and we're providing transport to anyone who needs it."

"Done," Masika said, and turned away from him, touching behind her ear to get that process started.

Kamau looked at one of the holo feeds before him,

which showed the mound from ground level. The mound approached in a way that seemed almost leisurely, blotted out the sun, and then the camera shot tilted abruptly and was cut off.

Looking at a wider shot, Kamau saw people running from the Uhuru Memorial Park where the mound had first begun to grow. Local police were arriving, as well, stopping their silent electric cars well away from the mound and aiming pulse rifles.

They fired, but to no effect.

Then an exit formed in the side of the mound and Jenregar individuals began marching out. They had their own weapons, and returned fire. Police officers fell, some of them vaporized by the Jenregar bolts, others only wounded.

More Jenregar exited, this time by the hundreds. Kamau, horrified, turned to Masika: "Get the police on the line — they've got to tell those officers to pull back!"

But for some of those officers, it was too late — the Jenregar closed in on them, and before most of them could retreat, the mass of Jenregar fighters was upon them, stinging one officer after another, their acid doing its deadly work.

Soon all the officers near the still-expanding mound were lying still, their bodies slowly dissolving — slowly enough, in fact, that within the next minute the mound overtook them. *I'll bet it's absorbing their bodies*, Kamau thought in disgust, *making them part of itself.*

He asked Masika, "How are we doing with the evacuation plan?"

"All the city's trolleys are moving in as close as they can, and the light rail. I've even diverted a maglev from the Kampala-Mogadishu run — it's holding here to get as many people on board as possible."

"And is everyone getting the word to evacuate?"

"As far as we know. But I'm afraid someone's working inside one of these offices and hasn't heard anything — or is playing around in one of the outer areas of the Memorial Park and isn't accessing their newsnet."

"A terrible fact we will just have to accept, Masika."

"I've been looking into how these mounds are growing in other cities. Most of them take over a large circular area downtown and start sending out Jenregar fighters."

"So the entire city comes under attack?"

"Not just yet," Masika said. "The fighters seem to create a perimeter circling the mound — the equivalent of several blocks. After that, they'll go out on scouting excursions or maybe probe for weaknesses in any military units around them."

"So after this initial expansion, we may be safe for awhile."

"As safe as we might be living in a city whose center has been destroyed — a city occupied by acid-injecting aliens."

"The important part," Kamau said, "is that we may have some breathing room here soon. We will have little time to mourn our dead — and we must must work as we never have before to help the living."

Nathan Carlsson arrived in the midst of a chaotic scene in Newton Habitat's main control room. It was organized much like a starcraft's bridge, complete with artificial grav since it was located at the stationary center of the "north" hub of the rotating habitat, which would otherwise be a zero-G area. The front of the room was dominated by control panels and readouts. At the rear was a window overlooking the cylinder of the habitat. Flatscreens and holos also showed scenes from the interior of the habitat as well as the space around it. On one such screen, Nathan saw magnified images of Unity and Jenregar craft maneuvering for advantage as each tried to blow the other out of orbit.

Nathan went right to Adam Garrick, who was standing in front of a sensor readout at one end of the room. Technician Reiko Nylund, who'd called Nathan earlier, was working the controls. "What's the latest?" Nathan asked.

Adam said, "This firefight is lasting longer than anyone expected. My understanding of orbital mechanics is limited, but I know it takes a lot of energy to keep reversing course to make one firing run after another."

"But they're still getting closer?"

Reiko spoke up: "Just about five thousand K right now."

Nathan asked Adam, "Should we call an alert?"

Adam rubbed his chin for a moment, said, "I suppose we could. I'd hate to interrupt a lot of people's sleep cycle if it turns out there isn't any danger."

"Adam, we have to look at worst case scenarios here. I'd rather disturb everyone's sleep needlessly a hundred times than fail one time to warn them of a real threat."

"I suppose you're right. Do it however you think best."

Nathan turned to Reiko. "We'll make the message simple. 'Possible Jenregar incursion imminent. Evacuation possible. Stand by for instructions."

Reiko nodded and said, "I'll send that out over everyone's datalinks, their personal comms, and into every A.I in our little world here."

"Oh, and turn on the lights. Let's make it daylight."

"Is that wise?" Adam asked. "We've never done that before. It might confuse people."

"The part about not having done it before will let everyone know the seriousness of what's going on. And if we have to evacuate, better to do it in daylight."

"I suppose you're right, Nathan. But I so wish this wasn't necessary."

That's been our problem, Nathan thought. *Wishing instead of planning.*

RAMIRA ESPINOSA SAT IN THE DARKENED BAR GRASPING A Queensland Fourex beer. *The galaxy and nebula themes on the walls are pretty irritating*, she thought. *But enough beers will take care of that.* She said to Miyanda, "So what's your job?"

Miyanda's drink was soda water with lime. "I'm a rescuer."

"You rescue people like me dumb enough to get stuck in this city?"

"You're certainly not dumb, Ramira. I've seen your records."

Ramira felt dumbfounded and embarrassed. "There are records about me?"

"Prostitution is legal and regulated here. Mr. Fernandez kept very detailed records of your activities under his employment."

Ramira laughed. "You call being made to fuck or blow any stranger who walks through a doorway 'employment?'"

Miyanda placed a hand on Ramira's arm. "I'm sorry. I realize our system doesn't always work as it should. Mr. Fernandez had to pay taxes on the income you...generated for him, and so the government monitors that pretty well. It doesn't do as good a job when it comes to inspecting conditions for sex workers."

"So now you have to find me a job."

"That's the idea. These things happen, and we don't want the Confederation to get a bad name."

"You want a good name? Just let me leave."

"I'm afraid it's not that easy, Ramira. Then people would come here and eat our food and live in our hotels and then leave without paying for anything."

"That's not such a bad life, you know. Much of the Earth lives that way."

"Much of Earth -- beggin' your pardon -- is made up of whiners who don't know what it's like to have to work and virtheads who don't even know what it's like to live in reality. You can't just walk away from your job anytime with no economic consequences."

"I'm not going to become a whore again."

"You really shouldn't use that word, Ramira. It devalues the work you did."

"I *want* to devalue that work. I'm sorry that doesn't fit in with your pie-in-the-sky ideas of what being a 'sex worker,' as you put it, is all about."

"I see."

"I was brought here under false pretenses. Diego would beat me if I hesitated to do what he wanted. I'd like to call him a son-of-a-bitch, but that would be an insult to bitches. My only regret is that he's not right here in front of me, with my fingers around his throat and my knee against his balls."

Miyanda said, "Lady, remind me not to get on your bad side. Well, at least I have somewhere to take you. One of the few places still hiring right now. Though the transportation getting there isn't as glamorous as you may be used to."

Eventually the Junior NCO, Scar, and Bandage settled into bed in various rooms of the house, each of them with his or her rifle close at hand; Thomas couldn't help noticing that the Junior NCO laid himself down while grasping his weapon to his chest. *Does he keep it close as protection against us or against the other soldiers?*

Perhaps a bit of both.

Thomas felt surprised that the soldiers hadn't throw him or his father out of their respective bedrooms. And he found himself wondering — *Where did Wounded Eye go to?*

He received his answer when he stepped outside for a breath of fresh air before heading to bed. Wounded Eye stood just outside the house, keeping guard; presumably he and the other soldiers would trade watches throughout the night. *Do they expect him to sound the alarm if the Jenregar masses come roaring over the next hill?* Thomas wondered.

Wounded Eye turned abruptly at the sound of Thomas stepping onto the wooden porch, pulse rifle at the ready. Thomas expected a threatening comment, but Wounded Eye merely grunted, lowered his weapon, and looked away from Thomas.

Movement in the northern skies attracted Thomas's attention as several stars moved in formation — *A meteor shower?* he wondered.

But no — a couple of those stars *changed course* and went off in radically different directions. *Not meteors*, Thomas realized — *spaceships, perhaps even starships.*

As he watched, five or six of those craft wheeled and spun about one another, executing movements he knew the Human body could never withstand. *Except such ships have inertial dampening fields*, Thomas thought. *They can use the power of gravity itself to protect their crews from the extreme forces involved.*

Why can't they use such powers to save us from the Jenregar?

Thomas saw that one star among those that appeared to be battling one another remained stationary. *One of the orbital habitats?* he wondered. *It would seem to be in the right portion of the sky.*

Another realization came: *Perhaps the very battle to save us appears right over my head.*

<hr>

Nathan Carlsson tried to keep his attention focused on a dozen monitors at once in Newton Habitat's control room, as the battle among Unity and Jenregar craft drew closer. There, not a thousand K distant — energy bolts thrust back and forth, visible in the vacuum of space only if they struck their targets.

And many of them were striking their targets, both Human and Jenregar.

On other monitors, Nathan could see plenty of activity within the habitat itself. People had begun to gather in groups outside their homes and in the city square. The resolution was good enough that he could see the worry in their faces, the uncertainty.

Nathan told Adam, "We've got to *do* something. We can't just let people stand around and wonder what's going to happen."

Adam spoke with an edge in his voice that Nathan had never heard before. "What would you have me do? I can't turn the Jenregar away on my own."

Nathan fought to keep the exasperation he felt out of his voice: "No, but you can *lead*! Give these people something to do — figure out the order in which we'll evacuate people, let them volunteer at the hospital, anything! We're hopelessly behind in our planning as it is!"

Adam thought for a minute, rubbing his beard, then turned abruptly to Nathan and said, "I've about had enough of your second-guessing me. I think I'd like to — "

After a few moments, Thomas witnessed the sight of one of the stars blooming brightly for an instant, then fading once again to its previous illumination. *A Jenregar craft, I hope.*

The habitat shuddered beneath their feet, and on one of the monitors, Nathan saw an energy bolt pierce their world's skin at an angle inside the tech area and exit out the ag side. Nathan's heart jumped as he saw the remains of several buildings — and the bodies of several people! — sucked out of the hole on the tech side. The ag side saw more people, several rows of crops, and at least one farmhouse disappear.

"Oh my God!" Adam exclaimed, as he slapped his hands onto the side of his head.

"WARNING — HULL BREACH," came the alert from the habitat's comp.

Nathan turned to Reiko, who was at the main control panel, and told her. "Confirm that the repair nanotech is online and working."

Reiko punched some controls, reported, "It is — but it's going to take several minutes to get even a basic seal on both those holes." On the monitors, Nathan could see people near either of the breaches holding on \to corners of buildings, onto one another, trying not to be pulled into the holes.

Adam said to Reiko, "We've got to get hold of anyone working outside the habitat — can they rescue anyone who's gone out those holes?"

Nathan told Reiko, "Forget that — anyone not killed by the explosive decompression is heading away from here too quickly to grab before they asphyxiate or freeze."

Adam grabbed Nathan's arm. "You heartless bastard!"

Nathan jerked his arm away. "We should've planned for this sooner!"

"Gentlemen," Reiko said. "Might I suggest we concentrate on the actual disaster for now?"

Nathan made a final glare at Adam, then said, "You're right. How's the repair job going?"

Reiko indicated a monitor showing a closeup view of the damage in the ag sector. The outer skin of the habitat was starting, painfully slowly, to close up, with inner layers starting to mend themselves as well. The jagged ends of pipes and circuitry were also extending their reach to "heal" the breach and re-establish life support, water, and other services.

Nathan glanced at several other screens. "It looks like no one's in danger of being sucked out anymore."

"That's good," Adam said, "But we have to have a lot of injured."

"I'll get hold of Tana. She can tell us how many injured are coming into the hospital, and how we can help her."

But before Nathan could touch behind his ear to activate his datalink, the control room went dark — no internal lights, no monitors, not even backup systems — and the grav went out, as well. Nathan's stomach churned as his feet left the floor — he wasn't really a spacer and his body wasn't accustomed to zero-G.

He made his way toward an actual window at the back of the control room, bumping into someone — "Excuse me!" — and looked out into the same utter darkness.

"Oh, shit," he said. "Now what?"

THOMAS WAITED A FEW MOMENTS MORE, AND EVENTUALLY THE remaining moving stars settled into a straight-line path and descended as one toward the western horizon. The single stationary star remained, but Thomas could swear it seemed dimmer.

NATHAN TURNED HIS BACK ON THE WINDOW AND RAISED HIS voice: "Reiko — where are you?"

"Right here!" came her voice from a position to his right.

"Why the hell are all the lights out? And what about other systems?"

"The answer to both is 'I don't know.' And without any systems running at all, I don't know how to find out."

"We're supposed to have backups to the backups!"

"And there's not a one of them working!"

Nathan said, "I've got to get down there — see about the hospital."

"Go ahead," Reiko said. "I've got things here, if we can get the power back."

"What do you mean?" Adam said. "You can't just abandon your post here."

Nathan felt his way toward the seldom-used stairwell at

one side of the control room. "What am I abandoning? The control room's useless. For some reason, we don't even have flashlights here! Explain that! Down there, I can at least try to make myself useful."

"You're just trying to get to your family!"

"Hell, yes! Do you think I'm going to apologize for that?"

"Wait!" Adam insisted, but Nathan was already feeling his way down the dark stairwell. Normally the artificial grav from the control room continued part of the way down the stairs, but not now. He pulled himself down awkwardly, feet first, using the railing on the side of the stairwell. *I know most spacers would glide smoothly down head-first,* Nathan thought, *but I'm no spacer. And if the grav comes back on while I'm in the stairwell, I don't want my head breaking my fall.*

Without thinking, he touched behind his left ear to activate his datalink. Nothing. *Stupid,* he thought. *There's nothing to relay the signal.*

But I have to find out whether Tana and Randi are all right. The energy bolt didn't hit close to the hospital or to home, but still —

As Nathan continued down the long stairwell, the habitat's "natural" grav generated by its spinning grew stronger, until it reached a full G as he exited onto the floor of the cylinder. *Good,* he thought. *Some people have lights going.* He'd exited on the tech side, and saw the back-and-forth of flashlights as people made their way down the street, and inside several homes people had work lights going.

Thank goodness the hospital's not half a K away, Nathan thought. *I'll head there first — maybe Randi went there, too.* As he proceeded cautiously down the street, though, he had to wonder how extensive this power failure was. *If the lights are out, does that imply all the hospital's tech is out, as well? People dying because the systems keeping their bodies functioning have been disabled?*

And what about the habitat itself? Two large holes punched in its side, and then the power's out? How far did repairs get while the power was still going?

How much air have we lost? What else might happen that could turn this entire cylinder into a death trap?

I can't know the answers to any of those questions. All I can do is walk faster.

IMMEDIATELY OUTSIDE THE FRONT DOOR OF THE HOTEL Angelina stood a bicycle rack. Miyanda lifted a bike from that rack and indicated another one to Ramira. "I had this one dropped off for you. You do know how to ride a bike, don't you?"

"*Please*," Ramira said. "You're not seeing me at my best. I can cope with most situations."

"Fine," Miyanda said as she hopped onto her bike and rode toward the eastern part of the city. Ramira managed to keep up without wobbling too much.

As they left the hotel district and entered a neighborhood devoted to small businesses and governmental offices, Ramira couldn't help but think, *This'll be easy. Here's a floral shop, an emotion shaper's, a clinic -- there has to be something I can do.*

On the horizon, however, loomed the Jenregar mound at the center of Santarem. Ramira couldn't figure out why, on the one hand, the Jenregar didn't seem to be making any more incursions into the rest of the city and, on the other hand, Human authorities didn't seem to be doing anything to defeat them.

Miyanda stopped in front of an art gallery called Temporal Expressions, which featured a storefront with everything from incredibly detailed holos to time sculptures. It was small, looked old, but seemed to have a prime location here in the tourist area, not to mention an excellent view of the Tapajos River, which was just a couple of blocks over. "I've placed a number of clients here before," she said.

Ramira asked, "Just how many people get stranded in this city?"

"More than you'd think. In fact, I've others to see this morning. The manager and owner at Temporal Expressions is Esteban Navarro. You should get along with him quite well."

"What about the bike?"

"There's the rack. No one will take it. You've seen how strict we are with the law here."

"Even during a Jenregar attack?"

"Well — you've got a point, there. We'll hope for the best."

"Fine," Ramira muttered. "It's not my bike, after all. Wish me luck."

"You won't need it." A wave, and Miyanda continued eastward.

As Ramira entered the gallery, a tinkling bell announced her presence. The building was only about five meters across, but went back farther than she'd realized at first. A small figure of a discus thrower on a pedestal in the middle of the room caught her eye. It was a time sculpture, made of pliable porcelain that twisted its upper body backwards, little muscles straining in its legs, arms, and torso, then extended its arms, twisted forward again, and froze at the instant it would have made the throw, its feet never actually lifting off the pedestal. Then the thrower moved back to its former position and the sequence began again. The pedestal identified it as "Persistence."

"Do you like it?" The voice from behind startled Ramira. It belonged to a tall, thin man, probably in his seventies, who was stepping into the room, a cane helping with his slow gait.

She recovered quickly enough to respond, "Yes. Very much."

"I'm Esteban Navarro, and I run this place. How may I help you?"

"I'm Ramira Espinosa, Mr. Navarro, and I'm not a customer. I'm looking for a job."

Mr. Navarro placed both hands on top of his cane and leaned forward for a closer look at her. "I bet Miyanda sent you here." He leaned to one side to look past Ramira and through his front window. "Yep! Recognize those cheap city bikes anywhere."

Ramira said tentatively, "She told me she's placed people with you before."

"I notice she didn't stick around for introductions."

"She said -- "

"She had another client, I know. There's always another client. What can you do?"

"Well, I guess you'd say I'm good with people. Know how to please them. How to react to someone's mood."

"Hmm! And if my grandmother had a blue tongue, she'd be a lizard."

Ramira decided to let that phrase just flow right past.

Mr. Navarro indicated a small counter to one side of the room. "Could you stand there and greet people when they come in?"

"I can do that."

"Great -- first, let's make you familiar with some of my wares." He indicated the pliable porcelain discus thrower. "This is a recent Solheim."

"A name I actually recognize," Ramira said. Kelsey Solheim was one of the most accomplished artists of the post-Great Human War period. "I can't decide, though, whether I like moving art."

Mr. Navarro smiled. "Some people do find them distracting. I think it's marvelous, though." He tottered on shaky legs as he spread his arms wide. "I think everything in here is marvelous. That's why I devote myself to it all. Now look at this next work."

Ramira leaned in for a better look at a detailed holo a couple of meters wide and three deep. It depicted a red landscape -- rust-colored dirt leading up to tall mounds with rounded edges that were glowed crimson in early morning light. "Looks like Mars," Ramira said. "Wait a minute -- the sky's a pretty vivid blue." She looked at Mr. Navarro. "That's not likely, is it? Oh, and look -- this green vegetation certainly isn't likely. Unless it's someone's vision of a terraformed Mars."

Mr. Navarro said, "It's not. These are the Olgas. They're about thirty K from Ayers Rock in Australia."

"And beautiful. I hope I'd get to go there someday. And look -- this is another work that exists in time as well as space, isn't it? I can make out the wind moving the grass and shrubs."

Nr. Navarro said gently, "That's why we're called Temporal Expressions."

"Oh. Yeah."

"If you'll excuse me, I have some work to do in the back room. If I can acquire more good works for this place, maybe I can fight the recession. Which is more than the stock market is doing."

"What if someone comes in and they ask a hard question?"

"You holler for me and I give them an easy answer."

"Fair enough," Ramira said.

The whole thing ended up being academic, though. No customers came in for the first few hours Ramira sat in the main room. She wound up contenting herself with catching glimpses of cargo barges and sailing boats as they made their way up and down the river.

By late afternoon Mr. Navarro hadn't made a single sale. *You have to have customers to sell something*, Ramira thought.

Finally, the bell tinkled again as the door to the shop opened and an actual customer arrived. *Unless it's another of Miyanda's clients*, Ramira thought.

The woman seemed to be about the same age as Mr. Navarro, and her gaze swept across the room slowly, taking in each of the artworks in turn. Then that gaze reached Ramira, who made sure to give the woman her brightest, most open smile.

The woman's eyes swept right past her without acknowledgment, and Ramira's smile faded.

I wonder if I should try to sell her something, Ramira thought. *I don't think it's time to "holler" to Mr. Navarro just yet.* "May I help you, Ma'am?" she asked.

The woman's head turned toward her slowly, methodically, as if a mannequin had spoken and she couldn't quite believe it. Ramira heard Mr. Navarro calling from the back room: "Ramira -- you need any help out there?"

The customer said to Ramira, "Thank you. I was just looking."

Apparently she was looking for the door, because she went right to it and left, the little bell seemingly mocking Ramira: *See, I have a job and can do it right every time.*

Mr. Navarro came into the room just as the customer was leaving. *Oh, damn,* she thought, *I've failed, and right in front of him.* "Mr. Navarro, I'm sorry."

Mr. Navarro leaned on his cane with both hands again and said, "For what?" He glanced out the front window and said, "That's Cecilio Luna. She comes in here about once a week, never buys a thing."

"You...know her?"

"We're acquaintances. You say she was here and didn't say a thing?"

"Not until I spoke to her. Said she was just looking."

"Didn't ask for me? That's unusual."

"She came in, looked around, and I didn't get her to buy anything, she just looked around, and -- "

"Now, don't get all upset. It's all right."

"I just want to be a good worker, I just want a chance to prove I am. *And get out of this godforsaken place.*

"Ramira, most people who come in here just look. That's the nature of the place."

"I couldn't help but notice you've not sold a thing in all the hours I've been here."

"I'm not sellin' groceries, you know." Mr. Navarro indicated the artworks all around him with the tip of his cane. "If I sell one artwork in the course of a week, I'm doing well."

"How do you get by?"

"Do you realize how much that Solheim discus thrower is worth?"

"Uh...no idea, actually."

"Enough to keep this place running and me in bread and water for about six months."

"Oh."

"Oh, indeed. It's the same for about everything in here. I don't need to sell many things in a single day or even a single week. Well, it's just about knock-off time."

Ramira tilted her head to one side. "What are we knocking off?"

"Why, work, of course. It's five o'clock, and I've no special appointments. And the pubs have been open for hours."

"Sounds good to me."

"I'll see you tomorrow, then. And don't worry, you're doing fine."

"Uh...Mr. Navarro?"

"Yes?"

"When do I get some money?"

"Your first check is issued after you've been here two weeks."

"Two weeks?"

"Maybe you'd best talk to our friend Miyanda some. About checks and budgeting and stuff."

Ramira said, "I don't even know how to get hold of her."

"She's right outside. See you tomorrow!"

KAMAU'S MOUTH FORMED A HINT OF A SMILE AS HE FACED Masika as they stood in the middle of his small office and watched her reaction to his decision. "Governor Kimathi — " she began.

"Please, whenever we're alone, it can be Kamau."

"Very well, then — Kamau — I can't take over from you. Especially not during this crisis."

"It is especially during this crisis that I must devote myself to science rather than government." Kamau took a step toward one wall and waved the holoscreen to life. An image of intertwining strings of nucleotides appeared. "What do you see here?" he asked.

"It resembles the Human double helix," Masika said. "But it seems to be quite different in its details."

"Quite different, indeed. This is Jenregar DNA, or whatever we might call its equivalent." Kamau indicated one strand of material that was much more deeply braided than Human DNA. "Here, we believe, is the area that controls the Jenregar pheromonal responses. This may be the key to understanding those responses and, ultimately, defeating them."

"So that might involve, for instance, sabotaging their own responses to a Human presence, as Mike Christopher did on Korolev Habitat, and on that Jenregar ship where he actually rescued a man."

"That certainly is a possibility. But my immediate goal is more ambitious — to communicate with the Jenregar."

Masika's eyes grew wide. "How could you ever consider that? These beings have killed dozens, hundreds of people right here in the city. Around the world, they've certainly killed tens of thousands."

"And the world's military machine is fighting them as hard as it can. I understand that, and wouldn't expect anything else. But I've spent my life as a mediator, as someone who brings people together."

Masika said, softly, "These aren't people."

"They're intelligences. They're starfarers. We've learned to communicate with the Cetronen, Sobrenians — even methane-breathing Drodusarel. Could the Jenregar be so different?"

Masika shook her head. "I fear they might be."

"I learned about biological systems by doing much of my own field work, both here on Earth and on other worlds. I learned about diplomacy and mediation from the great Ambassador Kasinda Obote. He did everything from making peace between tribes killing one another with spears and knives to being Earth's ambassador to the Moon during the Troubles there. And what do you think both those experiences have taught me?"

Masika's cheekbones seemed to stand out even more. "I've heard you say it enough times. There's always common ground. There's always a solution."

"*Yes*," Kamau said. "It's up to us to find it." He tapped the side of his head. "The solutions are in here — " He placed his hand over his heart. " — and in here."

"With all respect, I'm not sure the Jenregar has a heart — at least not in the subjective sense you mean."

"Heart or no heart, I must search for it — or whatever equivalent it has. But that will require a lot of hard work. I can't do this and run the city at the same time."

"What if I'm not up to it?"

"Nonsense. You were always my choice to succeed me. Although I'd hoped — and expected — I would simply step down at the end of this term and support you in the election."

"I never realized that," Masika said.

"It's been my intention ever since Nyaga died." Kamau's husband, Nyaga Abasi, had died two years earlier. Though he'd been eleven years older than Kamau, rejuv had kept him young and spry — until a sudden heart attack took him one morning.

"I...can understand that."

"But events have overtaken us." Kamau took Masika's hands. "Will you help me?"

"You know I will."

"Excellent. You will run things — leaving me free to do what I know I must do to help save our city."

"And the world, if you're right."

"So it may be. And as hard as I intend to work, I wouldn't turn down a good bit of luck."

BEFORE NATHAN GOT MORE THAN A FEW STEPS DOWN THE street from the rim of the cylinder, a couple of people approached him, flashlights swinging back and forth. As they drew closer, he recognized Emma Hord and Laura Kellerman, exo-biologists who made Newton Habitat their home base when they weren't conducting research out in the field. "You've got to help us," Emma said.

"What's wrong?" Nathan asked.

Laura pointed back the way they'd come. "We've got people trapped in a house just down the street from us. No tech, we're digging by hand or using scraps of wood."

"They sent us out to find help," Emma said.

But I've got to find out what's happened to Tana and Randi, was Nathan's first thought.

His second: *I've got people nearby I know need my help. How can I turn my back on them?* "Let's go," he said.

When Nathan first arrived at the collapsed house, everything seemed hopeless. He saw a bare-chested man using a splintered wooden board as a lever to try to lift part of a collapsed wall from a woman trapped in the rubble of her house, who was screaming in pain. Another man, his face and clothing covered with dirt, was trying to reach in and inject the woman with nanotech that would relieve her pain even as it began healing her, but despite his best efforts, he couldn't quite reach her.

And he's risking his own life in the process, Nathan thought, *if that wall collapses again*.

Nathan dug through the remains of the home, found another long board, and slipped it beneath the rubble, hoping that adding his strength to the other man's might possibly make the difference.

For Thomas, sleep came only intermittently; he would begin to drift away into that blessed unconsciousness only to have the slightest sound jerk him utterly awake — a rustling of clothing against bedcovers, a distant clank of metal against metal, repeated coughing.

Then Thomas would lie there awhile, all his senses on high alert. Paradoxically, now he would hear nothing unusual; eventually his body would begin to calm, and he would drift away again.

Then a floorboard would creak, or another round of coughing would begin, and the pattern, having established itself, maintained its integrity for that full, restless night.

Finally there came a time when Thomas opened his eyes and found himself squinting against the morning sunlight. He almost called out to his father in concern — he couldn't recall a time when Jiang Shun hadn't arisen before the sun, eager to walk into the fields, scythe in hand, and give himself up to those eternal rhythms.

Then he heard raised voices outside, one of them his father's. Thomas threw on his clothes and hurried toward the front door.

As Thomas stepped outside, he squinted against the early-morning sun as it rose to his left. Immediately before him stood Scar, looking down at the old woman, Han Ling, who knelt before him. The top of her head oozed blood, and her shoulders shook.

Jiang Shun stood behind her, his hands outstretched, pleading with the soldiers: "Forgive this old woman — she did not know better!"

The sun cast sharp shadows across Scar's face. "She will learn — we will not allow anyone but soldiers to have weapons in this village! Certainly not to threaten us with them!"

"If you must strike someone again, strike me," Jiang Shun said. "I will take responsibility for her."

Before Thomas could speak or act, Scar raised his weapon high and struck the side of Jiang Shun's head with the stock.

"Baba!" Thomas yelled, and ran to his father as he fell to the ground, apparently knocked senseless. Scar reversed the pulse rifle and aimed it directly at Thomas even as he cradled his father's head in his lap. "Say the wrong word, little man," Scar said, "and your father will find himself choking on your ashes."

Thomas bit back the harsh, angry words that threatened to pour from him, more out of concern for his father than himself. *If I die here*, he thought, *who will take care of him?*

From behind Thomas came the Junior NCO's voice: "Private! Stand down!"

Scar flashed an angry glance toward his superior, and for a moment Thomas thought the man would switch his aim toward the Junior NCO. In the next instant, though, Scar, his features reflecting an intense frustration, lowered the pulse rifle.

The Junior NCO stared down at Thomas and his father, then at Han Ling. Then he turned to Scar. "Get the others. These people need medical assistance."

"But I — " Scar sputtered.

"*Get the others*," the Junior NCO said. Reluctantly, Scar shouldered his rifle and started toward the rear of Jiang Shun's house.

The Junior NCO knelt next to Han Ling, who looked up at him with a fierce anger showing in her eyes. "I apologize for this man," he said. "He has seen too much — as we all have."

Thomas dared to look the man right in the eyes, and overcame his natural reticence to challenge someone directly. "We would gladly have helped you if you came to us with respect. Instead, you take an old man's home as your own, eat his food, treat him as you would a slave. And you beat an old woman to the ground."

The Junior JCO stood. His posture stiffened. "We do what we must." He indicated Han Ling's rifle. "You see how this one welcomed us. You call her 'old woman,' but her rifle could have killed any one of us."

Han Ling didn't look up at the soldier, but said, "Not if you leave our village alone."

The Junior NCO said, "Old one, I respect you. But I will not allow you to harm us." The other three soldiers approached, each of them with pulse rifles at the ready, speaking furtively among one another.

Thomas saw that the Junior NCO looked at his charges with thinly disguised disgust. He waved them forward and indicated Han Ling and Jiang Shun. He told his soldiers, "Take this woman and this man's father into their homes. Do *not* harm them any further."

Scar started to speak up: "You'd let this woman — "

"Do *not* harm them further! You will follow my orders!"

Thomas sat quietly as the soldiers he thought of as Bandage and Scar lifted Han Ling beneath her arms and helped her rise. Bandage put an arm around the old woman, who leaned against her as they headed toward her home. Scar took Jiang Shun's arms and Wounded Eye his legs, and they lifted him up and took him into his home. Thomas gave the Junior NCO a final glare, then followed the others inside.

Chapter 7

For Nathan, the next several hours meant:

Muscles straining and aching, especially his back, in the continued effort to extract people from their collapsed homes.

Emotions soaring as he helped pull a woman who ran one of the habitat's wineries, Mary McClure, from what was left of her home. Emma Hord and Laura Kellerman carried her toward the hospital on a makeshift litter.

The hospital! Just where Nathan wanted to be.

But he was needed here, and worked without rest, without food or water, beneath as many small lights as people in the neighborhood could find, cursing Adam Garrick and himself and everyone in the habitat who'd never considered that everyone within Newton Habitat could find themselves cut off from the tech they counted upon every moment to sustain their lives.

Some attempts to help failed, such as when the lonely cries of Scott Ephram, a medical researcher Nathan knew was supposed to be brilliant, began to fade. Nathan and the bare-chested man worked desperately — blood ran down

Nathan's chest and arms from a dozen cuts inflicted by wood, stone, and glass, he blinked as sweat stung his eyes, and his breathing became so rapid he feared he might hyperventilate.

And his back! He could tell it was threatening to give out on him, but he didn't dare slow his efforts to reach the man.

By the time they reached him, Scott's body was still and lifeless. Despite all that effort, they didn't pull his body from the rubble; instead, at the sound of other faint cries for help in other homes, Nathan and the other man whose name he didn't even know traded looks in the dim light of fading flashlights and headed toward their next rescue attempt.

Eventually, though, Nathan found himself stumbling away from beneath those lights and sitting his ass down on the ground — *Only for a moment of rest*, he told himself. *Only a moment.*

Meteor strike, Nathan thought. *That was the only threat we prepared for. See it coming, plenty of time to get ready. Plenty of time to evacuate or set up backup systems or whatever else we needed to do.*

And Earth's right there, only half an hour away. Take a look outside our habitat, and it fills the sky — looks like you could reach out and touch it. Billions of people right there, an infinite resource we can tap.

Only Earth's kind of distracted right now. Jenregar mounds forming in its cities, Jenregar starcraft in its skies.

And where does that leave Newton Habitat?

RAMIRA BOUNDED OUTSIDE AND EMBRACED MIYANDA. "MR. Navarro's *so* nice! This could work out really well!"

"That's why I sent you to him. And the work load's easy."

"I feel like I'm pretending to work."

"Wait for that first payday. You'll feel like he's pretending to pay you."

"I guess I should've asked how much it would pay."

"You should have. Not that it would've made a difference. Especially since the hotel wants some money, and wants it today."

"Well, I don't have any, so they're not going to get any."

Miyanda said, "You really don't understand, do you? They're going to throw you out."

"Well, that's great! I *want* to be thrown out."

"No you don't — because being homeless is illegal here. The moment that Keyes fellow turns you in to the authorities, you'll be put in jail."

"Then they can't do that!"

"Why can't they?"

"Because I need somewhere to stay."

"That's not their problem."

"Then whose is it?"

"Yours! The hotel's only interested in paying customers."

"How do I get to be one of those?"

"You're on the right track. You've got a job, you've -- "

"They're worrying about this when the city's under attack by aliens?"

Miyanda said, "And yet life goes on, somehow. You can decide whether that's efficient or crazy."

"Living in a market economy is a lot more 'real' than reading about it. I feel like I'm drowning."

"Now you're getting it! That's called a motivator. Baby steps, then. Let's take you to a bank and see if we can get you a loan."

KAMAU KIMATHI WAS IN HIS LAB ON THE OUTSKIRTS OF Nairobi, in the middle of dictating his latest theory about how the Jenregar hive mind kept its control over millions of individuals when his back threatened to give way.

It was as if he'd been in a trance and abruptly returned to consciousness. Kamau was standing in one corner of his research lab on the outskirts of Nairobi. He'd set it up to his own exacting specifications, and was surrounded by all the equipment he'd anticipated needing — microarray sensors, genomic sample analysis tech, and dozens of other devices designed to scan, poke, and prod samples of Jenregar remains. *I'd like a live Jenregar to examine,* he thought. *No, change that — to interrogate, we'll say. You examine something that's dead or non-sentient. That isn't a participant. I have to know what does a Jenregar individual feel, what does it really want, what is its relationship to the hive mind?*

None of that mattered, because a live Jenregar was not forthcoming soon, he knew. If ever.

But none of that was foremost in his mind now. As Kamau grimaced against the pain running up his back and into his shoulders, he made his way toward the only comfortable chair in the room, which unfortunately was in a far corner. With each step, he braced himself with one hand against a lab table or a piece of equipment sturdy enough to support his weight.

Finally he reached the chair and settled himself into it — a process nearly as painful as walking had been. *Rejuv aside,* he thought, *today's one of those days when I'm feeling every one of my 92 years.*

His body having demanded his attention, Kamau returned the favor and took stock: *My legs are aching, my hands feel as if they're about to curl up into claws, and my eyes feel as if they're on fire.*

This search for an answer is taking its toll. I concentrate so intensely that I didn't even realize I'd been standing so long, that I'd barely taken my eyes off monitors and readouts for — damn, the better part of six hours.

I also have to pee really bad. And — I'm starving. Tackling either problem would mean getting up again.

Might as well resign myself to it.

Kamau tried to stand, but his back protested sufficiently that he settled back down into the chair. He thought, *This is where, in bad holodramas, someone comes in and sees me and demands I work less, telling me I won't do anybody any good if I kill myself.*

But I'm smarter than that. If 92 years have given me any wisdom at all, it's to be self-aware — to know my limits and hold myself to them.

Kamau got his feet under him and pressed his hands firmly against the chair arms to raise himself up. This time, the pain emanating from his back was muted.

I won't do anyone any good if I collapse in the middle of my research. I have to remember how suddenly it happened to Nyaga. But — just a little longer, Kamau thought. *Then I can rest.*

"I appreciate that you didn't hesitate to call me," Doctor Beverly Kwan told Thomas. She indicated Jiang Shun's still form on his bed as she gathered up her dermal mender and medical nanotech injector. "I expect him to recover pretty easily — I managed to transition him from unconsciousness into sleep. He needs that more than anything else. Oh, and he'll want to eat when he wakes up."

"Thank you, Doctor. I appreciate that you...didn't hesitate at what you had to do."

Dr. Kwan placed her equipment into her little black bag. "Use nanotech to help heal him? Don't underestimate your father's intelligence, Thomas. He knows the difference between honoring traditions and letting someone suffer needlessly."

"Even himself," Thomas said.

"Correct," Dr. Kwan said.

"What about Han Ling? Did they injure her badly?"

"A nasty cut and a big bruise — she could've easily had a concussion, but I looked in on her, mended the cut, got some tech into her, and she wants to take on these soldiers again." Dr. Kwan leaned in close to whisper. "She even has another shotgun."

"I wonder who should fear that possibility more — us or the soldiers."

Dr. Kwan smiled at that, then looked around and spoke more softly, as if the soldiers hovered just over her shoulder. "What will we do about these soldiers? We can't let them just take over the village. And we can't forget about the Jenregar — the latest reports before the newsfeeds shut down had them approaching closer to the village by the hour, unless they change course again — something they've done several times in the last day or so."

"How long until they arrive, if they continue to move this way?"

"Days at the most. Perhaps a few hours. I'm concerned about my grandmother — my Nai-nai. She's still in Zhengzhou. But the last time I spoke with her she assured me she's safe."

"But how safe are we? We must evacuate the village."

Dr. Kwan said, "These soldiers seem determined that

we'll stay here. Do they intend to fight the Jenregar here — make a final stand?"

"These cowards who picked a fight with an old woman? No. Although, perhaps I've made an unfair assessment of the one in charge — the Junior NCO. So far, he has found enough bravery to keep the others in line."

Dr. Kwan's voice turned bitter. "So that, in turn, they can keep us in line more efficiently. I suspect they want to see which direction the Jenregar will take. If it heads this way, the soldiers will count upon the mere presence of this village to slow its advance."

"In the meantime, they have plenty of food and shelter rather than trying to live off the land."

"Exactly." Dr. Kwan nodded toward Jiang Shun. "Take care of your father. By tomorrow afternoon he will have recovered. He'll want to make plans."

"Plans? For an evacuation, you mean."

Dr. Kwan raised an eyebrow. "Do you really think the soldiers would allow that?"

"What other plans could he have?"

"I don't know. But I also would never believe he would simply allow his village to lie beneath the heels of these soldiers."

"If I prayed, Doctor, I would pray for that. But I have no idea what he might do."

Dr. Kwan picked up her bag and favored Thomas with a brief smile. "Don't worry, Thomas. The important thing remains that *he* knows."

The doctor left, and Thomas sat next to his father, to remain with him until he woke up.

Chapter 8

A HAND CLAPPED DOWN ON NATHAN'S SHOULDER AND HE brought his head up with a gasp. *I didn't even know I was asleep*, he thought. *If that makes any sense.* He'd drifted off with his head and arms resting on his knees. "It's Nathan, right?" a rough voice said.

"Yeah." He got his feet under him and stood up. He could barely make out the dirty features of the bare-chested man silhouetted against the muted lighting from the continuing rescue efforts.

The man held out his hand to shake. "Bob Weiss."

"Ah! I've heard of you — of the Weiss winery, of course."

"That's us. Listen, we've got a fellow, Frank Burrows, needs to go to the hospital. Looks like both legs are broken, he may have a concussion, and probably internal injuries." Bob pointed to his right. "We found a supply cart you can take them in."

"Listen, if you still need me here — "

"Nathan, you've done a helluva job. But you're exhausted. Get Frank to the hospital. See how your wife's doing. Get some rest yourself."

"All right," Nathan said. "I will. Thanks."

"We'll split a bottle when this is all over."

"Which can't be soon enough." Nathan headed over to the supply cart Bob had indicated. Frank Burrows appeared to be asleep or unconscious, lying there on the flat surface of the cart, with only a thin lip around it to keep him from rolling off. Nathan took hold of the tall metal handle at one end of the cart and began to push. That turned out to be difficult as he navigated through some of the rubble — the cart would stop short against a pile of bricks or wood. Turning the cart around and pulling turned out to be easier.

Staying on the street was more difficult — with very little light, Nathan had trouble even staying on a straight track at first. Fortunately, by the time he had gotten a few hundred meters from the damaged and destroyed homes, the debris cleared up and the road ahead became clearer.

That was when Frank woke up. "What happened? Why am I bouncing around — it hurts!"

"I'm sorry, Frank. I'm Nathan Carlsson. You've been hurt pretty badly. Try to stay still, and I'll get you to the hospital."

"Carlsson, huh? Aren't you the Assistant Supervisor?"

"I am."

"Then how the hell did this happen, huh? Tell me that!"

"I wish I knew, Frank. It shouldn't be this way."

"A mystery, huh?"

"You might say that. But one we're going to have to solve pretty quickly."

"It's a good thing I'm lying here unable to move."

"Why's that?"

"Because, Nathan, if I could get up on my feet like a man I'd punch you in the face."

"Sorry you feel that way. We're doing our best."

"Well, your best isn't goddam good enough, now, is it?"

"Apparently not, Frank. Try to lie still. We should be at the hospital in just a few minutes."

"I'd put *you* in the hospital if I...if I...." Nathan saw Frank go limp, and hoped to bloody hell he was only unconscious. He pulled the cart that much faster.

To Ramira, the interior of the Q-T Savings and Loan smelled like the cleantech was set on "high." Despite the sunlight cast onto its marbled walls and pristine floor, she couldn't detect a single dust mote in the air, nor a single scratch on any surface. *I guess they can afford it*, she thought. *After all, this is where all the money is.*

Miyanda sat down beside her across from the loan officer, a man named Jackson King, who was looking at a shielded holo readout. Ramira asked, "I suppose those are my records?"

Mr. King didn't look toward Ramira. "Yes, of course."

Miyanda raised her hand just enough for a warning gesture. *I know, be quiet*, Ramira thought. *I don't want to starve, after all.*

"Well," Mr. King said. He turned off the holo, folded his hands on his desk, and faced Ramira and Miyanda. "Miss Espinosa, your situation is certainly unusual."

Miyanda spoke up before Ramira could. "You've helped me in such circumstances before."

Mr. King gave Miyanda, then Ramira, an institutional smile. "I certainly have. And I admit, I've never had occasion to regret it." He produced an actual physical sheet of paper that he slid over to her. "Things are tough with the recession, and all. But take a look at that."

Ramira checked out the dense paragraphs, looking for

clear meaning in them and largely failing. She was grateful that Miyanda was turning the document slightly so she could look over her shoulder. *Certainly she'll keep me from falling into an even bigger pit than the one I'm trying to climb out of*, she thought.

Miyanda pointed to a number at the bottom of the page. "This really isn't sufficient," she told Mr. King.

"It's the best we can do, Miyanda. You know how little the woman makes over there in that shop. You know our policies. Who else makes such loans at all? My hands are tied."

Miyanda turned the document toward Ramira. "I suppose it'll have to do. And the interest rate's not so bad."

Ramira said, "Oh! I know what interest is. I have to give back more money than I'll get, to pay these people back. Which is how the bank makes its money. But that means it's going to take me even longer to get out of here."

"That's actually a pretty good summation," Miyanda said. She told Mr. King, "We'd like some crisp, new bills as part of the loan."

Ramira asked, "So I should sign, then?"

Miyanda let out a sigh, but nodded. "It's the best we can do for now."

As they left the bank and retrieved their bikes, Ramira asked Miyanda, "Are you hungry? We can go back to the hotel and have something sent up."

Miyanda gave Ramira a wan smile. "That's a habit we're going to break. Very expensive."

"Oh. This whole business with money is very complicated. And that bank loan -- it's all designed in favor of the system, isn't it? Nothing favoring regular people."

"I'm proud of you," Miyanda said. "You're starting to

understand a market economy. Now you'll learn about how to buy the cheapest food."

Miyanda led the way and peddled across the edge of a market area with plenty of stands featuring fresh vegetables, meats, and fish. Miyanda glanced back as they left the market behind. She must have seen Ramira's quizzical look, because she said, "Many of us came from lower-tech environments, and we still enjoy what you can get at these kinds of markets. And before you say anything, replicators really aren't the same."

Ramira curled her mouth in frustration at Miyanda stealing her words from her. Finally they stopped in front of a building with a brightly lit sign above the door proclaiming it as Lerner's Market. "So how's this place different?" Ramira asked as they stashed their bikes.

"This is one of those details. Usually I'd say we should buy from that open-air market. Raw materials are a lot cheaper than the pre-packaged meals we're going to get here. But you wouldn't be allowed to cook anything in your hotel room, or to install the equipment for it. These packaged meals heat or chill themselves."

They entered the store and Ramira was confronted with aisle after aisle of products, mostly in boxes featuring brightly colored graphics and promises of culinary bliss -- pastas, steak, chicken, various types of focaccia, curry, and a number of meat pies. She picked up one of the latter. "So eating this stuff is cheaper than the hotel meals?"

"A damn sight cheaper," Miyanda said. "When you move out of the hotel and get a place of your own, that's when we can start you cooking from scratch."

Ramira glanced up from her meat pie box. "Wait a minute. What's that about a place of my own?"

"The hotel's expensive too. It's going to take weeks or

months for you to save up enough money to buy your way out of here. I can help you find an apartment, and you can put a lot more money toward that ticket."

"Damn. I thought I'd be here a few days. Is Mr. Navarro really paying me that little?"

"Sure he is, and your expenses can eat up your money. The hotel room, food, utilities, all kinds of stuff."

"Utilities?"

Miyanda said, "You have to have energy provided to your apartment for lights, appliances, everything. And you'll have to pay at least a month's rent in advance, and a deposit against potential damage."

"Is *nothing* a public service in this place?" Ramira plucked several more boxes from shelves and began piling them up in her arms. "Some of this stuff looks pretty good. Especially this curry."

Miyanda gently took a couple boxes from her and returned them to the shelves. "We need to talk about a budget."

Ramira shrugged. "Let's do that while we eat."

A FRIGHTENED SHOUT AWAKENED KAMAU. HIS EYES BLINKED open and he wondered why his face was so cold, why he was staring so closely at the white, pristine floor of the lab. "Governor!" was the first word he could make out, and then someone hovering over him was shaking his shoulders. "Wake up!" the voice he recognized as Masika's told him. She continued, "We need a med team here in Governor Kimathi's lab right away."

Kamau struggled for words, could only come up with: "What...?"

Masika rolled him over onto his back. "You mean what happened to you? I don't know. I just found you here on the floor."

"I was working. In fact, I was just thinking that I needed to take a break."

"Uh, huh. And how long ago was that?"

"Oh, I don't know. Maybe five or six hours."

"And when did you start this morning?"

"Not *so* early," Kamau said. "Maybe six o'clock."

The three members of the med team, two men and a woman, pushed a smart gurney into the room. Masika stood to let them get close to Kamau. Down went the gurney, and it folded itself down onto the floor and an enticement field scooped him right up, taking care through medical nanotech and sensors not to disturb his head or neck in any way.

Damn, Kamau thought. *I was just about ready to head for the bathroom and then the commissary. Guess now I'll have to wait.*

Chapter 9

That night, Thomas lifted the soup spoon to Jiang Shun's mouth, but his father wouldn't have any of it. "Give me that spoon," he said as he raised himself to sit up in the bed. "I won't have my son feeding me like a child."

"Careful, Baba — don't burn yourself on the bowl."

"I know how to eat soup after seven decades."

Thomas handed over the spoon. He asked, "Tell me, Baba — what happened this morning before I awoke?"

"The soldiers forced me out into the fields even earlier than usual — 'Get to work,' they said. 'We must have plenty of food to eat.'"

"They will certainly not remain for the full harvest."

"They must assert their power, these soldiers. They joined the army for the wrong reason — to wield that power over others, rather than protecting them. They would not let me get you up — they wanted you to remain at the house to fix their meals and perform whatever other chores they could come up with."

"And Han Ling?"

"She went out to hunt her pheasants. That one soldier...the one who ended up striking her...."

"I call him 'Scar.'"

"Yes. He dragged her out of the woods and back into the village. I tried to protect her. You saw the rest. We must get these soldiers out of our village."

"How can we do that, Baba? You can't even get through to the army base."

"Actually, my son, I received a message from them just before that confrontation with the soldiers."

"Can they come help us?"

Jiang Shun shook his head. "They cannot. The soldiers at the base must spend every action, every thought, on how to save Zhengzhou from the Jenregar. They cannot spare anyone to come here."

"This makes me think back to my own journey from the city. What I saw along the way — mangled bodies, people with terrible injuries from the acid the Jenregar individuals sprayed onto them — we should've realized the army could never help us."

Jiang Shun took a sip of soup, then told Thomas, "I never said they couldn't help. Only that they couldn't spare any soldiers."

"I don't understand, Baba."

"They have a way we can help ourselves. And perhaps we will find the best path that way, after all."

"You enjoy playing the stereotype of the inscrutable Chinese man, don't you?"

"If it irks you sometimes, my son, then perhaps I do. It lets you know to keep respecting me."

Thomas hesitated for a moment, then decided to speak: "I know you want me to call you Baba. And I've done so."

"I thank you, my son. You know how the old traditions mean so much to me."

"Then I must make a similar request. I'd like you to call me 'Thomas,' and not just 'my son.'"

Jiang Shun stared at his son for a long time. Then he said, "Calling you 'my son' is actually my compromise. I would prefer to call you by what I consider to be your real name — Deshi. It pleases me in its traditional sound."

"Baba — I've respected your request. And I find it surprising how much I enjoy calling you that. Please accept my request, as well."

For a moment, Jiang Shun looked as if he smelled something distasteful. Then he glanced up at his son and said, "Very well...Thomas."

"Thank you, Baba."

"I...hope we can live long enough to call each other by our preferred names for a long time." Jiang Shun raised his bowl and sipped the last of his soup. "The soldiers haven't bothered you?"

"They've left me alone tonight. I think the Junior NCO has some shred of humanity within him, and has insisted upon it. But what shall we do tomorrow, Baba?"

"As for you — you shall wait. Perhaps we can do something in the morning."

"Then you should get some more rest, Baba."

"I will. There is much work still ahead of us today. And tomorrow morning, Thomas, I will make sure to get you up."

Thomas couldn't help but wonder whether his father's had more meaning than they seemed to on the surface. But it appeared Jiang Shun had drifted off to sleep again, and he was determined not to disturb him for now.

As Nathan pulled the cart carrying Frank toward the receiving area of the Newton Habitat Hospital's emergency room, his heart sank when he squinted against the glow of backup lights and saw how many people were waiting outside. Some sat on stone benches, a few were being supported by healthier companions, and still more were sitting or lying on the surrounding grass.

A woman standing just before him held her bleeding arm close to her chest. She moaned softly. A man on one of the benches sat hunched over, hands on his head, which was lacerated in half a dozen or more places, as blood flowed down his face and dripped onto the ground. A closer look at one of the bodies lying in the grass, and Nathan knew he'd never move on his own again.

He looked back at Frank's prone form, which was lying as still as the man on the grass. *Someone has to be doing triage out here*, Nathan thought. *I have to find help for Frank.*

And I have to find Tana.

The pathway toward the receiving area was a slight grade, and Nathan found himself straining to pull Frank's weight on the cart with any speed. In the next moment, he found himself unable to keep gaining ground at all. Fearful of letting the cart roll backward, Nathan began to turn it around, aiming to push rather than pull, intending to keep himself behind the cart so it wouldn't roll away from him.

Halfway through the spin, however, he heard a voice behind him — a familiar one, but with an unfamiliar tone: "Sir, can I help you with that?"

"Tana!" he cried, and now he *did* almost let the cart go in his surprise and relief.

"Nathan! My God, I didn't even recognize you!" They

propped the cart against their legs and went in for a quick embrace and kiss. "I didn't know what had happened to you — I couldn't get hold of you. I was so tempted to leave the hospital and go looking for you."

Together, they began pushing the cart toward the receiving area. "I know," Nathan said. "I have to admit, I only left the control room because I felt useless there — I couldn't help on the technical end. And when I tried to get to you here, I got sidetracked helping people out."

As the doors to the E.R. parted, Tana waved once to a couple medical assistants just inside the door. She spoke calmly but forcefully: "This patient goes to the front of the line. Full diagnostic — full nano-spread." The assistants took the cart, and Frank into the depths of the E.R.

"He's not dead?" Nathan asked.

"Not just yet. I could see his breathing's pretty shallow, and he's took some pretty big bumps. But he would've died if you hadn't gotten him here when you did."

"Damn. I was afraid I'd failed him. I was afraid..."

The next thing Nathan knew was that the floor was rising up to hit him in the head and that for some reason Tana's voice this time wasn't calm and was a damn sight more forceful than before, and his only wish was that he could make out her words.

As Ramira and Miyanda entered the Hotel Augustina's lobby, each loaded down with shopping bags from Lerner's Market, Mr. Keyes motioned for them to approach him. When they reached the desk and put down their groceries, Mr. Keyes said in an even, quiet voice, "We will require a payment sometime today, Miss Espinosa, or we'll have to approach certain authorities."

Miyanda grinned at Ramira and said, "Give him some of those crisp, new bills."

Ramira reached into a pocket and produced them. She stared at the currency for an instant, as she realized what these simple pieces of paper meant to her, then reluctantly handed them over. Mr. Keyes's eyebrows raised, he took the bills, examined one against the light from a window, rubbed it between thumb and forefinger, then counted them and put them away. "Excellent, Miss Espinosa," he said. "We'll expect more of these soon."

Ramira and Miyanda picked up their shopping bags. Mr. Keyes asked, "Are those self-heating meals?"

"They are," Ramira said. "Well, except the ones that are self-chilling."

Miyanda said, "There's no rule against them in your hotel, Mr. Keyes."

"You're correct. I was just going to tell you those curries are delicious."

"Thanks," Ramira said, giving Miyanda a knowing look. "Maybe I'll have one tonight."

"Excellent choice."

Ramira made for the lift, with Miyanda right behind her. A few minutes later, sitting across from Miyanda at the one small table Ramira's room featured, she took a taste of the curry. "Hmm. We were both right. It *is* good."

"Ramira, I'll try to find you a flat, though affordable housing's pretty tight right now. You just keep working at Mr. Navarro's. But I think you might want to consider a second job."

Ramira used her tongue to move a glob of food to one side

of her mouth. "I don'd...*don't* have a problem with that. Work me as hard as you can. You don't know how much I appreciate this. I know you're going far beyond what the job must require."

Miyanda paused mid-bite. "I'm pretty driven by my job. And — I don't have much else to do. There's no one to go home to."

"No husband?"

"None."

"Boyfriend -- girlfriend?"

"Nope."

"Anything casual?"

"I'm not a casual woman, Ramira. It's all or nothing for me."

Ramira said, "I wish I knew what I was. I haven't had the chance to allow someone to be interested in me when it didn't mean money was about to change hands."

"I'm sorry, Ramira."

"I like Mr. Navarro. I like his artworks. But if you can find me another job, too, that would be great. I want out of here."

"You know, it hurts me a little when you keep saying you want to leave here so badly."

Ramira looked at Miyanda. "I'm sorry. I don't mean it that way." She indicated her own package of warm curry. "This would be a feast in the town I came from."

Miyanda put down her fork. "But isn't it the replicator economy there that's kept people down?"

"It's a series of dictators that's done it. They keep the replicator economy so no one starves, everyone has a roof over their heads — we don't have it so bad that we riot. But it gives them a way to control us. They keep a true democracy from forming, and even keep a tight hold on information."

"But you got out," Miyanda said.

"I thought things would be better here. I was wrong. Didn't you ever consider going somewhere else? A replicator economy that has more freedoms, like Brazil? That's where I want to go. I'd be free."

"To do what? Exist? Fill space?"

"Live. Travel. Have whatever meals you want, whenever you want."

"There's no risk there. I like that I can survive in this kind of system if I'm given half a chance."

"It's difficult for me to understand that," Ramira said.

"You've been through hell, Ramira. I know that. But that part of your life is over. You're not digging ditches. You're not doing something totally mind-numbing. And you're right, Mr. Navarro is a marvelous man."

"He noticed you didn't 'stick around for introductions,' as he put it. That you say there's always another client."

"That's because there is. So I refuse to let you hurt me anymore. I'll have my revenge on you, and get you the hell out of here as fast as I can. I should have something for you tomorrow night after you leave Mr. Navarro's."

"Sweet revenge," Ramira said. "And on me. I can't wait."

***

KAMAU RETURNED TO HIS LAB AFTER THE BETTER PART OF A day spent in bed rest, and Masika was right by his side. "You can get back to your own job," he told her. "I know you have better things to do than babysit me."

Masika shook her head. "The most important task ahead of me is making sure you stay healthy. You could be the key to defeating the Jenregar."

Kamau paused next to an equipment table and ran his hand down the side of a dissecting microscope. "I need to be alone, so I can concentrate. It's how I do this kind of work — no distractions. I don't even play music."

"Oh, you'll be alone — as long as you don't count the comp program I've established."

"What — you're spying on me?"

"You bet I am," Masika said.

"This is exactly the kind of thing I was thinking of the other day. It's like a bad cube drama — someone comes in to save me from myself. And the worse part is, this means you don't trust me."

"Oh, I trust you, all right — trust you to work too hard, for too long a time, and wind up in the hospital again."

"I should feel insulted," Kamau said. "But there's just one problem with that."

"You know I'm right."

"That's the problem. So will you be looking over my shoulder the entire time I'm in here?"

"Not at all. In fact, the comp mostly just monitors your lifesigns. And how often you eat. And get a drink of water. And a bit of rest."

"My God, Masika, does it monitor when I take a big poop?"

"If we wanted it to. I don't intend to call up that information. But if you push your body too far like you did the other day, it'll let us know." Masika touched him on the shoulder. "We're all counting on you, Governor."

Kamau placed his hand over hers. "You're the governor, now."

Masika smiled. "You don't get away that easily — once a governor, always a governor."

"Well...thanks for the concern. And...I'm ashamed to say...I haven't been checking the news nets. How's the fight against the Jenregar proceeding?

Masika closed her eyes tightly.

But that doesn't keep you from seeing an unpleasant truth, Kamau thought. "Is it so bad?"

Masika looked at Kamau. "We've lost the center city. But at least the mound doesn't seem to be growing much more. It's a pattern that seems to be reflected around the world."

"What are they waiting for?"

"No one knows. Maybe they're just waiting to see how Humanity reacts."

"Then we have to provide that reaction," Kamau said. "Thank you for all you've done. Now let me get back to work."

Kamau waited until he heard the door close behind Masika to bend over his equipment and continue his search for something, *anything* that would allow him to communicate with the Jenregar.

Chapter 10

I CAN'T BELIEVE A TRIP ON A PLANET'S SURFACE TOOK THIS LONG, Mike thought as he and Jeremy exited the underground terminal of the Brussels-Luxembourg Railway Station just an hour or so after local dawn. From the time they'd boarded the maglev train in San Diego, transferred to a different train in Juneau, Alaska, transferred again in Novosibirsk, Russia and Athens, Greece, it had taken just over twelve hours for them to arrive here, with little opportunities for decent sleep or a meal other than snacks.

They left the towering glass and metal of the station, and the sleek sounds of arriving and departing maglevs behind — fortunately, Earth Unity HQ was located in the old European Parliament's main building right above the maglev station.

"Thank goodness we're finally here," Mike said as they entered the main lobby. More bright surfaces, more glass.

Fatigue and strain showed in Jeremy's voice: "No one's happier about that than me."

Mike thought, *I've lost count of how many times I've held*

my tongue, given that he had to be rescued from a Jenregar ship, and that he still has no idea what's become of his wife.

Once we're done with this briefing, it'll be good riddance to one another.

Before Mike could even begin the search for someone in authority, a woman exited an elevator to their right and walked directly to Mike. Her handshake was brief but strong. Chestnut eyes seemed to pierce directly into his consciousness. "I'm Neriah Fulton," she said in English, moving quickly to shake Jeremy's hand as well. "I'm kind of a 'floating diplomat' here. A non-specialist, you might say. I do whatever's needed, and right now what's needed is to find out what the hell the Jenregar are up to and what we can do about it."

"We're here to help," Mike said.

"Anything I can do," Jeremy told her.

"Excellent, gentlemen. Let's get started."

Neriah took Mike and Jeremy to a briefing room and introduced them to two other people, Damian Rivera and Luisa Torres. "They were rescued from a Jenregar mound in Madrid," Neriah told them. "As you can see, they were both...changed...by the Jenregar."

Damian's mouth had been altered to make it much smaller than the Human norm. His speech was halting, and sounded as if he was mumbling, but Mike's datalink translation of the man's Spanish also helped: "The Jenregar took me into that mound. They started working on me...without anesthetic. Apparently it's how they perform surgery on their own individuals, without regard for the pain they cause."

Neriah said, "Apparently the hive mind only receives information and some sensory impressions from its individuals. Any painful sensations aren't included."

Mike said, "So the hive mind doesn't know, and doesn't care. That fits in with what we already know about them. Individuals aren't important — only the group."

Luisa held up her left arm, which had been made into a Jenregar-like limb — a biological hydrostat which maintained its shape through the pressure of internal fluids, much like a worm or an elephant's trunk. "That's how they changed me, as well. I passed out from the pain more than once."

Jeremy said, "They'd just started working on me. They poked and prodded. I tried to look them in the eyes, develop some sort of rapport with them, but I realized they can barely see. They didn't care how much they hurt me."

Neriah asked, "How far did they get with you?"

"I thought at the time they were torturing me. I screamed at them, tried to let them know I'd tell them anything I wanted, but they didn't listen — I realized they couldn't understand me, weren't even trying."

Luisa reached out with her right hand, the one that was still Human, but Jeremy pulled his arm away from her. "Sorry," he said. "I know you're being sweet, but I can't stand to be touched right now. Only Julia. That's the only person I want touching me."

He's suffering from post-traumatic stress, Mike thought. *He's going to need major therapy whether his Julia returns safely to him or not.*

Jeremy continued: "I've told you all I can. I'm not an expert on xenobiology. I'd like to get some rest."

"You deserve it," Mike said.

Jeremy stood, and his features held nothing but disdain for Mike. "You don't determine what I deserve. You're not even a real person."

Neriah said, "Jeremy — that's amazingly unkind to the person who saved your life."

"It's all right," Mike said. "I'm used to it. I expect nothing better from him."

Neriah stood and told Jeremy, "We have quarters here in this building. I'll show you there." She asked Mike, "How about you?"

"I'm OK. I can go some more. I'd like to find out a few more things from Damian and Luisa."

Jeremy and Neriah departed. Mike told Damian and Luisa, "It looks as if the Jenregar is trying to develop a way to transcend its own abilities. It nabbed Jeremy from a Human ship, and it looks as if it was examining his eyes. And I saw a Jenregar individual with eyes that resembled a Human's. It was one of the most eerie sights I can imagine — scared the shit out of me."

Damian said, "We know the Jenregar is developing augmented eyesight so it can better detect Humans who infiltrate their mounds."

Luisa nodded. "We saw evidence of that in our own mound in Madrid."

Mike said, "I think any solution we find to defeating the Jenregar is going to be biological, not military. They're trying to combine our Human advantages with their own — use our own abilities against us. We're going to have to figure out how to use their abilities against them."

Damien ran a finger along the edge of his lower lip, as if still examining how the Jenregar had mutilated him. "They have been merciless toward us," he said. "We must be the same toward them."

Luisa said, "I want to kill them all."

Mike felt he had to say the word. "Genocide?"

"You're not the first one to use the word. It is what they would do to us, isn't it?"

"Yes, I'm afraid it is. The Jenregar doesn't pacify, it doesn't occupy. It doesn't assimilate. It kills and move on."

"Then we must do that first."

Mike had nothing to say for a moment, and Damian and Luisa also sat silently. *We have to think not only about what we may have to do*, Mike thought, *but what we may have to become.*

THE NEXT THING THOMAS KNEW, SOMEONE KEPT SHAKING HIS shoulders. He blinked open his eyes, said, "What — "

Jiang Shun stood over him. "Thomas, you must remain very quiet."

Thomas couldn't help grinning at the sound of his preferred name. But he sobered quickly: "The soldiers — " he whispered.

"We must act before they have a chance to wake up."

"The sentry — "

"Don't worry about the sentry."

Thomas got out of bed, began dressing. "Baba, why do you have your scythe?" Realization arrived. "You want to kill them in their sleep!"

"I don't *want* to, Thomas. But follow me."

As they entered the living room, however, the Junior NCO stood there, his pulse rifle trained upon Thomas and Jiang Shun. "Perhaps I don't sleep as soundly as you'd hoped," he said. He raised his voice: "All soldiers — report!" After a moment, when no one arrived, he shouted even louder: "REPORT!"

Now Thomas heard movement -- the creaking of a bed

in the next room, a couple of grunts, and what sounded like someone stumbling into a piece of furniture.

The Junior NCO rolled his eyes and sighed deeply, but never took his eyes — or his aim — off Thomas and Jiang Shun.

Finally Wounded Eye and Bandage entered the room, dressed only in their skivvies but carrying their pulse rifles. Thomas saw the mean-looking knife still strapped to Wounded Eye's right leg. Both raised their rifles and trained them on Thomas and Jiang Shun. Wounded Eye leaned back against a wall as if he could barely stand.

They will surely kill us, Thomas thought. *One small movement of anyone's trigger finger, and we become dust.*

The Junior NCO told Jiang Shun, "Drop that scythe."

Jiang Shun laid it gently on the floor.

The Junior NCO told Wounded Eye and Bandage, "I told you not to fraternize in that way. We will speak later." To Jiang Shun and Thomas he said, "Explain yourselves."

Jiang Shun spread his arms wide. "I only have two words to say."

The Junior NCO raised his pulse rifle higher and pointed it at Jiang Shun's head. Thomas gasped, he could feel the blood pulsing at his neck.

"What two words?" the Junior NCO demanded.

Jiang Shun said in a raised voice, "*Silent Dragon!*"

Thomas heard electronic sounds from ahead of him and to both sides — *the soldiers' pulse rifles!* he realized.

The front door flew open and Han Ling burst through the doorway, shotgun at the ready. The unconscious body of the sentry, Scar, sprawled across the doorway behind her, with Beverly Kwan standing over him holding a nanotech injector. Han Ling exclaimed, "Drop those pulse rifles and get on the floor!"

The Junior NCO reacted first, aiming his pulse rifle at Han Ling and squeezing the trigger. Nothing happened. He looked down at his weapon and his eyes went wide. "Fearful Presence!" he told the rifle. "Fearful Presence!"

Bandage's weapon wouldn't fire either — she told it, "Mighty Warrior!"

"Victorious Hero!" Wounded Eye said to his rifle, and when it wouldn't fire, he reached down and pulled his knife from its leg sheath.

Jiang Shun snatched up his scythe in the same instant that Wounded Eye's hand drew back to throw the knife. The scythe flew across the room and its tip impaled Wounded Eye's hand to the wall behind him. His screams chilled Thomas.

Bandage flipped over her rifle to grasp it by the barrel and rushed toward Han Ling, intending to brain her with the shoulder stock.

Han Ling, though, didn't hesitate — she fired her shotgun directly at Bandage's legs. Bandage yelled in pain and fell to the floor.

The Junior NCO let his pulse rifle drop to the floor. Jiang Shun indicated him, saying, "We'll tie this one up."

"No," the Junior NCO said, as he gingerly pulled his pulse pistol from his holster using two fingers and handed it to Jiang Shun. "Let me help you with the wounded. I won't give you any more trouble." Thomas couldn't help but think the man looked relieved of a burden.

Han Ling moved the aim of her shotgun toward him. "A promise you'd best keep," she said, and the Junior NCO nodded vigorously.

Beverly Kwan indicated the still form of Scar, still lying in the doorway. "This one should stay out for awhile — I dosed him pretty well. I'll run ahead to the infirmary to prep for these other two."

Thomas said, "Baba, I must apologize — I didn't have enough faith in you — the army gave you the deactivation keywords for their rifles!"

"You can thank a paranoid military that would never want its own soldiers to carry out an insurrection."

As Thomas, Jiang Shun, and the Junior NCO carried Bandage toward the infirmary, with Han Ling training her shotgun on a still moaning Wounded Eye, more movements of stars, almost directly overhead, caught his eye.

Thomas, even while straining under the load of the squirming form of Bandage, said, "Baba, look — the stars!"

Those stars didn't just wheel around one another jockeying for position — they grew larger by the moment.

Jiang Shun said, "What do Jenregar ships look like? Have they targeted our village?"

But those "stars," even as they grew larger and brighter, never resolved into the forms of anything resembling a ship — instead, Thomas had to squint against their radiance as they headed toward the eastern horizon, then disappeared.

As that brilliance began to fade, Jiang Shun told Thomas, "Whatever that brings, we will worry about it later. We have work to do."

⁂

HE HEARD FROM A DISTANCE: "NATHAN? NATHAN?"

He found himself emitting a high-pitched groan, then felt embarrassed by it, and refused to try to say anything, fearful of what noise he might make next.

"Nathan? Can you hear me?"

Yes I can, he thought, *and you're damn irritating. I was sleeping perfectly well —*

Then, with a start, he realized: *No, I wasn't. I — did I faint? That's more embarrassing than the groan.*

Nathan opened his eyes and saw Tana staring down at him. He was lying in a hospital bed. Her smile was luminescent, her fingers ran through his hair, and the tracks of dried tears were faintly visible on her cheeks.

The next realization: the power was back! Otherwise, he'd never have been able to see the paths those tears had taken. "How long have I...."

"Been out?" Tana asked. "Just a few hours."

"I didn't get a chance to ask about...about Randi."

"She's fine. She's here, in fact."

"In the hospital?"

"I felt safer with her here," Tana said. "She's actually helping — she's one of my best traffic cops out in the hallway as new patients come in."

Nathan had never felt such relief — that his family was all here, together, and safe — *Or as safe as anyone in this habitat can be*, he thought. "How long has the power been back?"

"About forty-five minutes. It's saved some people's lives, I know — though we're still swamped. In fact, I just peeked in here for a minute. I have to go."

"Patients...still coming in?"

"They're still finding people in the rubble. And we already had plenty we haven't gotten to yet."

Nathan tried to sit up, but his head began swimming and he laid back down.

"Let that be a lesson to you," Tana said.

"The lesson is to do it more slowly," Nathan said, and eased himself up again. He let out a deep sigh. "There. All better."

"You're not headed out to try and rescue more people, are you?"

"I've got to get back to the control room."

"Adam already called. Said to tell you he has everything under control."

"Shit," Nathan said, swinging his legs onto the floor. "That's what I'm afraid of."

"Well, we *could* use the bed."

Nathan kissed Tana on the cheek. "Something tells me some undue influence got me this one in the first place."

"Sometimes 'wife' supersedes 'doctor.' Just be careful."

Nathan paused at the door. "Oh — how's Frank?"

"Who?" Tana asked.

"The guy I brought in on the cart."

"Oh! He's pretty beat up, but he'll be fine. You saved his life getting him in here."

"Well, that's one," Nathan said. "Let's see if we can add a few more to that." He blew a kiss toward Tana, who caught it as he left.

THE NEXT MORNING, RAMIRA ESPINOSA WAS UP BY SEVEN-thirty, got onto her bicycle by eight-thirty, and peddled toward Temporal Expressions. *Don't want to be late*, she thought. *I want to give Mr. Navarro a good impression.*

It was eight-forty-five when Ramira pulled up in front of the shop. The front door was locked, and she rapped on it quietly with her knuckles, then louder when Mr. Navarro didn't answer. Finally he shuffled from the rear of the shop, leaning more on his cane than he had the previous day. He unlocked the door and let her in. "You could've rung the bell, you know," he said.

His gruff tone brought a rush of blood to Ramira's face. "I'm sorry," she said. "I didn't want to disturb you."

"It's too late for that."

"Mr. Navarro -- what's wrong?"

He whipped around and waggled the end of his cane at her. "Something wrong? You can't know how much is wrong. Any more than you can know what it's like to have a bum leg and not be able to afford to fix it."

"Mr. Navarro, please. If there's anything I can do to help..."

"Not unless -- but no, you're young." He started to walk away from her. "You don't know anything about this."

Ramira placed her hands on her hips. "Try me."

Mr. Navarro spun around and nearly pointed the cane at Ramira again. But his stance became unsteady and he struck the floor with the cane even as Ramira moved to steady him. "I'm all right," he told her.

"Maybe you should come back here and sit down," Ramira said. She took him by the arm.

She didn't know what to expect in the back room; even in the little time she'd spent with the old man, she'd seen him appear from or disappear into it enough times that it held a touch of wonder for her. *I guess I expect it to be some sort of lair, dark and mysterious, where I can barely hear the furtive noises of unseen creatures.*

But it wasn't. Instead, it was a bright white room, beautiful in its simplicity, that held only a comp console and a chair. The walls were bare except for the one immediately in front of the console, which sported a holo projector.

Mr. Navarro sat at the chair behind the console. "I'd offer you a seat, Ramira, but these old bones...."

"That's all right. So what's the problem? Nothing with the shop, is it? Nothing stolen?"

"Goodness, no. It's...Mrs. Luna. Cecilio."

"She's not sick, is she?"

"No. You have to understand -- what I told you before -- we're more than just acquaintances. I'm sure she wanted to see me yesterday when she came in here. But you were here, and I imagine she wanted to speak with me alone."

Ramira's face broke out in a wide smile. "Why, Mr. Navarro -- you didn't have to hide your girlfriend from me."

Mr. Navarro looked at the floor. "She's not my girlfriend. We've never even touched other than to shake hands."

"You mean, no kisses?"

"None."

"No hugs?"

"Certainly...um...Certainly not!" Mr. Navarro said. "Everything between us has been perfectly proper since her husband died."

Ramira muttered, "Perfectly boring, you mean."

Mr. Navarro propped his hands on top of his cane and glared at Ramira. "I said you were young."

"Don't change the subject. You told me nothing was stolen."

"Nothing *was* -- oh, you're going to tell me my heart was."

"No, *your* common sense. If I'm so young, that makes you so old that you should know better than to love someone and not do anything about it?"

"How do you know I'm in love with Cecilio?"

"Because it's the one thing you're not talking about."

"Are you so wise in the ways of love?"

Ramira said, "Only when it involves other people."

"Then perhaps you'd do something for me."

"Name it," Ramira said.

"GOVERNOR KIMATHI," THE COMPUTER VOICE SAID, AS KAMAU leaned over a micro-sensor array trying to wrench secrets from a piece of Jenregar flesh. "You really should sit down a moment. Perhaps have some lunch."

"I'm not the governor anymore," Kamau said. "Go away. I'm busy."

"Governor, your vitals tell me you need to rest a moment. And you haven't had anything to eat or drink since early this morning."

"Thank you for the suggestion. Please go away."

"I must make the suggestion again," the comp said. "If you do not comply with that suggestion, then I must insist. And if I insist, a message goes directly to Governor Bilali."

Kamau stood straight, but at the cost of a flash of pain headed down his back. "Now listen here — you leave her out of it."

"Then you must comply."

Kamau hung his head and turned off the sensor array. *How can I live with this frustration?* he wondered as he shuffled toward a table in one corner of the lab. Only two chairs were pulled up next to the table, and he sat in the nearest one. He told the replicator in one corner of the table to make him a lunch of fruit juice and ugali.

He had to admit, the replicator made great ugali — it was a standard Kenyan dish — cornmeal cooked into the consistency of dough — but it reminded him of the way his mother used to make it. *Do they have a way to determine that?* Kamau wondered. *Is this another way they're trying to keep me happy?*

Kamau rolled a lump of the ugali into a ball and dipped it into the vegetable stew he most enjoyed with it. He thought, *If so, I gladly accept it, even as frustrating as it is to take a break from my work.*

Just as he finished his meal, and began to rise to head back to work, the door chime sounded. *Who could that be?* he wondered. *Most anybody I know would just walk right in.*

He raised his voice just a bit to say, "Come right in."

The door slid open to reveal a tall, dark-haired woman who looked at Kamau with an odd expression Kamau couldn't quite place. "How may I help you?" Kamau asked. "Are you in the right room?"

"I believe so. Governor Kimathi?"

"I keep telling people I'm not the governor anymore, but they don't want to believe me. But, yes, I'm Kamau Kimathi."

The woman stepped forward to shake his hand, but her grip was also tentative, as if, being 92 years old, he was some sort of wilting flower.

He also noticed her hand was webbed. And that she had some kind of nasty scar on her forehead.

The woman said in Spanish-accented English, "I'm Carrie Molina. I've been asked to help you in your research."

Kamau let his hand fall away from Carrie's, and stood as tall as he could, though even at his full height he couldn't quite look down at her. *I haven't lived over nine decades and had my relative success as a politician without being able to sense someone's mood,* he thought. *But this woman has too many of them for me to pull apart and examine separately just yet.* "Ms. Molina, I'm afraid you've been misinformed. I hope you didn't come a long way. I prefer to work alone."

"Oh, I knew that coming here. And I *did* come a long way — from Unity HQ in Brussels, in fact. A trip that should take about two and a half hours took me about as many days — and that's considered pretty fast, considering all the maglev lines that the Jenregar have disrupted."

"All the same, Ms. Molina — "

"Please, Governor, call me Carrie."

"I'll call you Carrie if you'll call me Kamau." *And drop a couple of those masks you're wearing*, he thought.

"OK, I can do that."

"I can do that, *Kamau*?"

"Uh, yes. I can do that, *Kamau*."

"I still don't want an assistant."

Carrie indicated the micro-sensor array. "How how much has your research on Jenregar body parts revealed to you?"

Kamau glanced toward the instrument, then back toward Carrie. "A few things. But not as much as I'd hoped, actually."

"All the same, your work has already captured the Unity's attention. How'd you like the real thing to work with?"

"What do you mean, 'the real thing?'"

"I mean a real, live Jenregar."

"You can do that?"

"I can."

Kamau raised a finger and waggled it at Carrie. "If you can't come through with that, young woman — I'll have you riding back to Brussels in an instant. And not on a maglev — it'll be a broken-down bus on the most pothole-ridden road I can find."

"I *can* do that, Gov...Kamau. If I can't, I'll arrange for that bus myself."

Kamau took a step forward and shook Carrie's hand again. "Then I guess I'm welcoming my new assistant."

Carrie's smile at his acceptance was so sincere that Kamau started to believe her various moods could be attributed to nervousness. *But I can't be certain*, he thought.

I'll have to watch this one carefully. And for now —Kamau narrowed his eyes and stared at Carrie. "The Unity wouldn't be approaching me if it didn't want something in return."

"You're right. But they want something from me, as well. Can we talk about that once the Jenregar arrives?"

Kamau considered that. "If that's your wish." He tilted his head toward the micro-sensor array. "At least that lets me get back to work, for now."

Apparently Carrie could take a hint. She excused herself and left the lab without saying another word.

Chapter 11

After a couple more hours of debriefing, Mike took Neriah's suggestion of grabbing a few hours sleep in quarters the Unity provided. When he woke up, it was nearly night. *I'm out of sync,* he thought. *In more ways than one. I've got to figure out what to do next.*

For now, he ordered a hot meal and sat in his suite and ate it alone. No company, no music, just his own disordered thoughts. Afterward, he stood on a balcony overlooking the lights of Brussels and wondered how long it might be until this great city saw a Jenregar incursion.

Here at the center of Belgian, European, and Earth Unity government, Mike was all too aware of the weight of history embodied within the very architecture of this city. *And it's only the smallest part of Human endeavor and achievement,* Mike thought. *Everything I am physically may come from that goddam ectogenesis tank, but all the rest that makes me Human — science, music, logic, love — comes from this planet. Deny it, and I'm denying the Sibelius Violin Concerto, Victoria Falls, and the late city of Florence. It's as if the Earth's grav has been reaching out to me all these years, unseen, unfelt, but slowly and inexorably drawing me back to itself.*

Until returning to Earth has made me realize I love this world after all — despite people like Jeremy.

I have to find a way to help save it.

The door chime sounded. Mike took a deep breath. *Not even a single night of peace,* he thought, *whoever this is, whatever they want.*

He went to the door. "Who is it?"

"Neriah. It's urgent."

He opened the door and Neriah's crestfallen expression and slumped shoulders told him something was very wrong. "What's happened?" he asked.

"It's Jeremy's wife," she said. "She's dead."

"Is it confirmed? How do we know that?"

"We found the starcraft that she and Jeremy took from Costaguana. It was burned out inside, cast adrift. Most of the passengers and crew were never even taken off of it. Julia Sheffield was one of them. We've seen her body, confirmed her ID through DNA, prints, retina, everything."

"Dammit," Mike said. "Does Jeremy know?"

"Not yet. I'd like you to go with me to tell him."

"Why me? I'm the last person he'd want to hear something like that from."

"Like it or not," Neriah said, "you *did* share an awful experience the last few days. You both know the Jenregar and what it's capable of. In the heat of emotion...maybe he'll remember something we can use."

"That's kind of cold."

"So's a world where Humanity isn't the dominant lifeform anymore."

"All right," Mike said. "I'll come with you. Do you know where he is?"

"We do," Neriah said. "And you're not going to like it."

Mike had read about virt parlors, and seen cubes of what they looked like. But he wasn't prepared for the reality of it when he and Neriah entered the large, sterile, and pristine room located in a structure that was just a short walk from the European Parliament building.

Dozens, hundreds of dark green coffin shapes were laid out in a large room, each on a pedestal placing them chest-high. Silence ruled — no attendants were in sight and the tech involved both in maintaining each virt client and in delivering each one's preferred fantasy to his or her receptacle was utterly quiet.

Perhaps given the coffin-like shapes of each receptacle, Mike had expected the place would reek of dust and decay, but the scents that greeted them were surprisingly fresh and natural, as if they were walking across a grassy landscape or down toward a beach.

"Not what I expected," Mike told Neriah, as they walked down the line of receptacles, "but I still can't approve."

"Now, now. We can't all be famous explorers. Or even unknown Unity diplomats. And I've been known to indulge myself for an hour or two sometimes."

"Nothing wrong with that. But this is different. There's something wrong with a planet where a high percentage of its inhabitants would rather live in a fake reality for days at a time."

"You won't find an argument from me there." Neriah stopped before one of the receptacles. "Here he is."

Mike examined the readouts on the side of the receptacle. "Vitals look good. All in all, he seems pretty calm in there."

"Which I suppose is the point," Neriah said. "I wonder if he's with Julia."

"In his fantasy, you mean?"

"Yeah. None of our business, of course, but...."

"Let's get this over with," Mike said.

Neriah touched a control on the side of the receptacle. Its top half slid aside, revealing Jeremy lying there on his back, arms folded, earphones cupping the sides of his head, dark goggles covering his eyes.

"This seems primitive," Mike said. "Why can't he just be on a holodeck?"

Neriah said, "Those are fine for training or it you're immersed in something that takes place within a single room. But if you're traveling cross-country or just inside a large building or a starcraft, you need more space. In this case, it's virtual space."

"Should we wake him?"

"Opening the receptacle closes the virt program. He'll come around in a moment."

Sure enough, Jeremy began to stir; even through the darkened goggles, Mike could see his eyes fluttering. His hands fell to his sides for a moment, then Jeremy groaned and he took off the headphones and goggles. He looked up at Mike and Neriah. "The *hell* with both of you! You have *no* idea what I was experiencing in there — no right to interrupt it."

Neriah said, "This is important."

"It had better be — " He sat up expectantly. "Is it Julia? You've heard from her, haven't you?"

I really didn't want to witness this, Mike thought. *As much as I dislike the man, I wouldn't wish this pain upon anybody.*

"Jeremy," Neriah said. "We haven't heard *from* her. We've heard *about* her."

"That means...she's dead, isn't she?"

Neriah cleared her throat. "Yes. I'm afraid she is."

Jeremy clasped his hands over his eyes and began to weep. "I knew it," he muttered. "The goddam Jenregar. I *knew* it. I...I was with her just now. In the virt. It was our honeymoon — *on* the Moon. Watching the Earth go through its phases in the same spot in the sky day after day..."

"I'm sorry," Neriah said.

"And — in the goddam virt, I was so happy — but none of that happiness carries over once you leave it. It's as if it's all a wonderful dream — but nothing more." Jeremy fell silent for a moment, then asked, "How did it happen?"

As Neriah explained the circumstances of the discovery of Julia Sheffield's body, Mike stood silently. He couldn't find any words, and didn't want to intrude upon Jeremy's grieving, anyway. After a time, Jeremy swung his legs over the side of the receptacle. "I want to hurt them," he said. "I want to kill them all."

"Then *think*," Neriah said. "Is there anything you saw while you were on that Jenregar ship that might help us?"

"I...had to wonder how they were getting Human and Jenregar genetic material to bond together. I don't know much about biology, but wouldn't they be pretty different?"

Mike said, "We still don't know that much about their biology. We don't know if it uses some analogy to our own DNA, or whether there's another way of transferring characteristics down to the next generation."

Jeremy slid down to the floor and stood on shaky legs. Neriah started to grab his arm, but Jeremy waved her away. "Why are you here, Mike?"

Mike hesitated, and Neriah broke in: "I asked him to be here."

"Have a look at the freak, huh, the virthead?"

Mike said, "Jeremy, I'm here the same reason as Neriah

— is there anything you know that can help us fight the Jenregar?"

Jeremy said, "The only thing I can think of is to copy what they're doing. They're becoming more Human in a way. We have to become a bit like the Jenregar."

"I was saying the same thing with Damian and Luisa. We have to figure out how to use their abilities against them."

"You make it sound so academic, Mike. Just what I'd expect from an artificial Human. What do you know of real grief and suffering?"

It was all Mike could do to keep from reciting a litany of his own life's tragedies, large and small, from being targeted for a beating by a group of three other 17-year-old boys at school, to being sentenced to death *in absentia* from countless pulpits of various religions to going on an exploratory mission to witness two star systems colliding that ended in the death of his longtime lover. *But I won't be that petty*, Mike thought. To Jeremy, he only said, "This isn't about what you think of me."

Jeremy said, "What do you know of real sacrifice? What would you ever be willing to commit to, to save the world — or at least, the world that matters most to Humanity?"

Sacrifice, Mike thought. *That's it!* He looked at Jeremy, then Neriah, and said, "That's exactly right. That's what it's going to take to really hurt the Jenregar."

Neriah asked, "What do you mean?"

"Sacrifice. Listen, Damian and Luisa suffered tortures almost beyond understanding — not just the pain and suffering, but being made into something that's almost *not Human*."

"Damian's mouth," Neriah said. "Luisa's arm."

"Exactly right. We have to sabotage the Jenregar's most

distinctive feature — how it uses pheromones to communicate with itself and adapt its surroundings."

Neriah said, "Like somehow giving its individuals a message telling them to retreat from Earth, or something?"

"When I took them on at Korolev Habitat, we sprayed some of the Jenregar individuals with pheromones that signaled all the others that they'd died. They ran all over themselves, half of them trying to carry the other half into the recyclers."

"They won't fall for that trick again," Jeremy said.

"You're right," Neriah said. "We have intel that shows us they've taken precautions against any attempts to spray their mounds — plenty of sensors, force screens — we have to come up with a different way of delivering those pheromones, or whatever we use."

Mike said, "And I'd bet we could sure come up with plenty of new ones — dozens or hundreds, maybe — keep the Jenregar guessing, and so busy that it can't adapt quickly enough to fight us effectively."

Neriah asked, "But how do we target them?"

"We know the Jenregar are looking to experiment on more Humans. But what if we, say, infected some of those Humans with bio-weapons — something that could spread through a Jenregar hive before they could stop it?"

Jeremy said, "Like a disease, or at least one of those pheromones — something that would damage them or keep them from fighting."

"The only problem," Mike said, "is that you're looking at a suicide mission — in fact, worse than that, because you're essentially going to be tortured and mutilated before you die."

They stood in silence for a moment, among the virtuality

receptacles. Then Mike noticed Jeremy was looking all around, as if seeing those long rows of receptacles for the first time. Jeremy said, "Hear me out. It seems to me that what would make a lot of people hesitate to take one of these missions is the part about the torture. Doesn't that seem right?"

Mike said, "The part about dying makes me hesitate. But I take the point. There are things I might die for. But I'd want it to be quick and painless if at all possible."

Jeremy slapped the side of his virt receptacle. "*Here's* your answer. You don't have to have a big chamber like this to lose yourself in a virt. We do it this way because people spend hours and days in them. We monitor people's vitals, we make sure they're hooked up to food drips and that their waste flows away from them — don't look at me with that disapproving expression, Mike, virt addiction isn't what we're talking about here."

Mike asked, "So what *are* we talking about?"

"We can implant chips inside people that can run virt programs. You said it yourself — it's a suicide mission, so we don't need them hooked up to a receptacle to monitor their vitals or take care of them. They can be running the most intense virts we can give them, and they'll never realize where they are or feel a bit of the torture. We take volunteers — "

"It's still a suicide mission," Mike said.

"But it's not a suicide plus torture mission. Even so, I don't suppose you'd want to volunteer."

"I have to admit, I don't. I hope to live a little longer. And I'd like to think we can find another way to do this — one that doesn't require people to sacrifice their lives."

"Maybe you can," Jeremy said. "Or maybe you just have to find people who don't have that much to live for."

"You can get past this, Jeremy," Neriah said. "I know it's difficult to lose your wife, but — "

"No, it's more than that." Jeremy looked at Mike. "I guess you were right, Mike. It looks like I've been fooling myself. The greatest virt tech in the world, making me feel like Julia was right next to me — I could see her, smell her, touch her — but when it ends, it isn't enough." He tapped the side of his head. "In fact, I found it pitiful. I found *myself* pitiful."

Mike said, "But Jeremy, Neriah's right. I've been through this, myself — losing someone I was close to. Given time — "

"No," Jeremy said. "Time's up. And I'm going to show you how a *real* Human reacts to a threat against his homeworld."

DR. BEVERLY KWAN DIDN'T SUBSCRIBE TO THE SAME LOW-tech philosophy as most of the rest of the village — Thomas and Jiang Shun placed Bandage upon a hospital bed that immediately showed readouts of her vitals and suggested a series of meds to prevent infection, nanobot protocols to begin repairing the wounds to her knees, and pain suppressants and sedatives to ease her to sleep during the entire process.

"Approve," Dr. Kwan said, and the bed's systems went to work, inserting IVs and making injections.

Thomas heard a strange sound, a sort of chittering, but told himself he had too active an imagination.

Dr. Kwan moved on to Wounded Eye, who sat on an adjacent bed, holding his mangled hand and staring wide-eyed. The Junior NCO went to him. "The doctor will take good care of you," he said.

"Until she injects poison into us," Wounded Eye told him.

The strange sound outside grew louder, and Thomas took a couple of steps back toward the infirmary's entrance. The eastern sky glowed red, and he hoped that glow emanated from the sun, and not some sort of Jenregar weapon. He saw nothing else unusual, but thought he smelled an odd odor, something he couldn't place.

The Junior NCO said, "She strikes me as a better person than that." He glanced at Dr. Kwan, who smiled in an attempt to reassure Wounded Eye. "She strikes me as a better person than any of us."

"Go ahead and lie down," Dr. Kwan said. "I've wanted to look at that eye, as well."

Han Ling pushed the Junior NCO toward an exam room. "We'll lock you in here," she said, "so you don't cause us any more problems."

Hours later, with their patients settled in under the baleful eye of Han Ling, whose shotgun remained at the ready, Thomas's curiosity won him over and he stepped outside the infirmary. He felt grateful that sunlight, not some Jenregar construct, illuminated the clouds to the east and directly overhead.

Then Thomas turned his gaze downward, into a landscape still swathed in darkness. The more his eyes adjusted, the more his horror grew, as he saw revealed a landscape filled only with dead, wilted wheat, brown grass, and trees that appeared as if they sagged beneath their own weight. Even the air smelled of dust and decay.

Jiang Shun came out of the infirmary and stood next to Thomas. "Baba, don't look," Thomas said. "You shouldn't see such a tragedy — "

"I have already seen it," Jiang Shun said. "I looked outside while you continued to help the doctor."

"Who has done this?" Thomas asked. "Who would destroy all your work, and the work of all the other men and women who have kept the old ways?"

"You might find yourself proud of me in a way," Jiang Shun said. "I checked through my datalink after the Junior NCO re-activated our newsfeed."

Thomas watched his father's features, silhouetted against the rising sun, and saw a deep sadness come into his eyes, watched his forehead furrow, his head bow. Thomas said, "Our own people have done this?"

"It feared the Jenregar might turn this way — and our leaders sent missiles that exploded in the air just before impact."

"They released the substance I smelled all night!"

Jiang Shun said, "It has something to do with chemicals and pheromones — an attempt to alter the Jenregar's body chemistry — render them helpless. It's worked against them before. But this time, it did not."

"But those chemicals and pheromones did kill our crops."

"They did," Jiang Shun said. "And I have more. It seems that the Jenregar turned away from our village just moments before the missiles fell. Everything that happened here — the soldiers taking over the village, our overpowering them — the crops dying — none of it means anything."

Thomas looked out at the newly desolate landscape, which the rising sun revealed in more detail each moment. He turned toward his father, made a fist with his right hand and cupped it in his left. He bowed deeply. "It means I learned to call you Baba. You learned to call me Thomas.

And it means not rogue soldiers nor Jenregar nor the loss of our crops can steal our community."

"'Our' crops?"

"Yes, Baba."

Jiang Shun indicated the desolate, brown landscape before them. "But what shall I do now?"

Thomas didn't have an answer.

Jiang Shun spoke again: "I suppose people somewhere need to eat, and must do without replicators, at least for a time. Somehow, somewhere, I can plant new crops."

Thomas said, "And it seems a knowledge of biology will help us fight the Jenregar — a much bigger, and more important battle, than the one we fought today."

"Such responsibilities may take us apart again, Thomas."

"Not for long, Baba. Not even in a world turned upside-down, that we must find a way to right again."

RAMIRA ESPINOSA GOT ONTO HER BIKE AND PEDDLED TO MRS. Luna's house. It was a small cottage at the edge of the Tapajos River, with five stone steps taking you up a slight slope to a neatly manicured front yard, and plenty of creeping vines making their chaotic paths up, down, and around the sides of the house. Out front was a large porch Ramira decided must be perfect for watching the sailboats ply up and down the river in calmer times, and in back she could make out a large vegetable garden.

Does she garden for pleasure or to make ends meet? Ramira wondered. *These market economies perplex me sometimes.* She leaned her bike against a white picket fence, an artifact that until now she'd only read about in stories. A soft breeze off the river tousled her hair and she ran her fingers through it to get it out of her eyes. Behind her, a cargo ship cut through the water, headed downriver. The ship's insistent splashing meant Ramira nearly missed the sounds coming from the rear of the house. *She's back there right now*, Ramira thought.

Ramira bounded up the stone steps and made her way around the side of the house, where a narrow sidewalk, also of stone, led the way. As the sound of the cargo ship faded, she could make out scraping noises and a female voice humming a bouncy tune. When she peeked around the corner, she made out Mrs. Luna, dressed in well-worn clothing, on hands and knees, digging in the dirt with a trowel. A small pot of plants Ramira recognized as coneflowers sat next to her, apparently about to join another set that constituted about a quarter of the small garden. Ramira also saw purple day lilies, fingermoss from the Human-colonized planet Seura, and various flowering shrubs.

Ramira dragged one foot to make a scraping sound against the stone, and emitted a quiet cough. Mrs. Luna looked up at her, but didn't seem startled. She got to her feet, still holding the trowel, and gave Ramira a suspicious look. "Yes? How may I help you?" she asked. But before Ramira could answer, Mrs. Luna folded her arms and looked at her with narrowed eyes. "I recognize you. From the store. Mr. Navarro sent you, didn't he?"

"Yes, Ma'am."

"You tell him," Mrs. Luna said, "I'm no more interested in charity than he is." She aimed the trowel at her as if it were a disruptor. "You go right now and tell him that, hear?"

Ramira felt deflated. "Yes, Ma'am. I will."

Mrs. Luna turned her back on Ramira, went down on hands and knees again, and resumed her work. She wielded the trowel with much stronger thrusts than before, and Ramira could see the tension in the muscles of her neck and shoulders.

Ramira went to the front of the house, retrieved her bike, and contented herself for now with what was actually a pleasant ride along the bike path next to the Tapajos River, as she paced another cargo ship headed, of course, downriver. The small waves it created broke behind her, their lazy rhythms an oddly calming influence. For the time being she was content not to think, but only to pedal, and on the downhill slopes merely to coast.

AS CARRIE MOLINA ENTERED KAMAU'S LAB, SHE SAW HE WAS in his usual stance, leaning over what she could see was a readout of the nature of Jenregar pheromonal responses. *I hope he can accept everything I have to tell him*, she thought. *He's brilliant, but he can be feisty.*

And I have to figure out how to reconcile our very different goals regarding the Jenregar.

"I haven't had a chance to tell you a couple very important things, yet."

Kamau only slowly looked up from his work. "Oh? What might those be?"

"Well, one is that I recently had a Jenregar implant removed from my forehead."

"I admit I noticed it. But I thought I'd wait to see if it was something you wanted to talk about."

"I do. It seems that implant, while it was still planted in my head, allowed me to detect the presence of Jenregar individuals — it gave me a rather basic link to the rest of the hive."

Now I've sparked his interest, Carrie thought, as Kamau's eyes brightened and he turned his back on the readout he'd been studying. "That's...extraordinary. So, if I may ask — what did it feel like? Did it give you any insight to the Jenregar's feelings or motivations?"

Carrie shook her head. "None at all. It was simply a fact. If you're wondering whether I felt some sort of emotional or maybe even mystical connection to the hive — the answer is that I didn't."

Kamau rubbed his chin. "Hmm. That's disappointing. I wonder, though — perhaps you weren't connected as completely as an actual Jenregar individual would be. If you'd spent more time there — "

"Kamau, if I'd spent any more time in there I'd be dead. Just like my father." At a questioning look from Kamau, Carrie continued: "He was there in the mound — in Madrid. Tortured as the Jenregar experimented on him. Dying when I had to leave."

"I'm so sorry, Carrie. I didn't realize you had such a personal connection to this."

"Personal enough that I know I was as connected to the hive as any Jenregar individual. You see, after that implant was installed, I was able to sense my father's presence the same way I could that of the Jenregar. He had an implant similar to mine. But between us — as you might expect — the connection was very emotional."

"As it was not among the Jenregar."

"That's right," Carrie said. "No individual feelings or motivations to appeal to. I'm sorry."

"You have no reason to be sorry, Carrie. You've been through a horrific trial. But — you told me you had a couple of very important things to tell me. What was the other one?"

Carrie said, "Today's the day."

"The day for what? Have I forgotten an appointment?"

"*The* day!"

"You mean — "

"Yes!" Carrie said. "A Jenregar is being delivered here in just a few moments."

"You didn't tell me!"

"Kamau, I only found out myself. Chinese authorities managed to capture a Jenregar individual a city called Zhengzhou — apparently at significant loss of life to their own troops. They're sending it to us."

Kamau said, "About time the Chinese did something effective. So far all I've heard of is rumors of their own soldiers running away from battle and the government destroying their own peoples' crops."

"I've heard even worse from my Unity sources. That China may have nuked one of its own cities to destroy a Jenregar hive."

"I do not want to believe that."

"I wish I *didn't* believe it. Be that as it may, the Unity has managed to get a shuttle to fly low and fast out of China, and it's avoided being detected by the Jenregar. It should be landing here in just a few minutes."

"I've not had a chance to prepare — "

Carrie said, "You've done nothing *but* prepare since you resigned as governor."

"So what's going to happen?"

"The shuttle lands outside the lab, here. The Jenregar's in a secure holding area in a transport module aboard the shuttle. "We're going to get our first look at it just a few minutes after it lands."

"Then it'll be brought into our lab?"

"Actually," Carrie said, "there's going to be a lot of

activity here overnight. This wall's over here's going to be knocked down — "

"What? Who authorized that?"

"Well — the Unity kind of decided that on its own." Carrie waited for Kamau's reaction. *I can see he's torn*, she thought. *This is what he's waited for, maybe never thought he'd get to see — a real, live Jenregar for a subject. But he's made this lab a place of comfort for him — and changing it in any way puts that in jeopardy.*

Kamau said, "I suppose the Unity knows me as well as I know myself."

Carrie said, "What do you mean?"

"We could stand here and argue about my personal space here in the lab, and how it's been violated, or we could just go and see this Jenregar. Because that's how that conversation would end anyway, and we might as well save time."

Carrie couldn't help but grin at that. "I suppose that's so." She started to say more, but didn't as the whine of the shuttle's gravitics came into earshot.

Kamau indicated the doorway. "Then let's go see our Jenregar."

Carrie led the way outside, but made sure to maintain a slow pace for the sake of her 92-year-old colleague. *I can only hope I'm that spry when I reach that age*, she thought, *even with rejuv treatments.*

A warm afternoon greeted them as they left the main laboratory building. Security guards flanked the main entrance. A half dozen more guards were coming down a ramp on the side of the medium-sized transport shuttle, even as the shuttle's engines were shutting down. They were all heavily armored, and carrying much larger and more powerful pulse rifles than Carrie had ever seen before.

The guards arrayed themselves all around the shuttle. The one closest to Carrie and Kamau indicated the ramp behind him. A metallic-sounding voice came over a speaker in the guard's helmet: "You can see the Jenregar individual now — for five minutes only."

As Carrie let Kamau lead the way up the ramp, she said, "I wonder why just five minutes."

"Knowing the Unity — with all respect, Carrie, since you work for them — it's probably just arbitrary."

"I work *with* the Unity sometimes, Kamau. Not *for* them."

"Ah. A subtle difference, but one I appreciate."

At the top of the ramp, they took a right down a narrow corridor. At the end of that corridor was a room about four meters square. It nearest wall was transparent.

On the opposite side of that wall stood a Jenregar. She'd been closer to several of the species, of course, but she'd always been fighting them or fleeing from them in those other encounters. *I've never had the chance to consider one in "cold blood," so to speak,* she thought. *And that phrase seems appropriate — I feel as if a cold fluid is easing down my spine.*

The Jenregar was an adult, as usual not quite a meter tall — not imposing due to its size, by any means. As was common among Humans, the first feature she looked at on the Jenregar's face was its eyes — but they were small and narrow, clearly secondary organs. No external ears, only recessed flaps of skin that moved to gather in sounds. The mouth functioned only to ingest food, not to convey speech.

The Jenregar stood up straight, its body a hard carapace, limbs tentacle-like, maintaining their body shape only through the pressure of internal fluids.

It didn't react at all to Carrie or Kamau staring at it.

Carrie could barely hear Kamau's first words: "Now that

I'm actually staring at such a being, I wonder how I could possibly communicate with it."

Carrie said, "I can't believe you're looking at this...creature...with such a sense of wonder."

Kamau looked at Carrie. "Why not?" he said. "It's an example of a species that has become an enemy to Humanity, that's true. But it, and the others like it, must have something in common with us. Its own fears and dreams — its desires."

"I'm sorry, Governor, but it *doesn't* have to have any of those things. I respect what you're trying to do, but my own interests run, I guess I'd have to say, parallel to yours."

"You just want to kill them more effectively."

"They killed my father. They tortured him first, then they killed him. I had to abandon him in one of their mounds so I could survive and try and kill as many of these bastard things as I can."

Kamau said, "I wish I had comforting words for you."

Carrie turned her attention to the Jenregar again. "Either way, your work is vital. We have to know much more about how the Jenregar think — how commands from the local queen are received and interpreted — *if* they're interpreted at all."

"None of which will be possible if we can't communicate to this Jenregar individual."

"I approve of curiosity for its own sake, Kamau. I suppose you'll use any breakthroughs as you see fit — but I can't imagine you communicating with this...thing."

"I won't hide anything from you. Anything I learn, you'll know, too."

"Even if you find a way to commit genocide against an intelligent Galactic species?"

"Even then. I hold my trust in knowledge for its own

sake. I know Mike Christopher has already come up with one potential weapon against the Jenregar. I have to hope our efforts lead us to the better, more peaceful path."

"I hope you're right," Carrie said. "As long as that better path also leads us to a way to save Humanity."

Chapter 12

Mike and Neriah stood on the tarmac of an out-of-the-way corner of the Brussels Starport, watching from about two hundred meters away as a line of thirty people waited to board a large personnel shuttle. The wind whipped across the wide expanse of the landing pad, roaring just loud enough that Mike leaned in close to tell Neriah, "I can't believe the Unity found this many people for a suicide mission."

These volunteers, along with hundreds of others launching elsewhere, were to be dropped near selected Jenregar mounds to be "captured." Any attempt by anyone to enter with energy rifles or explosives or other more "traditional" weapons would be instantly killed, but the hope was that the Jenregar wouldn't be able to detect the nanite protocols implanted within these Humans' bodies.

Once the Jenregar started working on them, their bodies, having passed the usual Jenregar safeguards, would release pheromones that would give various commands to the Jenregar individuals — instructions to dismantle their hives, or to consider other Jenregar individuals as sick or damaged, and dispose of them. As Mike had suggested, those and dozens of other commands would bring chaos to the otherwise unified Jenregar hive mind — or so it was hoped.

Neriah looked stricken. "I can't believe I proposed it to the Unity — and that it accepted the idea. Or that a few of these volunteers decided to forego the virt chip."

"Are they so desperate?" Mike asked as the line moved forward to enter the shuttle. "Do they have so little to live for?"

"Some are that way. Damaged somehow. Others consider it their patriotic duty to their homeworld."

"Then they're better than I am."

"Don't say that, Mike," Neriah told him. "You've risked your life plenty of times. Look, there he is."

Jeremy Sheffield moved forward slowly as the line advanced. He looked toward Mike and Neriah and gave a casual salute. Neriah waved back and, after a moment's hesitation, so did Mike. *Though I doubt my gesture provides him with any comfort*, he thought.

Mike told Neriah, "I wonder what his Julia would've thought about him doing this."

"I don't know anything about her. Maybe she'd be horrified. Maybe she'd be proud."

The final person boarded the shuttle, and within moments its gravitic drive lifted the craft from the landing pad. As it arced away to the west, Mike said, "We all come to an end eventually. At least Jeremy won't suffer. I wish I could be so certain of that whenever my time comes."

Neriah asked, "So what's next for you?"

"I suppose we'll see how this plan works. That may take a while. In the meantime, I have a personal trip to make."

THOMAS JIANG AND HIS FATHER SAT IN THE SMALL COURTYARD of Jiang Shun's home after a long day of work in the fields and the village. With all their crops destroyed, Jiang Shun had insisted upon performing maintenance on all the village's equipment, from the simplest plow to the most advanced automated harvester. "One day we'll work these fields again," he said, "and we'll be grateful this equipment will be ready for use."

Thomas couldn't argue with that, but he was unused to physical labor, and was glad to be able to sit and have a beer.

The western sky held only a faint glow, and Thomas knew he'd be headed for bed soon. *In my old life in Zhengzhou,* he thought, *I'd have been home a couple of hours ago, and maybe ready to head out to a party. Who knew the life of a research biologist could've seemed so special?*

Jiang Shun lifted the small tankard of beer from the short table between each him and Thomas, leading Thomas to lift his drink and take a long, refreshing sip. Afterwards, Thomas said, "So much has changed, in only a matter of days."

"And, despite the loss of our crops, some news is for the better," Jiang Shun said. "I hear the Jenregar are being pushed back in some places. The maglev is running to Zhengzhou again."

"But no one's using it to return to the city, Baba. It runs empty that way, and still full coming out."

Jiang Shun waved that concern away. "Bah! Things will become better soon."

"I can only hope you're right, Baba," Thomas said and polished off his tankard of beer. "But what will we do now that we've put away our farming equipment? Can we even stay in the village?"

Jiang Shun said, "I fear we may have to leave for awhile. We need to eat."

"I hate to become a refugee," Thomas said, "especially after we won out over the soldiers."

"Those were not great soldiers. The Junior NCO was the only one with a worthwhile heart. If we're to be forced off our land, at least it's by the Jenregar — a more worthy opponent."

A knock came at the door, a hollow sound from a couple of rooms away. "Who could that be?" Jiang Shun wondered. Thomas started to rise, but his father beat him to it and headed toward the door. Thomas was just starting to ponder whether he wanted another beer when he heard Beverly Kwan's voice — he couldn't make out her words, but she sounded upset. Thomas rushed to the front door, where Jiang Shun was just letting Beverly into the house. One look at her face, and Thomas's heart felt as if it skipped a beat — her eyes were wide, she was breathing so quickly Thomas feared she might hyper-ventilate, and her hands were shaking.

"Sit down, sit down," Jiang Shun told her. "Can I get you something to drink?"

"No, no, thank you," Beverly said as she sat. "I've just received serious news through a medical channel from Zhengzhou. It was cut off before I could receive too many details — two terrible things have happened." She looked up at Thomas. "I had to talk to someone. And perhaps ask for some help."

"Of course," Thomas said as he sat across from her. "What can we do?"

"It's my grandmother, Nai-nai. I thought she was getting

out of Zhengzhou. But she was caught up in a crowd. Nai-nai's legs were hurt — she's 82, very spry, but she had to go to the nearest hospital. But they only kept her a day — put her back out on the street."

Jiang Shen, standing behind Thomas, asked, "Why would they do that?"

"There's no room," Beverly said. The Jenregar are being pushed out of some places around Zhengzhou, but that just means they're moving into other areas. Including near that hospital. There are so many casualties coming in they're making patients who aren't in serious condition leave. A family — the Liaos — nearby saw her hobbling down the street and took pity on her. She's staying with them."

"What do you know about that family?"

"Very little. All I have is the name. I'm hoping they can help get Nai-nai out of the city."

"You can't count on that," Thomas said. "Do you want to go get her?"

Beverly grasped Thomas's hands. "Would you help me? I'd be forever grateful."

Jiang Shen said, "I'll get that pulse pistol we took from the Junior NCO."

Thomas stood. "No, Baba. You need to keep running this farm."

"What use is a farm without crops?"

"It tells everyone who you are and what you're capable of. As does the presence of those troops you managed to defeat. No, you're too important to the village."

"Son, I can defend Beverly better."

"Against what? Dozens of Jenregar falling upon us? I'm going to take a weapon, but I don't fool myself that I can actually protect us against them. But I know these city people since I've become one of them. I can deal with them better."

Jiang Shen's shoulders fell, and he looked toward the floor. "I suppose you're right, Thomas." He told Beverly, "My son is the best chance you have of getting your grandmother back. I'll be awaiting the three of you right here."

"Wait a minute," Thomas said. He asked Beverly, "You said two terrible things have happened. What was the other?"

"Oh!" Beverly said, and covered her mouth with her hand. After a moment, she lowered her hand and said, "I feel so selfish. We focus so much on what's important to our own lives, often neglecting thoughts of others. It's what happened to Xiamen." That was a city on the southeast coast of the country, facing the Taiwan Strait.

"Have the Jenregar attacked it, as well?" Thomas asked.

"Worse than that," Beverly said. "They were just starting to build their mound when it's said a nuclear weapon struck it."

Jiang Shen clenched his fists and stomped his feet on the floor. "Who did this? What other country would dare take it upon themselves to attack us that way, even if the true target was the Jenregar? Our national sovereignty — "

"You don't understand. It wasn't an attack by another country. It was a *Chinese* weapon. We did this to ourselves. All the Jenregar there were destroyed. But a city of over five million Humans died along with them."

Jiang Shen's expression turned cold and hard as that of a statue. After a moment, he turned and went without a word into his bedroom, closing the door quietly behind him.

"I'm sorry, Mr. Navarro," Ramira said when she returned to Temporal Expressions. They were in the main room of the shop. No customers.

Mr. Navarro leaned on his cane and grasped Ramira's shoulder. "Ah, no worries. You did your best. Oh, but I'm such a coward. Why would I send someone else to do the job I should do?"

"If there's any other way I can help out...."

"You've done well by me. I've no complaints. I only wish you could do better for yourself. Take the rest of the day off -- I'll be sure to pay you for today. And any day you find a better-paying job than being here, be sure to take it."

"Miyanda is trying to find something more for me."

"Then I'll see you when I see you. I can only do so much, but I'll keep you as cashed up as I can."

"Thanks, Mr. Navarro," Ramira said. "You sure everything else is all right?"

"I suppose."

"Which means it isn't."

Mr. Navarro gave Ramira a wry glance. "You know me too well, even though it's been such a short time. I'm so worried about the Jenregar. That mound in the middle of the city keeps growing. It doesn't seem as if they're sending as many of their troops out as they were. But the government doesn't seem to be doing anything to fight them."

"I've wondered about that. I worry about it all the time. And not just for myself. My bother Matias is depending on me, too. I so want him to be proud of me."

"I understand those feelings. And that's not all, Ramira. I didn't tell you the whole truth about how well this store does financially. I owe money. Everything I have is tied up in this shop. And with the recession, no one's buying. You're lucky to have a chance at any job at all, Ramira. People don't have jobs, so they don't have money to spend, so businesses can't hire anyone."

"Which means no one has money to spend, and the cycle continues."

"You're starting to catch on. The banks -- the only loans they're giving out right now are predatory ones that keep people in debt forever."

"Uh, oh."

"What's that?"

"Nothing," Ramira said.

"If you're determined to leave here, make it soon. I don't know how bad things are going to get. The military's been anticipating another Jenregar push farther into the city."

"What about you? What are you going to do if that happens?"

"I don't know," Mr. Navarro said. "But I know I'd never leave these artworks behind. They're my life."

"Everything's getting so desperate."

"You don't even know how desperate, Ramira. The government's even asking for volunteers for suicide missions now — something about infecting the Jenregar mounds from inside."

"Who would ever consider that? You'd either have to be incredibly dedicated, or have nothing left to lose."

"I fear we may have no shortage of such people soon," Mr. Navarro said.

Ramira sought more words but found none. She headed outside, got onto her bike, and peddled toward the hotel.

Chapter 13

Hours after watching Jeremy's departure, Mike got himself onto a maglev train that was leaving Brussels headed for Calais, France, where he would switch trains to head toward America. The trip wasn't even two hundred kilometers; even allowing for acceleration and deceleration, Mike knew the trip wouldn't take over ten minutes. Neriah had promised him that in the time since he and Jeremy had taken their roundabout journey across much of the planet, many routes closed to them earlier had opened up.

I intend to take the short way back to America this time, Mike thought. His next thought was, *Poor Jeremy. Every time I think of him, my thought's the same. I hope he didn't suffer.*

Not many people were on board the automated maglev as it pulled away from the Brussels-Luxembourg Railway Station. *Either people are afraid of getting stranded,* Mike thought, *or are sticking close to their families right now.*

Can't say as I blame them either way.

Though I have little concept of what a real family would be like.

Mike leaned back in the form-fitting seat and tried to keep his ears focused on what little sound was transmitted into the cabin; he considered it a minor example of "white noise" that he hoped would let him clear his mind. He kept his eyes focused on the small display on the unoccupied seat in front of him that showed the maglev's progress — a thin green line that stretched steadily from Brussels toward Calais.

Somewhere beneath the town of Bergues, France, only forty kilometers from his immediate destination, Mike heard the sound of the maglev's propulsion fading. That didn't seem unusual; they had a lot of momentum to kill before reaching Calais. Then a calm female voice announced, "The Calais maglev tunnel has been blocked; all passengers, regardless of destination, please prepare to leave the maglev train."

Now what the hell's going on? was Mike's immediate thought.

The few other people in the cabin with him began looking around; obviously, they were confused, as well. Mike decided to take the chance that an actual Human or even a particularly responsive A.I had spoken: "What's caused the blockage? Will we be safe in leaving the train?"

A man in his twenties sitting across the aisle from Mike said, in French, "You'll never get an answer." Fortunately, Mike had only recently, when he was first approaching Earth, decided to have most of the planet's major languages downloaded into his datalink.

After several moments of continued silence, Mike said, in English, "I guess you're right."

The man, who apparently had at least basic translator tech implanted within him, stuck out his hand. "Terry Needham. You sound as if you're also from America."

Mike shook Terry's hand. "I am, though not lately. Mike Christopher."

Terry's eyebrows raised and his eyes widened. "The spacer?"

Mike fought not to frown. "Yes," he said. "That's me."

Terry flashed Mike a wide smile. "Don't look so perturbed. "I'm a big fan."

"Uh huh."

"No, really — the way you got the effort to save Splendor going — and that trip to Moruteb! The sights you saw — worlds crashing together, fish living at the base of a dry cliff, other lifeforms living in a world's rings — it's amazing!"

"It was," Mike admitted. "But also keep in mind we lost two crewmembers on that trip."

"Including your shipmate, Linna. I'm sorry — my enthusiasm for your work — it's easy to forget the Human toll."

No it's not, Mike thought. *Not when you've lived it.*

The train came to a complete halt, and the overhead lights went out for a second, came back on immediately, went dark again, this time for a longer period, then back. Mike stood and told Terry, "We'd better get the hell out of here like the A.I said."

Mike headed toward the exit at the opposite end of the train car. Without thinking, he found himself at the head of the line of people, as he placed a hand on the disruptor at his hip. *Careful, now*, he told himself. *You're not leading a mission onto an unknown world. Next you'll be checking the atmosphere and grav before stepping outside.*

The train car's doorway slid open, revealing what must have been a seldom-used station — dirty walls, scuffed and stained floors. *And I don't even want to guess what some of those stains might be*, Mike thought. As he stepped from the car, his grip on his disruptor tightened, but he didn't pull it just yet. The only smells were a mixture of mold and something metallic.

Terry's voice from behind him: "Where the hell are we?"

Mike looked all around for a cube or flat display, or even an old-fashioned sign. As he looked toward an unmoving escalator, he saw several rectangular shapes, lighter than the surrounding walls, where some kind of display might have been, but they were obviously long gone.

"Just one way to find out, I guess," Mike said. He looked back at Terry and the five other people gathered around. "Anyone here have law enforcement or military background?"

The others looked at one another, then back at Mike. A couple shrugged or shook their heads. "Guess not," Mike said. "Anyone else armed?"

Another negative response. Terry told Mike, "How the hell did you get onto the planet with a gun?"

"Well, for one thing, I didn't bring my disruptor, just a stunner — it won't kill anyone. For another, I didn't exactly arrive through customs, and the Unity has given me some privileges as far as getting through security checkpoints. Either way, I guess I'll go up top, see where we are, and try to find out what's going on." Several people nodded to Mike or one another, and all of them seemed willing to let Mike be the one to take the risk.

As he started toward the escalator, though, Terry's hand slapped down on his shoulder, and he shrugged it off. "Don't do that."

Terry's eyes went wide. "Sorry! Do you want me along, too?"

"Listen — I'm not a police officer or a soldier, but I know what it's like to walk into a potentially dangerous situation.

I'll do best if I don't have any distractions walking right next to me."

Terry's mouth curled in frustration. "Well, if you put it that way — "

"I do," Mike said, and continued toward the escalator.

As eagerly as I anticipated this, Kamau thought as he and Carrie prepared to examine the Jenregar individual, *I can't help but feel my lab is being violated.*

The Jenregar stood impassively in the far corner of Kamau's facility, within the same four-meter-square enclosure that had been moved from the Unity shuttle. Two Unity guards stood on opposite corners of the enclosure, fully armored, helmets concealing most of their features, holding pulse rifles close to their chests, staring as impassively as the Jenregar.

Kamau leaned close to Carrie and whispered, "The guards make me as nervous as this Jenregar does. I tried to talk to them a minute ago, but they told me they're not supposed to speak to me."

Carrie said, "They don't want to get too friendly. If that Jenregar gets loose, they're supposed to try to kill it. But if it got to one of us first and stuck us with one of those stingers, they'd have to shoot us, as well — as a mercy to us."

"I see. Then I suppose I'll do my best to ignore them, as well. All right — have you seen the surveillance holos from overnight?"

"Just a few minutes' worth."

Kamau said, "This Jenregar never moved at all — didn't sit down, didn't look around or show any curiosity about its surroundings, didn't eliminate any body waste. And what do we think it eats?"

Carrie shrugged. "There's so much we don't know about them. This one hasn't been fed in days, apparently. We certainly don't know what to feed it. That's why the Unity took the chance with the shuttle to get it here — the thought was that it could die of starvation any day now."

"Then we've got to find out how it feeds, and what it feeds on."

"I have no sympathy for it, Kamau. It dies when it dies."

"I'm not speaking from sympathy. The longer it lives, the more we can learn. We've never had a live Jenregar to study before."

Carrie let out a long sigh. "You're right. I'm sorry. I let my anger get the best of me."

Kamau placed his hand on Carrie's shoulder. "I understand. I would feel the same way if I were in your situation."

"You're being quite gracious in working with me."

"We have the same goal, Carrie. Saving our own species."

"Let's get to it, then. Is there any equipment I can help you with?"

Kamau went to a desk filled with several types of sensors, some of them crystalline blocks that passively accepted information from all around them, others sharp and metallic that sent out streams of radiation, sound, and even subspace waves that actively probed their surroundings. "All these should work fine from right here," Kamau said. "None of them emits anything harmful to Humans — or Jenregar, as far as we know."

"Although if we *did* find something simple that harmed them — "

"You know my feelings about that," Kamau said. "But we discover what we discover. The step after that will be to try a mixture of pheromonal cues."

"Trying to learn their language, so to speak."

"Exactly."

"So what's first?" Carrie asked.

Kamau touched a control on the back of one of the crystalline blocks. "First, a passive sensor. What can we learn without interacting with this Jenregar?"

"You think capturing it and throwing it into a shuttle and bringing it across two continents isn't interacting?"

"No experiment is perfect. We aren't interacting with it *right now*, at least as far as we know." Kamau activated the passive sensor. "Let's see what we can find out."

Kamau ran a battery of tests on the Jenregar individual, first using only passive sensors. They registered the being's presence, its weight, which was about half that of a Human adult, and the minimal heat it emitted from its body.

No sign of significant brain activity that would indicate advanced intelligence or the capacity to make its own decisions, Kamau thought.

Kamau knew Carrie was watching him with growing concern. Finally she asked, "Anything significant?"

"I told you I'd share everything with you. This Jenregar is barely what I would call sentient. Your average dog or cat would rate higher on the scale."

"Thus confirming that they act largely on instinct and pheromonal instructions from the hive mind."

"Perhaps." Kamau considered for a moment. *I do what I have to do*, he thought, and fired up equipment that aimed more invasive energies at the Jenregar.

It continued to stand impassively. Then Kamau began

working the equipment that would pump various pheromones into the Jenregar's environment.

Still no response from it, Kamau thought after a moment. *I don't understand some of the results I'm getting. And who knows how long this Jenregar will last? We have to find out something substantive soon.*

I'm going to try to evoke a response I may soon regret.

A few more pheromonal cues pumped into the Jenregar's air, and Kamau waited.

Still, no response.

A warning from Kamau's datalink, and he leaned back from the bank of sensors. He let out a deep sigh. "Problem?" Carrie asked.

Kamau shook his head. "I've got to rest awhile. If I don't, the comp will start bitching at me and then start shutting down the lab."

"Oh."

"I suppose you might need a break as well." He indicated the corner of the lab where a table and chairs stood next to a replicator. "I could use a glass of juice. Why don't we sit together for a time and we can discuss what I've learned so far today."

A few moments later, Kamau took a sip of his fruit juice and was staring far away, past Carrie's presence. She hadn't touched her hot tea yet.

Finally he said, "I'm disappointed in what I've learned."

"How so?"

"All my theories about communicating with the Jenregar have involved immediate pheromonal responses."

"Meaning — ?"

"Meaning, I've been injecting pheromonal cues into the atmosphere of that room."

"To do get it to do what?"

"I tried one to get it to stand down — to relax, take in its surroundings, allow itself to listen to us."

"And this is something that's worked before."

"We've used it in the suicide attacks that have been penetrating their mounds — and it's worked there."

"But now the Jenregar just stands there."

"*So* frustrating!" Kamau said.

Carrie took a sip of her tea. "So...does that imply that it understands context?"

"What do you mean?"

"That it knows it's in a cage, surrounded by Humans, and that any pheromonal cues can't be coming from the hive mind."

"But that negates the nature of those kinds of cues," Kamau said. "The whole idea is that the Jenregar wouldn't be able to help itself."

"You mentioned 'one' of those cues. Were there others?"

Kamau stared at his glass as he gripped it with both hands. "There was one other. And I'm ashamed of using it."

"Ashamed? I've not known you that long, Kamau, but I can't imagine you doing something you'd be ashamed of."

"This is a sign of how desperate I've become. I tried to instruct that Jenregar to attack us."

Carrie asked, "How...how could you be so careless? If that thing had somehow gotten out of that enclosure, you could've endangered all of us."

"Carrie, don't worry. I trust in the security of the enclosure. The Jenregar couldn't get out."

"And you — you didn't even tell the guards what you were doing, did you?"

"They are already at high alert. What precautions could they take that they are not already doing?"

"Wait a minute — so that's not what you're ashamed of?"

"Of course not — I'm ashamed of trying to connect with this Jenregar in a manner that uses violence."

"We could've all been killed!"

Kamau said, "You forget how many of my countrymen and women I've seen killed — torn apart by these beings. So do not lecture me!"

"I'd think seeing that would make you all the more aware of the possible danger we're in."

"It makes me aware that any danger is worth the risk."

"But it has to be an *informed* risk. I'll risk my own life to find a way to defeat the Jenregar — hell, I've already done that several times over. But that's *my* decision."

Kamau's shoulders slumped. "You're right, Carrie. I apologize. It's just...."

"I know. We're desperate. But that may be one thing the Jenregar is counting on. Desperate people make mistakes. But we don't have the time to afford a lot of mistakes."

After a moment, Kamau said, "We should get back to work." When Carrie started to speak, he held up a hand and she kept quiet. Kamau said, "From now on, I really will let you know everything I'm about to do. You can inspect my equipment. If you have an objection, let me know, and we'll work it out."

"I appreciate that, Kamau."

"It only makes sense. How can we hope to communicate effectively with the Jenregar if we cannot do so with one another?"

———

THE NEXT MORNING, THE SKY DAWNED BRIGHT AND CLEAR. Thomas and Beverly packed food bars, bottled water, first-aid kits, and a change of clothes into backpacks. Jiang Shen gave Thomas the pulse pistol and provided him a quick tutorial on its use. "You're probably right, that you couldn't hold off a crowd of Jenregar," his father told him. "But you might slow them down just long enough to get yourself and Beverly out of a dangerous situation."

Beverly muttered, "Or turn them away from us and toward someone who's not putting up a fight."

"This is war," Jiang Shen said. "And in war, tragic things happen. And terrible decisions have to be made." He wiped his eyes. "I suppose we learned that yesterday, didn't we?"

Thomas said, "Baba, we don't know all the details of what happened in Xiamen. Perhaps our leaders saw a chance to win a quick victory. Perhaps our situation is more desperate than we know."

"I would gladly sacrifice myself to destroy the Jenregar." He pointed at Thomas. "But should I sacrifice you?" He moved his hand toward Beverly. "Or you?"

"I...have no answer to that, Baba."

Beverly gave Jiang Shen an obviously forced smile and said, "We'll try and come back without getting killed by aliens or having to make terrible decisions."

"I hope that's true," Jiang Shen said. "Be careful. I'll walk you to the station."

"Please stay here," Thomas said. "You have your work here to do. We have ours."

As Jiang Shen regarded his son, he pursed his lips, tilted his head to one side, then gave a slow nod. "Very well. You're on your own until I see you again."

Thomas shook his father's hand, Beverly gave him a quick embrace, and they set out through the village. Few people were about just yet. Thomas smelled the familiar aroma of rice porridge as they passed one home — another reminder of a traditional China that still existed here, separate from the faster-paced, Westernized, bacon-and-eggs China of the cities. *And how has that China, in the form of Zhengzhou, fared?* he wondered. *What have the Jenregar done to it?*

The walk out of the village, past the now barren fields of neighboring farms, to the maglev station wasn't a strenuous one; the hills along the way were seldom steep, and the air was brisk enough to keep Thomas and Beverly comfortably cool as they proceeded.

Thomas found he had little to say as one step followed another, and that made him self-conscious — *Shouldn't I have thoughts to share with Beverly?* he wondered. *Will she think I'm doing this purely out of a sense of duty and not —*

— not because of how I feel about her?

Having asked the question of himself, Thomas had no answer. He trudged onward, step by step.

The morning after Ramira had made her failed visit to Mrs. Luna's home, Mr. Navarro's voice came over the comm in Ramira's hotel room. "I hate to bother you like this," he said, "but I need you to come in early — I need your help desperately!"

Ramira put aside her dish of warm curry. "What do you need me to do?"

"The Jenregar are headed this way. I need to get everything out of the store as quickly as I can. Can you help me load up?"

"Of course I can," Ramira said. "I'll be right over."

Ramira rushed downstairs and started toward Temporal Expressions on her bike.

As Ramira approached the shop, she saw the mound at

the city center had reached its highest level yet. At a couple of places near Temporal Expressions, she saw smoke rising from burning buildings.

Ramira immediately flashed back to that horrifying night when she and Diego and Julian were running from a Jenregar horde. But she cast that image out of her mind as she peddled onward.

At the shop itself, Ramira expected to see a chaotic scene -- Mr. Navarro working valiantly to get all his wares out of his store, smashed artworks on the street, perhaps a shouting match between him and authorities trying to get him to leave right away.

Instead, he saw a perfectly calm Mr. Navarro calmly carrying boxes of artworks out to a mobile storage rig sitting in front of the shop.

A skidding stop on her bike, and Ramira, out of breath, said, "I got here as quickly as I could."

Mr. Navarro put down the box he was carrying and clasped Ramira by the shoulders, then took her into a strong embrace. "Just by showing up, you're helping me more than you could know."

Mr. Navarro let her go and Ramira saw Mrs. Luna coming out of the shop. She came up next to Mr. Navarro and took him by the arm. He laid his hand over hers. Mrs. Luna said, "It took an emergency this big for him to call. Naturally, I came right over."

Mr. Navarro said, "More than anything, Cecilio is keeping me calm. She had a little money put away. Convinced me to let her use it to hire this storage rig. You should've seen it -- all automated, pallets and boxes and netting that animate themselves and grab and wrap things and packed most of them away."

Ramira said, "It...looks like you didn't need me here at all."

Mrs. Luna smiled at Ramira. "My dear, I can tell by the look on your face you're wondering what's going on. Well, these artworks have stood between me and Esteban for years. I understand their beauty, but he's so devoted to them..."

"My heart had no room for anything else," Mr. Navarro said. "But after this close call, I'm closing the shop, selling most of the artworks, and we're leaving the Confederation."

"But — the recession," Ramira said.

Mr. Navarro said, "There's not a recession everywhere. My heart was never really into selling this things. Whenever I'd sell one, I'd just buy another one, sometimes something even more expensive."

Mrs. Luna said, "But the Jenregar, you might say, focused Esteban's mind on what was really important."

Mr. Navarro looked at Mrs. Luna. "Now I can't wait to get out of Santarem."

"Actually, we're leaving the Earth entirely," Mrs. Luna said. "Going to Minerva Habitat. No more worries about money, Esteban and I can be together, he and I can appreciate what's left over from his collection together -- he can even have his leg healed."

"I'm keeping the cane, though," he insisted. "I've gotten mighty used to it."

Ramira felt her heart near bursting with joy for her friends -- Minerva was a habitat devoted to art and philosophy, a replicator economy where Mr. Navarro and Mrs. Luna could live a life free of the need to work to survive. "I'm so happy for you. But Mr. Navarro -- the artworks you hold on to will be worthless there."

Mr. Navarro's expression revealed a deep contentment. "No, Ramira. They'll be worth exactly what they should be."

"And, my dear," Mrs. Luna said. "We'd like you to come with us. *That's* why we called you here."

Ramira stood there blinking and wasn't able to come up with words for a moment. "What...what do you mean?"

"What we mean," Mr. Navarro said, "is that we want you to join us in Minerva Habitat. I know Brazil was your first choice, but wouldn't Minerva suit you just as well?"

Ramira's heart soared. "Of course — of course it would! Oh — what about Matias?"

"Your brother? We'll contact him and bring him along, too."

Ramira embraced Mr. Navarro and Mrs. Luna in turn. "I'm so happy. I can never thank you enough."

"Join us and carve out a happy life for yourself," Mrs. Luna said. "That's all we'd ever ask in return."

Chapter 14

Mike trudged up the frozen escalator, stunner in hand, keeping an eye at the top of the steps. All he could see was the ceiling of a shelter and a bit of sky. Strain as he might, he heard nothing that indicated what he might be about to encounter out there.

Step after step. He slowed as he neared the top of the escalator. Finally, as he climbed the last several steps, he realized where this station was.

The English Strait.

Toward the middle of the last century, nanotech had been used in a terror attack which emptied the English Channel of water and raised walls of earth high enough to keep the seas from rushing back in. What was once England's Shakespeare Cliff was now a sloping plain. The French city of Sangatte had been destroyed.

At one time, there had been thoughts of reclaiming the channel, allowing the seas to rush back in, but over the decades the strait came to be seen as a monument of sorts to a time of terror that had largely passed when the replicator economies arrived and relatively few Humans suffered for lack of food, clothing, or shelter. Provide the basics, most governments learned, and many political conflicts faded away. So did many governments.

Peering down the steep slope that led to the bottom of the strait, Mike felt as if he was looking out at a desert. Even the slightest wind blew dust clouds across the barren landscape and, Mike knew, formed many small dunes out there that then would drift apart and reform in a different shape elsewhere.

Mike could see small patches of green in a few places — hardy plants eking out a precarious existence. Life was tenacious, even in the harshest climates.

On the northeastern horizon, he could just make out the earthen wall that kept the North Sea at bay. The southwestern wall holding back the Atlantic Ocean was far over the opposite horizon.

The terrorists nearly a century ago had picked this spot precisely — here at the Pas de Calais, the strait, like the channel before it, was at its narrowest point — not quite 35 kilometers from the French side to the British. It was more shallow than many people realized, only about 45 meters here where Mike stood.

Despite his circumstances, Mike couldn't help smiling: *That's all from a report I wrote in elementary school*, he recalled.

A sound behind him — Mike turned, and there was Terry Needham. Although he looked to be in good shape, he was huffing and puffing from the climb. Mike let out a deep sigh, but otherwise managed to contain his exasperation at the man; after all, Mike hadn't discovered any dangers here.

At least not yet.

Terry looked out across the landscape. "Pretty desolate," he said.

Mike only said, "Yeah."

"So what are we supposed to do now?"

"Any more announcements from the train?"

Terry shook his head. "Nope."

Mike touched behind his left ear to activate his datalink. "Mike Christopher to Unity HQ."

No response.

"Brussels, do you copy?"

After a moment, Terry asked, "Still no response?"

"None. This is Mike Christopher to any Unity base or starcraft. This is a mayday." Another moment, and Mike told Terry, "The Jenregar must be jamming our comm somehow."

"So we're stranded *and* cut off from communications."

"That's what it looks like. We should assume we're on our own for the time being."

Mike heard a crackling sound over his datalink. He pressed his hand over his left ear and said, "Yes, this is Mike Christopher. I can barely copy you."

"This...is Neriah — Mike, do you copy?"

"Yes, I do, now."

"The Jenregar have disrupted a lot of our communications. Better talk fast."

"We're at the French end of the English Strait, and our maglev stopped. No response from the A.I."

"Can you see Calais from there?"

"No — we're closer to the old Chunnel -- you know, the Channel Tunnel -- entrance near Coquelles."

"Well, Calais is under a dome. Just happened today. The area around it is swarming with Jenregar. If you haven't seen any so far, just wait. And as you've found out, a lot of maglev service is being disrupted."

"God *damn* it," Mike said.

Terry asked, "What?"

Mike waved his concern aside for the moment, asking Neriah, "Is there any way you can help us? A pickup, maybe?"

"Mike, I have to be honest with you — the Unity would do about anything for you, but I don't have any aircraft or spacecraft to spare. Not to mention that the Jenregar have gotten pretty good at establishing no-fly zones close to their domes. Let me see whether we have any other options, and I'll get back to you. Neriah out."

"Copy. Mike out."

Terry's expression was hopeful. "So are they going to get us out?"

"They don't have a way to do it. But they're going to see what else they can come up with." Mike indicated the strait. "And, we're not heading across *that*."

"It *would* be quite a walk."

"Not to mention that it's still supposed to be riddled with transformation mines and death-tech."

"I guess we'll have to find another option."

"That's the problem," Mike said. "The finding."

Mike headed back down the escalator to the group of passengers waiting next to the maglev train. All five looked up at him expectantly. "We've stopped at the English Strait," he told them. "There's no other transportation in sight. I've spoken to a Unity official, and although they don't have a way to airlift us out, they're going to try to find another way to help us."

A woman in her thirties came up to him. Her English had a French accent. "You're Mike Christopher, aren't you?"

"Yes, I am."

The woman pushed her shoulder-length brown hair

back from her eyes. "So you've been in...how do you say...tight spots before?"

"I have."

The woman looked around at the other passengers. "So perhaps you can help us?"

Mike smiled. "I'm just trying to survive, too, you know. And I'm actually used to dealing with totally alien worlds — not my home planet."

The woman went to Mike and shook his hand. "I'm Emily Bamford. I know your background, Mike. It seems to me the Earth you've come back to may be as alien a place as you've ever visited."

Mike considered that. "You may be right. As long as I think of it that way, I may be on familiar ground."

Emily turned to the other passengers and said, "We should all introduce ourselves. I'll go first. I'm Emily Bamford, I'm from Montpellier, and I'm a nano-engineer."

Everyone else, it seemed, either possessed their own datalinks or at least basic translator tech as they spoke the various languages among them.

"Terry Needham, here — I'm a hobbyist, with interests including target shooting, botany, and Elizabethan history. And I'm very happy to meet Mr. Christopher, here."

"Marie Keskali — I guess you'd say I'm a world traveler. I'm originally from Addis Ababa."

"Well...you have to excuse me, I'm really scared. Alexia Fontaine's my name. From Caen, right here in France, I've been visiting friends in Belgium, and I'm just trying to get back home."

"Raymond Ferris, from Le Havre. I choose not to work."

"My name is Steffen Shuster. I have no profession or major hobby, and I'm from Solingen, Germany. Now can we try to get out of here?"

"I hope so," Mike said, even as he thought, *I have no idea how to realize that hope.*

That's when Mike received another call from Neriah: "You said you were near the old Chunnel entrance. Can you make your way there?"

"I don't see why not," Mike said. "So far we haven't seen any signs of Jenregar around us."

"Don't expect that to hold true forever. A lot of our sensors are being blocked, but we know there are Jenregar within just a few kilometers of your position — fortunately, in the direction of Calais, and not between you and the Chunnel."

"What happens when we get to the Chunnel?"

"The entrances have been locked up for decades. But I just received the code to open them up — I've gone ahead and set them to open when a Human draws near. You're the only people for several kilometers around, so we don't have to worry about anyone else getting in. We're sending a shuttle through the service tunnel between the two main tunnels to get you — but last we knew, the way was blocked about ten K from the French side, so you'll have to walk that far."

Mike asked, "But aren't there supposed to be people living in there - folks who are really off the grid, you might say?"

"That's the legend — people who can hack into the doorway tech and go back and forth. Sensors give us contradictory readings. I guess maybe you'll find out."

"All right. We'll head that way."

"I'll keep in touch as much as I can, Mike," Neriah said. "But I can't promise our comm won't get jammed again."

"We'll get to the Chunnel as quickly as we can."

When Mike explained the plan to the others, Alexia

Fontaine spoke up. "But I'm not heading to England. I'm just trying to get back home right here in France."

And Raymond Ferris said, "So am I — the Channel Tunnel is the wrong way. I was to get off the maglev just a little ways down the line to go to Le Havre."

"Listen, folks," Mike said. "I'm trying to protect all of us. The Jenregar may be nearby. Alexia — Raymond — I'm taking the trip I'm pretty sure is safe. I've been inconvenienced too, and I'm a lot farther away from my destination. It should take us a few hours to rendezvous with our pickup, depending on how fast we walk. Once the Unity rescues us, then we can figure out how to get each of us to where we're going."

Raymond folded his arms and glared at Mike. "And if we don't follow you?"

Mike held up his hands in exasperation. "Then you're on your own. And I have no idea what might be ahead of you."

Alexia looked at Raymond. "I think we should listen to him," she said. "This may be our only chance to get out of here safely."

"Perhaps so," Raymond said. "But it's damned inconvenient."

Mike said, "So's being killed by a Jenregar swarm."

Raymond considered that. "All right, then. When do we go?"

"Right now," Mike said, and and led everyone up the escalator.

By midday Thomas and Beverly reached the maglev station. If not for the signs indicating its location, it would've been easy to keep walking past carefully-tended fields and small farm cottages and miss it entirely. The station sat in a depression between two farms, and Thomas and Beverly reached it by traveling down a long, steep escalator. The boarding area was narrow, and just beyond it lay two enclosed tubes about eight meters tall. The nearest tube, Thomas knew, was where the train to Zhengzhou would arrive.

They were alone in the station. Thomas helped Beverly off with her backpack, took off his own, and they plopped down onto a bench. "I didn't realize how tired my legs and feet were," Beverly said, "until I sat down."

"I heard the train's been running pretty regularly," Thomas said. "We should only have to wait a few minutes." The train, Thomas knew, only got up to a fraction of its 4,000 kph top speed to reach the city.

After a few minutes, a tone sounded and Thomas stood. "Here it comes," he said. He and Beverly stood holding their backpacks as the train approached. Traveling in a vacuum, the train didn't transmit any sounds as it approached, but Thomas could feel a low rumble beneath his feet which quickly subsided as the unseen train came to a halt inside the tube before them.

A broad doorway slid aside, and Thomas and Beverly entered the train. "Empty," Thomas said as the doorway shut itself behind them and the train began to accelerate.

Beverly said, "I didn't expect anything different. Who's stupid enough to head *toward* a city under Jenregar attack?"

"I guess we are," Thomas said. They passed up a computer station meant for train personnel and placed his own and Beverly's backpack into a pair of seats and sat with her across the aisle from them. He said, "And I don't even want to think about what happened in Xiamen."

"I can't help but think about it. We don't know how desperate things are in Zhengzhou."

Thomas started to touch Beverly's hand, but hesitated. He told her, "The Jenregar have been in Zhengzhou for the better part of a week, now. If the government was going to bomb it, it already would have."

Beverly gave Thomas a stern look. "You can't know that."

Thomas took a deep breath. "You're right. But we have to act as if it's not going to happen. Otherwise, your grandmother doesn't have a chance."

Beverly grasped Thomas' hand. "You're right. I'm sorry."

Thomas barely had a chance to squeeze Beverly's hand back before she withdrew it. *She was right yesterday*, Thomas thought, savoring the lingering impression of her touch. *Sometimes we focus on what's important in our own lives, neglecting thoughts of others.*

Except all my thoughts right now are of her.

Within instants, Thomas knew, the maglev train was eating up the distance that it had taken him a full day to cover on his journey out of the city. But then the train began to slow. "It's too soon for us to be back in the city," he said.

"I know," Beverly said. "Could it be stopping for someone else who's headed back there?"

Thomas shrugged. "I suppose so. I guess we're about to find out."

The train halted and the doorway opened. Beyond: bedlam. Thomas stood at the sound of screams and energy bolts in the distance. *Dammit, my own pistol's in my backpack. Should I dig for it?*

Before he could move, though, a half-dozen people entered the train. A couple of them pointed pulse rifles at Thomas and Beverly. A man dressed in the uniform of a transit officer went to the nearby computer console. "We don't want to hurt you," another man said as he stood in the doorway so the doors wouldn't close. "Just leave us alone."

"We don't have anything you want," Thomas said.

"Yes, you do — this train."

Beverly said, "We're headed for the city!"

The man at the computer console hit a final input with a flourish. "Not anymore," he said. "At least not on this train. You'd better get moving."

Thomas grabbed his and Beverly's backpacks and motioned for her to precede him through the doorway. As they stepped onto the platform, the doors slid shut behind them. Again Thomas felt the vibration beneath him as the train set out, this time back the way it had come.

They were alone on the platform, but as Thomas looked up toward the top of the escalator, which wasn't moving, he still heard distant screams and the sharp reports of energy bolts.

He looked at Beverly. "There's no other way out. And we're still several kilometers from where we need to be."

Beverly said, "Then let's go."

Thomas pulled his pistol out of his backpack, then heaved the pack over his shoulders. He started up the escalator, which rose the equivalent of a couple of stories. Only about a quarter of the way up, his legs began to protest — he'd been walking most of the morning, after all, and their rest aboard the maglev had been all too brief.

"Who do you think is fighting?" Beverly asked between huffing breaths.

Thomas said, "I'm not sure which would be worse — us fighting Jenregar or other Humans."

"I hate to say it — but I think we'd have a better chance against the Humans."

As they approached the top of the escalator, Thomas

could make out of the upper floors of several buildings, most of them appearing to be professional buildings rather than residences. Many of them had windows blown out, and narrow columns of smoke rose from a number of those windows.

Thomas motioned for Beverly to stay back as he peeked his head up from the last several steps. *I'm actually glad the escalator isn't working,* he thought. *At least it's not just depositing me right in the middle of whatever mayhem might be going on up here.*

"What do you see?" Beverly asked.

"A bunch of people. Looks like they're crowded around several bodies."

"Jenregar or Human?"

"Looks like Human. Looks like most everyone still alive has a weapon, too." He ascended the rest of the stairs and told Beverly, "Let's move on, but *not* in that direction."

They headed toward a thoroughfare that seemed untraveled at first. Thomas kept looking behind him, making sure that the crowd near the maglev station hadn't noticed them. *Though I doubt they were heading toward the city,* he thought. *They're not that foolish.*

The closer they came to the city, the more damage the surrounding buildings had sustained. Beverly pointed out one office building that had been leveled. "I knew people who worked there — government people who regulated nursing homes. They did good, important work. I hope they got out safely."

"I'm sure they did," Thomas said, wishing he had more than empty words to console her.

A few minutes later, Beverly said, "There's a bus coming up behind us."

"Thank goodness," Thomas said. He took a step into the

street and waved the bus down. It slowed, stopped. When its doors opened, the driver said, "You're actually headed *into* the city?"

Beverly said, "We're fetching my Nai-nai. She's hurt."

The driver waved them onto the bus.

"We appreciate this," Thomas said as he sat next to Beverly. "We were on a train that got hijacked."

"I've heard about that happening," the driver said. "Unfortunately, there's no one on those trains to prevent it." He reached down next to his seat and pulled out a pistol. "That's not the case aboard this bus."

Beverly said, "We're just thankful the bus line is still running."

The driver showed a crooked grin. "It actually isn't. I never drove a bus before today. But someone's got to help people get out before the Jenregar come through here or before...." The driver appeared to run out of words.

"We heard about Xiamen," Thomas said.

The driver nodded. "Yes. I did, too. And so I drive."

MR. NAVARRO TOLD RAMIRA TO CLIMB INTO THE FRONT CAB of the mobile storage rig. "It's programmed to take us to the starport."

"We're leaving *right now*?" Ramira asked as she climbed aboard the rig. "I have to check out of the hotel! The authorities at the starport will know I haven't paid my bill and I won't be able to leave."

"That's all being taken care of," Mrs. Luna said as she climbed in next to Ramira. "All your belongings will be brought along to the starport, and we'll pay your bills. Esteban has some buyers waiting at the port for us."

"This is hard to believe," Ramira said. She saw Mr. Navarro still standing in front of Temporal Expressions, his cane supporting him. In the distance, she could hear what sounded like military ground units drawing closer. In her mind, she could hear the chittering of massed Jenregar. She told Mr. Navarro, "We'd better get going. It sounds like the Jenregar are getting closer."

Ramira could barely make out Mr. Navarro's voice: "I suppose you're right. Can't start the new life without driving away from the one we have." Mr. Navarro, with a little help from Ramira pulling on his arm, climbed into the rig. He tapped its dashboard with his cane. "To the starport, now! Make it snappy!" As the rig started forward, though, Mr. Navarro said, "It actually doesn't know 'snappy' from any other speed. It just knows to take us to the starport."

Then Mr. Navarro looked back toward his store. "Oh, no!" he said. "You can't do that!" He slammed his cane against the dashboard much harder this time, telling the rig, "Stop! Stop right now!"

"What's happening?" Ramira demanded.

Mrs. Luna looked back at the store from her side of the rig. "It's the Jenregar — they're overrunning the neighborhood — including the store!"

Stuck in the middle position, Ramira couldn't lean over enough to stare backwards. "But we can't stop — we'll just be killed."

"The army's there," Mr. Navarro said. "But the Jenregar are forcing them back. Emergency stop!"

The rig came to a leisurely stop and Mr. Navarro jumped out, breaking his landing onto the pavement with his cane. "Get away from my store!" he shouted, though the Jenregar were too distant to hear him and could never have understood him anyway.

Ramira leaped out right behind him, but the first sight of the Jenregar since that fatal night with Diego and Julian elicited a rush of fear that almost made her stumble. *Those crablike bodies, those writhing tentacles — they combine so many features that just disgust a typical Human.*

Or at least this *typical Human.*

Running up behind Mr. Navarro, Ramira was confident she could catch up to him within a couple of strides, but wondered how difficult it would be to drag him back into the rig.

Movement off to her side — *Dammit,* she thought, *if Mrs. Luna isn't out here now, too. At least she can get back into the rig on her own once I retrieve Mr. Navarro.*

Though the Jenregar are getting pretty damn close.

Chapter 15

Mike and the others soon topped a ridge overlooking the Chunnel entrance. Clearly no one was maintaining the area; unmowed grass reached nearly to Mike's knees.

A steep slope ran down toward the entrance itself — two tunnels not quite eight meters across, through which what were then known as "high-speed" trains took people and vehicles at three hundred kilometers an hour.

Mike found himself grinning at the term "high-speed." *The maglev can make that journey in about a minute*, he thought.

Terry Needham, standing next to Mike said, "After the maglevs came in, this was actually a tourist attraction for awhile. But for whatever reason, interest waned. They took up the tracks leading here and closed everything up."

Marie asked, "How do we get in?"

"The entrance should open up on its own as get closer."

"It had better," Steffen said. "We could never open that large a doorway without heavy equipment."

Mike led the way down the slope toward the tunnels. Each of them was capped by a gigantic round doorway. As the ground leveled off, he found himself on a concrete platform, and it was a matter of only a few brief strides that led him to its edge. One larger step of about a meter and a half, and he was on the former track bed — the tracks themselves long gone.

He approached the nearer tunnel, the one on the left from his viewpoint. Terry was right behind him, still. This tunnel's the one that usually went from here in France to the U.K."

Mike drew closer to the tunnel entrance. "They said it was set to open for any Human who approached."

Even anticipating that, Mike took a surprised step back when the gigantic door began to swing open toward them. It revealed the interior of the tunnel, with its single track still running straight toward infinity, or at least toward England. As they walked into the relative darkness of the tunnel, Mike paused a moment to let his eyes adapt. *I should be surprised any lights are left working at all*, he thought, *with this going unused for so many decades.*

It grew even darker as the large door shut behind them. "That's a positive sign, everybody," Mike said. "At least the Jenregar won't be following us." He walked down the middle of the track, everyone's footsteps echoing slightly. Dust motes floated in the glare of the overhead lights, and the entire place had the musty smell of something left unattended for a long time.

He touched behind his left ear. "This is Mike Christopher to Neriah — do you copy?"

No response. "I shouldn't be surprised, I guess. Between the jamming and being underground, we might not get another signal through the entire time we're down here."

Terry raised his arm as if he was going to slap Mike on the shoulder, then seemed to think better of it. He still sported a wide smile, though, as he said, "I feel better now that we're here, though. Safer, like we're in some sort of fortress."

Or tomb, Mike thought. He was surprised to see raised walkways on either side of the track. "How often would those walkways be used?" he wondered, to no one in particular.

Marie Keskali said, "I've read about this. The one on the right is for maintenance workers. The one on the left was in case of an emergency evacuation — it leads to the service tunnel. And the two walkways together would keep a train from tipping over if it derailed."

"Neriah told me about the service tunnel — it goes between the two main tunnels."

"There are several cross-passages that can take us to it."

"That sounds great — that's where our ride is supposed to be."

Within just a few moments, they reached the first of the cross-tunnels, which was only 15 meters long, and entered it. They passed an equipment room that featured a series of secured doors. Mike couldn't help wondering what kind of quaint, obsolete machinery might lie behind those doors. *But this is no time for sightseeing*, he thought, though he realized Emily was also taking in their surroundings.

Another few steps, and they were in the service tunnel. No rail line here, just a tube five meters across, a bare floor with a single white stripe down the middle and a series of cooling pipes and cables overhead. It, too, seemingly reached toward infinity. *But just less than ten K that way, it's supposed to be blocked — who knows why — and that's our goal.*

Due to the close quarters, the echoing sounds of their steps and voices made their surroundings seem more claustrophobic now; confident as Mike was in Neriah's reassurances, he was eager to get himself and his charges the hell down this tunnel and to safety as quickly as he could.

It's all this talk of legends of people living here, of Jenregar hot on our trail — as unlikely as any of it might be, I know it's got me spooked, and I'm used to First Contact situations.

Maybe it's like Emily said — Earth's become as "alien" to me as anywhere else I've been. It's what comes of taking things for granted, thinking I know about this world and the people who live on it, when things are actually drastically different.

Terry, who inevitably had come up to walk next to him, told Mike, "You're doing a great job so far."

Mike kept his attention on keeping a steady pace. He looked back at the others — Steffen staring straight ahead, Alexia's head turning back and forth as if she were a rabbit surrounded by wolves, Emily calmly taking in this new environment. "I haven't done anything yet. Wait 'til we meet up with our rescuers."

Steffen spoke up: "Mike is correct. He has done much for us so far, but we are not yet out of danger."

Mike took a deep breath. *I wish he hadn't said that*, he thought.

That's when Alexia, who was bringing up the rear, started looking all around her. "So — what kind of danger — you think the Jenregar sneaked in here somehow?"

Mike said, "We haven't heard a thing about the Jenregar being in here."

"Haven't *heard* anything," Alexia said. "That means they *could* be here."

Mike halted and turned toward the others. "Listen, everybody — we need to focus. Right now that means focusing on one foot in front of the other. I don't know of any Jenregar in here —

Marie interrupted: "What about the rogue Humans who are supposed to live here?"

"Myths," Raymond said. "I've lived in this part of the world all my life and never seen clear proof of such a thing."

Mike held up his hands. "*Please.* One foot in front of the other. That's what I'm going to concentrate on for the next couple of hours." And he continued on. Behind him, he heard Alexia mutter, "That's what someone says when they don't know what they're talking about."

Terry fell back and told her, "You've got to take this man on faith. He knows what he's doing."

"He may come from the heavens," Steffen said, "but he is no god."

"He'll be the first to tell you that. In fact, one of his favorite phrases is that he's even one of the few Humans who can tell you with certainty a god didn't create him."

I have favorite phrases that people know about? Mike wondered. But he put that odd thought aside and forged onward down the service tunnel.

***

WITHIN HALF AN HOUR, THE BUS TOOK THOMAS AND BEVERLY near the neighborhood of high-rise apartment buildings where Beverly's grandmother was staying. They thanked the driver once again and headed down deserted streets filled with debris. Some of the tallest structures, some as many as thirty stories tall, appeared to have been the most conspicuous targets, whether for Jenregar or Humans, Thomas couldn't tell. *Probably both at some point,* he thought. A couple buildings had large chunks blasted out of their sides, with barely a single window unbroken. One such complex had burned to the foundation, and Thomas could only hope most of its residents had had a chance to escape.

"Their apartment building should be just ahead," Beverly told Thomas. "Oh, I so hope my Nai-nai is all right."

"I'm sure she is," Thomas said, wishing he'd managed to make that statement with more confidence.

The building they approached appeared in much better shape than most of those they'd seen so far. Rising twenty stories above the street, Thomas saw most of its windows were intact, and it didn't seem to have sustained any serious damage. He even saw clothing hung outside on balconies to dry, which he chose to interpret as a hopeful sign.

As they approached the main entrance to the building, however, a young man — not quite out of his teens, Thomas realized -- came outside, pointing a rifle at them. "Who are you," he demanded, "and what do you want?"

Beverly said, "We're here to see the Liao family — they're taking care of my Nai-nai for me."

The man's eyes narrowed, and if anything his expression became even more suspicious. "How do I know you are who you say you are?"

Thomas took a step forward, and the young man raised the rifle to his shoulder. Thomas raised his hands. He worked to keep his voice calm as he said, "Who else would know where she was?"

The young man lowered his weapon and rubbed his mouth in contemplation. "I suppose you're right." He tilted his head toward the doorway. "Go on in, then. They're on the seventh floor, first apartment on the right."

"More climbing," Thomas muttered, knowing that these apartment buildings seldom had elevators, and that decades of political change, from communism to capitalism to a non-market, replicator economy had never made things different.

Beverly pointed out, "Imagine how difficult it was for Nai-nai."

"You're right," Thomas said as he led the way up the stairs. "We have it pretty good compared to many."

The stairwell was dark and dingy; the steps were well-worn. Thomas, once again, had little to say as they approached the end of their journey. *And then we have to make our way back*, he thought. *Possibly carrying Beverly's Nai-nai much of the way.*

As they continued to trudge up the final flights, Thomas couldn't help thinking, *I hope I can find it within myself to do this. I hope I can get both of these women back to our village safely.*

Mostly, I hope I don't fail Beverly.

Finally they reached the seventh floor, which was as dim as the stairwell, with several hallway lights burned out or without power. *I suppose we should be glad there are any lights at all*, Thomas thought. He stood with his hands on his knees for a moment and caught his breath. He gestured for Beverly to knock on the door to the apartment. She did, but there was no response at first. She knocked louder, and finally they heard shuffling footsteps from behind the door.

The door opened to reveal an elderly woman who appeared to be barely supporting herself with a cane. "Yes, may I help you?" she asked.

Beverly said, "I'm here for Rachel Kwan -- "

"Your Nai-nai! Of course! Come in!" As Beverly and Thomas entered the small apartment, the woman said, "I'm Liao Jun. I live here with my sister. And we've been so glad to take your Rachel in."

And then Thomas spotted her — Rachel Kwan, Beverly's

"Nai-nai." But even as Beverly shouldered off her backpack and dropped it to the floor, Thomas was struck by how frail the woman seemed, sitting slumped in a rocking chair. Thomas had seen pictures of her, but this was not the old but vital woman from those images, standing tall, graying hair perfectly coifed, dressed simply but neatly.

As Beverly bent to embrace Rachel, it was clear she didn't dare squeeze her too tightly, for fear of hurting her. Rachel was thinner than Thomas expected, her clothes hanging upon her as if she'd lost weight recently and hadn't had a chance to buy new wardrobe. Her hair had turned utterly white. Rachel's hands shook as she returned Beverly's embrace.

Beverly kneeled next to Rachel, taking both her hands. "Nai-nai — you...don't look well."

"I must admit, Beverly...I'm not well. Age seems to have caught up with me, just at the worst time. But Jun has taken good care of me. Of course, she's had plenty of practice taking care of her sister."

Thomas asked Jun, "And where is your sister? We'd like to meet her and thank her, as well."

Jun indicated a closed bedroom door to one side. "She's sleeping now. That's mostly what she does these days. She's quite remarkable — made it to a hundred and two without any sort of life extension technology. But as you can imagine, even getting out of bed is a strain for her."

"I see," Thomas said.

But Beverly turned to Jun. "When I heard the 'Liao family' was taking care of Nai-nai, I thought...well..."

"That it was an extended family," Jun said. "A man and wife, several children ready to help out. That was it, wasn't it?"

"Yes. It was."

Jun placed her cane next to a straight wooden chair and sat. She folded her arms. "Well, it's just me and Liang and my great-grandson downstairs. I'm sure you met him. I'm sorry that we didn't conform to your expectations."

"Please," Beverly said. "That's not it at all. I'm so grateful for what you've done. It's just...."

Thomas spoke up. "We don't know how we're going to get Rachel back home with us. And don't you and your sister want to leave, as well?"

"My sister can't move," Jun said. "And I won't leave without her."

Rachel said, "And I've decided I'm staying with them."

Beverly said, "Oh, Nai-nai — you *have* to come home with me."

Rachel raised a hand and shook her finger at Beverly. "Actually, I don't. I've lived a long and satisfying life. I'm so glad you came here to see me one last time. But you can't imagine how difficult it was for me just to climb up seven stories worth of stairs. Going down wouldn't be much easier. And you both know how difficult it is to find a bus or train. You and Thomas should leave before this city goes the way of Xiamen."

Beverly embraced Rachel again. "Oh, Nai-nai."

Rachel stroked Beverly's hair. "Go, child. The longer you stay, the worse the goodbye is. And the more danger you're in."

Beverly stood, wiped tears from her eyes, and grabbed her backpack. She told Jun, "Thank you for everything you've done." She started out the door.

Thomas managed only to nod toward Jun and Rachel before rushing to catch up to Beverly, who was already making her way down the stairwell. By the time Thomas got there, though, he found Beverly leaning against the wall only a few steps down. She was sobbing uncontrollably, her hands covering her face.

Thomas's instinct was to reach out to her, but he didn't know how she'd respond. Finally, he thought, *The hell with it*, and touched her shoulder. When she didn't pull away, he touched her other arm.

Beverly stepped into his embrace, her arms clasping his back as she cried on his shoulder. He didn't try to speak, just let her cry herself out.

After a minute or so, Beverly calmed. She pulled away from Thomas, wiped her eyes again, and said, "Thank you."

That was the first moment Thomas allowed himself to think that he could find himself loving Beverly.

In fact, maybe I already do, he thought.

But his next thought: *That isn't what's important right now. And I can't let either of us be distracted by that possibility.* He asked her, "Are you ready to head out now?"

Beverly nodded. "Let's get started."

Thomas followed her down the stairs.

Thomas gave the Liao's grandson a nod as they left the building. He nodded back, the sole sentinel protecting the Liaos and, now, Rachel.

They walked in silence as they proceeded along mostly deserted streets. At one point a bus came up behind them. Thomas was about to flag it down, but in that moment he glanced at Beverly, who turned her head slightly toward the bus, then returned her gaze straight ahead, studiously ignoring the vehicle. Thomas let it go past, not quite understanding what Beverly was thinking, but somehow realizing it was important to her.

Eventually, though, Beverly stopped at an ornate fountain in a small public square. She sat at the fountain's edge, took off her backpack, and splashed water from the fountain onto her face. Thomas sat next to her. He saw Beverly looking wistfully back in the direction of the Liaos' apartment building.

Thomas said, "We should've asked the boy if he wanted to go with us."

Beverly blinked as if she didn't understand at first. Then: "The grandson?"

"Yes."

"He wouldn't abandon his own Nai-nai."

"Well...I suppose I didn't think of it like that."

"He's probably their only lifeline to the outside world — gets their food, any other supplies they need. And you saw how he's guarding that door."

Thomas said, "It's just...."

"I know. He's too young to die. But consider he's also old enough to know what he's doing."

"I suppose you're right. Uh...can we catch the next bus that comes past...if one does?"

"Of course," Beverly said. "You know, I just realized why I let that other one pass. With every step, I was making a different choice than that boy. I was abandoning my Nai-nai. I wouldn't accept the same responsibility he has."

As gently as he could, Thomas said, "That responsibility will likely mean an early death for him."

"I know. But...the guilt is flowing through me like a flood." Beverly's mouth curled up in a smile, but it didn't reach her eyes. "Funny the way we interpret things, isn't it? The way we order our lives. Sometimes it makes sense and sometimes it doesn't."

They took the next bus that passed.

Even as Ramira caught up to Mr. Navarro, a troop carrier appeared from a side street and a couple dozen soldiers disgorged from it and began firing pulse rifles at the Jenregar. Several of the Jenregar individuals went down, but wave after wave of them kept coming, marching right over their dead comrades to keep advancing toward the soldiers.

Ramira grabbed Mr. Navarro's shoulders from behind. "We've got to get back to the rig!" she told him.

Mr. Navarro's face was a study in horror as he struggled against Ramira's grip. "But my store!"

"You were leaving your store behind!"

"Not for these unthinking beasts to destroy."

"It's *us* they're going to destroy if we don't get out of here."

Mr. Navarro stopped struggling. "You're right — forgive me."

Mrs. Luna came up to them. "Thank goodness you caught him," she said to Ramira. She told Mr. Navarro, "Esteban, it's all right. Think of what's ahead of us, not what we're leaving behind."

They started back toward the rig. "You're right," Mr. Navarro said. "I've been foolish. I — oh, my God!"

Another group of Jenregar was coming at them from just beyond the rig.

Ramira had to grab Mr. Navarro once again, as he tried to rush toward the rig that contained all his artworks. "No!" she told him. "They're about to cut us off!"

"But that's our future in that rig! Everything I've committed to sell!"

The leading edge of the Jenregar in this new group was even with the rig now. Several climbed on top of it and began tearing at its roof and its sides.

Ramira pulled a struggling Mr. Navarro farther away

from the rig. "We've got to get out of here! Mrs. Luna, help me with him!"

But as Mrs. Luna drew closer to them, several Jenregar took a leap forward and were about to fall upon her — just as the soldiers turned and fired upon the Jenregar. Several Jenregar individuals fell, their carapaces bursting apart from the impact of the energy bolts.

Mrs. Luna ducked as she neared Ramira and Mr. Navarro —

— then an energy bolt struck her! Mr. Navarro exclaimed, "No!" as he wriggled free from Ramira's grasp and went to his knees next to Mrs. Luna. Part of her left shoulder was gone, along with her left ear. Blood oozed from the side of her head as Mr. Navarro reached out a hand toward her but apparently couldn't make himself touch her. He turned toward the soldiers: "God damn you! You're as bad as the Jenregar!"

Ramira tried to make her way toward Mr. Navarro, but after that first step she was knocked to the ground, and could only try to cover her head as she wondered whether it was Humans or Jenregar who threatened to trample her to death.

Chapter 16

When Marie Keskali gasped and blurted out, "What was *that*?" Mike realized he'd been walking and walking and allowing the monotony of their surroundings to lull him into not paying attention. *A rookie mistake*, he thought, and asked Marie, "What was it?"

"Up ahead — someone stuck his head out of one of the cross-passages."

"What did he look like?" Mike asked.

Alexia, her voice just barely containing her fear, asked, "It wasn't a Jenregar, was it?"

"They cannot get down here," Steffen said.

"I don't think it was a Jenregar," Marie said. "But I can't be sure."

Mike said, "We need to be doing less talking and more finding things out." He turned to Emily Bamford. "Let's you and I go ahead of the others a little bit. The rest of you, wait back here."

Emily looked surprised, but came along with him willingly enough. Once they were a little ahead of the others, she asked, "Why'd you ask me to come with you? I've hardly said a word."

"That's one reason why. The other is, I can see you've been paying attention, and that's what I need right now."

"Paying attention is what I do for a living. A bridge or a building doesn't construct itself -- though it may look like it if I do the work properly."

They drew closer to the cross-passage where Marie had seen — something. Emily said, "I think I can hear — "

Mike raised his hand and Emily drew silent. "Wait here," he told her. "If anything happens to me, try to get back to the others." He walked the final few steps to the cross-passage. He peered around the corner —

"Welcome, friend." A man in ragged clothing, with long, unwashed hair stood in front of a stack of ripped, torn, and dirty storage boxes. He held out his hands, presumably to show he was unarmed. "At least I hope you're a friend."

Mike kept his stunner pointed away from the man, but didn't lower it, either. "I hope I am, too. We're just trying to make our way to England."

The man looked amused. "Plenty of easier ways to do that."

"We were on one of those easier ways. But the maglev's blocked. And the Jenregar were close by. We had to get away from them."

"Alien *bastards*." The man look a hard look at Mike. "Did you even know we were in here?"

"We'd just heard rumors."

"Well, the rumors are true. Fortunately for us, you were much more than rumors the instant you opened that doorway — all seven of you. I have friends right behind me with two pulse rifles trained on you. I see you just have a stunner. And it doesn't look like the rest of you are armed at all."

I'm not about to confirm that for them, Mike thought. "I'm not here to hurt anyone."

"Or get hurt yourself, I suppose."

"That's right," Mike said. "We'd just like to move along."

From behind the wall of boxes, a voice said, "He looks familiar, Jason."

"*No names*," the man said. "Run his face."

Mike heard a few random sounds from behind the wall, and then the other man said, "Goddam! He's Mike Christopher!"

The man Mike now knew was named Jason leaned forward and peered at Mike as if he were on display in a glass case. "Damn if he isn't! We'd heard you'd come back to Earth — what are the odds you'd find yourself down here?"

"Better than either of us would've guessed, I suppose."

"Man, you are — one epic individual!"

"Thanks, I suppose," Mike said. "Does this mean we can pass?"

"We're just one outpost," the man said. "But we can get the word on to the others to let you through."

"Thank you." He turned to Emily. "Let's get everyone else through here." He and Emily waved toward the others, and they moved forward. "Go on with them," Mike told Emily. "I'll catch up."

Mike stood in the cross-passage as everyone else went past. He told Jason and his unseen friends, "Thanks again. We'll keep quiet about you, I promise."

"Welcome back to Earth," Jason said. "I suppose it's not so bad."

Mike gave a casual salute and said, "I hope you've found the life you wanted."

"It's a mixed bag, like most people's. But it's ours."

Mike nodded and hurried to catch up to the others. Steffen was bringing up the rear and slapped him, hard, on his back as he passed. Somehow it more acceptable coming from him than from Terry. "An excellent job," Steffen said.

Alexia managed a smile that couldn't erase the fear from her features — she told Mike, "Thank you for getting us past those terrible men."

Mike said, "They seemed quite reasonable to me."

Raymond spoke up: "They could've turned on us at any minute. *Still* could, in fact — now that they're behind us, they could squeeze us against some of their fellows before us."

"And place themselves in a crossfire," Mike pointed out. "No, I don't think we'll see any trouble from them."

Marie said, "I'm just glad to be moving on."

Mike worked his way up to the head of their little pack. Thankfully, Terry contented himself with a wide smile instead of a backslap or too-eager comment. He caught up to Emily and told her, "Thanks for your help."

"I didn't do much."

"I knew someone had my back. Sometimes that's enough. And that freed me up to really pay attention to what those guys were saying. We learned a lot."

"Such as?" Emily asked.

"They knew there were seven of us, and we never caught a glimpse of them until that Jason fellow got careless. That tells me they have sensors that detected us. And Jason had one of those other guys, 'run my face.'"

"So they're not as 'off the grid' as we might think."

Mike said, "I wouldn't be surprised to learn they've got replicators down here, sleeping quarters — they may have established an entire little society down here."

"Is our own society so bad?"

"There are always people who don't fit in, for whatever reason. Hell, I left the entire planet for a quarter-century. These guys are just forty meters down. I went *light-years* away — wait a minute — what's that sound?"

Mike looked behind them. He could barely make out Jason and the other two men, each of them armed with pulse rifles, aiming them in the distance at what appeared to be a solid mass filling the service tunnel.

Not solid, Mike realized. *A Jenregar swarm.*

Jason and the others opened fire. "Take the others to safety!" he told Emily, and rushed back the way they'd come.

⁂

THOMAS AND BEVERLY GOT OFF THE BUS AT A MAGLEV STATION just a few kilometers outside of Zhengzhou. They were its only passengers; Thomas had to wonder whether most people who wanted to leave the city had already managed to depart.

As the bus pulled away, Thomas took note of their surroundings. This was a different station from the one in which they'd arrived in the vicinity of the city, and Thomas carefully glanced into a nearby woods to the west and a low office building to the east. *I'm developing the instincts of a soldier*, Thomas thought. *Not that I'd ever be the soldier my Baba was. I'm only a biologist carrying a gun.*

He and Beverly started toward the usual escalator leading down into the station, but before they could make their way inside, Thomas heard a dull roar from straight overhead. He looked up and saw a gigantic fireball descending rapidly — with nothing to compare it to, he couldn't perceive how large it was or how close, only that it surely represented a terrible danger. Even as Beverly started to glance skyward, he grabbed her and they both leaped into a shallow ditch at the side of the road.

Thomas covered as much of Beverly's body as he could with his own, but chanced a glance back at the fireball. It appeared to approach the horizon — and erupted in a bright flash that nearly blinded him. He turned away from it and held Beverly as tightly as he could.

An instant of silent waiting, then the sound of the explosion was a physical force that swept over them, the earth writhed beneath them, a hurricane-force wind passed over them, and the air itself seemed to press down upon them. Thomas heard the rattle of debris overhead, and, more distant, the sounds of breaking glass and toppling trees.

Then the earth settled and the air grew calm. Thomas sat up. Off on the horizon, a vertical cloud rose over the city. As it reached a certain height, it expanded into a mushroom shape.

Beverly said, "They did it — they nuked Zhengzhou!"

"That wasn't a nuke," Thomas said.

"What do you mean?"

"You saw the fireball. We'd never have seen a nuclear missile approaching. I suspect that was a meteor or small asteroid thrown down onto the city from orbit."

"Poor Nai-nai."

"And Jun and Liang. And that young man who was the guard."

Beverly said, "How many people do you think were still in the city?"

"No way of knowing. But it had to be at least tens of thousands — maybe hundreds of thousands."

Beverly leaned her head against Thomas' shoulders. He hesitated a moment, but then took her into his arms. Beverly said, "What kind of world do we live on, where this can happen? What kind of country do we live in, where our own people can do this to us?"

"I don't know," Thomas said. "And I can't honestly tell you that we'll *ever* know."

"Thomas — you're all I have to hold onto now."

Thomas thought his heart skipped a beat. He felt himself fill up with sadness and joy all at once — sadness for Beverly and joy that she was reaching out to him in her moment of grief.

For now, he thought, *I'm grateful just to hold onto her.*

I can only hope it's enough for her, as well. I have to make sure I'm worthy of her.

RAMIRA RETURNED TO CONSCIOUSNESS SLOWLY; THE FIRST sensation she was aware of was pain throughout her body, especially in her head and left arm. *But at least I'm alive*, she thought. *And I can feel my arms and legs. That's a positive development.*

The pain made her groan, though, and Ramira heard a familiar voice: "Ramira?" Miyanda asked. "Are you awake?"

Ramira opened her eyes and saw Miyanda leaning over her, staring intently at her. Ramira squinted against the bright sunlight streaming through a window in what was clearly a hospital room. "Yeah," she said. "I'm awake. How long have I been out?"

"Just a few hours," Miyanda said as she ran her fingers through Ramira's hair. She could see the puffiness in Miyanda's eyes now — had she been crying over her?

"What about..."

Miyanda looked away from her. "They're...both dead."

"God *damn* it — I'm sorry. I shouldn't talk like that, no matter what."

"I couldn't even find out exactly how they died. I know the soldiers shot Mrs. Luna accidentally. But then the soldiers and the Jenregar came together and it was hand-to-hand fighting for awhile."

Ramira tried to shift her position in the bed but a sudden burst of pain stilled her. "I was crushed beneath them both."

"You had a fractured skull and two broken bones in your left arm. But someone got you here to the hospital and they kept you unconscious while they fixed everything. You should be able to leave here later today."

"And then what's next for me?"

"I hate to say it," Miyanda told her. "But you're right back where you started."

"Mr. Navarro's artworks?"

"Destroyed in the fight. And he never had the chance to pay your hotel bill. And now you've got a pretty whopping hospital bill to pay, as well."

Tears flowed down Ramira's cheeks. "I don't think I can do this."

"It may take some years," Miyanda said. "But you *can* do it. I can see it in you — you're very determined."

"I don't know where you're seeing it — because I can't find it within myself."

Miyanda took Ramira's hands in both of hers. "Sometimes it takes someone else to see our better qualities. Mr. Navarro saw them — *I* see them."

Ramira snatched her hands away and rolled over, turning her back to Miyanda. "I don't have those qualities. I let Diego make me into a whore. I know my brother Matias would be ashamed of me — might never want to see me again."

"That can't be true. He's the only family you have left —
"

"And I'm not worthy of him. He's better off alone."

"You know that's not true. Look at Mr. Navarro, how many years it took him to realize what was important — he had maybe an hour's worth of happiness with Mrs. Luna before he was killed."

"I screwed that up, too — if I'd kept him from leaving the rig — "

"You can't blame yourself for that. If I could just convince you...."

Ramira felt Miyanda's hand on her shoulder and shrugged it off. "Leave me alone."

Ramira heard Miyanda's heavy sigh. "Once you're out of the hospital, you'll feel better."

"Once I'm out of here," Ramira said, "I know just where I'm going."

***

KAMAU WENT BACK TO HIS BANK OF SENSORS AND OTHER devices, trying different settings that he hoped would elicit a response from the Jenregar before him. *But I'm just going through the motions,* he thought. *I'm so aware of Carrie right next to me, I'm being so careful to explain everything I'm doing, that I can't concentrate on the problem before me.*

It doesn't help that she's absolutely right. What have I become? It's one thing to risk myself, another to risk the lives of others.

A voice came over Kamau's datalink, and he took a step

back from his equipment to listen. It was Masika Bilali: "Kamau, I have terrible news."

"What is it?" Kamau asked, aware of Carrie's eyes upon him.

"The Jenregar mound is growing bigger. It's taking over more of the city, and especially spreading into residential areas."

"Is this just happening in Nairobi?"

"No. Every mound is doing the same thing — the China one, the Madrid one, which I know Carrie will be concerned about, the one near Chicago. The suicide missions aren't working as effectively as they did at first. But we're still recruiting people for them. It's all we know to do."

Kamau said, "So you want to know what progress we've made here. Well, I wish I had better news. I've hardly learned a thing."

"I know you want to communicate with these beings, Governor. And yes, I use your former title to remind you of the responsibility you've taken. If it comes down to these beings — these monsters — or our own people, I know which I'm choosing. Give me something to work with."

Kamau leaned against the equipment table. "I understand. I'll keep working. You may have to relax the comp's restrictions on me."

"I'll...do just that. At least a little bit. But you've got to take care of yourself to take care of your people — of all the Earth's people."

"I know. I'll let you know as soon as I have anything to work with."

"Make it sooner rather than later," Masika said, and then the connection was cut.

Carrie was staring at him. "What is it?"

Kamau told her, "The Jenregar mounds are growing bigger. That includes the one in Madrid."

Carrie put her hand over her mouth for an instant, then said, "The suicide missions?"

"Aren't working that well anymore. And yes, I know what Governor Bilali wants — the same thing you want. But how can I rationalize committing genocide?"

Carrie went to a holo monitor and told it, "Newsfeeds. Jenregar mound in Nairobi."

Instantly, several images of the mound appeared before them — some were news broadcasts, others were simple raw feeds without commentary. Carrie stepped forward and with the touch of a finger chose one of the raw feeds. "Let's get a sense of what's happening directly — we don't need anyone to tell us what we're looking at."

The holo was focused on a wide shot of the Nairobi mound, which was growing visibly as they watched. Soldiers at the edges were firing energy bolts at the mound, but to no effect. Jenregar troops appeared from several entrances in the side of the mound and gave return fire. Many of the Human troops fell. A second, then a third wave of Jenregar troops followed, catching up easily to the Human soldiers and stinging them. More Humans fell, and Kamau could see their bodies starting to dissolve.

He continued to watch as Carrie chose another raw feed, this one showing the encroachment of the Jenregar mound into a residential area. Homes collapsed beneath the oncoming mass of the mound, people ran, many with children in their arms, or towing carts filled with the few belongings they could grab in the moments before their home's destruction.

"Enough," Kamau said, but Carrie continued to stare at

the holo of the ongoing advance of the mound. Finally he shouted, "Enough! Clear newsfeed!"

The holo faded. Carrie turned to him, and Kamau expected her to lecture him about the hard choice he had to make. But she stood silently, hands folded, as if waiting for him to speak.

Finally, he did. "I understand now. I should have before. The Jenregar do not negotiate. They do not hesitate to commit genocide. Therefore, we must not, either."

Carrie came to him, her features revealing a surprising sympathy, and gripped his arm. "You don't have to think of it that way."

"Yes, I do. I cannot do one thing and call it another. But this is as if the Jenregar held a knife to my mother's neck. I would do whatever it took to remove the threat. The Jenregar is threatening the mother of us all — the Earth. I can justify killing as many of them as it takes to save her."

Chapter 17

Mike ran up beside Jason and began firing his stunner at the approaching Jenregar, his fire added to that of the other three men who were taking as many shots as they could from around the corner of the cross-passage. "You should've kept going!" Jason yelled at Mike as he joined them.

"I made sure everyone else did," Mike said.

"Not quite," said a voice from behind him.

Goddam it, Mike thought, as Terry Needham joined them. "What the hell do you think you're doing? You're not even armed!"

"I'm your backup — just like Emily was, earlier."

Mike fired several more shots. "You're just in the way!"

Jason turned to Terry and said, "Get the hell out of here!"

Then Jason was struck by a Jenregar energy bolt and went down. Mike pulled Jason's body back into the cross-passage, snatched up his rifle, and handed his own stunner to Terry. "Think you can shoot that in the right direction?"

"*Yes*," Terry said.

"Then do it!" Mike said, and began firing Jason's rifle toward the Jenregar.

Mike felt the warmth of Terry's first shot against his right ear. "Not so close to me!" he shouted.

"Sorry!" Terry said, as he moved over a step and kept firing.

And an energy bolt took Terry right in the chest and he fell straight down in the middle of the tunnel, as if he were a marionette whose strings had been cut. Mike pulled Terry back into the cross-passage, looked at the gaping hole in the man's chest, and could only shake his head. *He just wanted to be in an adventure with me*, Mike thought.

Mike heard a commotion behind him and saw several people running past the other end of the cross-passage, in the tunnel to England he and the others had used to enter the Chunnel.

One of Jason's companions said, "They're trying to get around behind the Jenregar. There's an equipment access that they can squeeze through."

Mike said, "Then we've got to keep the Jenregar occupied while they get there." He leaned around the corner again and shot several bolts from the energy rifle.

The Jenregar were only about fifteen meters from them when Mike saw, in the distance, several people coming out from behind the Jenregar. He, along with the other two men beside him, pulled themselves back behind the corner as the other Humans opened fire.

It was over just that quickly.

The woman who led the group that had ambushed the Jenregar was tall and athletic, her pulse rifle still held at the ready. She stepped around the bodies of the Jenregar she and the others had killed, walked up to Mike, and shook his hand. "I'm Alice Hensley. I appreciate you coming back to help Jason, here, and the others."

Mike looked down at Jason's still form. "Were the two of you close?"

"He's my brother."

"Your — oh, God, I'm so sorry."

"Some of us thought it was stupid to guard against a Jenregar attack. Now we know it wasn't. I just wish I knew how they got in."

"They haven't been in here before?"

"We've heard them at the French entrance — the way you came in. But no, they've never gotten in before."

Though it was the last thing he wanted to do, Mike went over to the pile of Jenregar bodies. "Some of these have arms that don't look like typical Jenregar arms."

Alice came up next to Mike. "How do you mean? I've never even seen one of these close up."

Mike kneeled and pointed at one of the dead bodies' arms. "Look here — Jenregar arms are normally almost like tentacles. They maintain their shape by fluid pressure inside them. But this one's arm is harder — it even has muscles, like a Human arm. I bet if we cut it open, we might find bones in there."

"I can do that," Alice said, and started to bend over the Jenregar body."

"No," Mike said. "With all due respect, these bodies need to be examined by exobiologists — we have people who are trying to find out all they can about the Jenregar."

"The better to fight them. But how the hell did they develop Human qualities? And why?"

"They recognize their limitations. They're trying to adapt themselves to the Earth — just as their hives are an attempt to adapt the Earth to themselves."

"Meeting somewhere in the middle."

"Exactly." Mike snapped his fingers and said, "I wonder — if they gave themselves Human DNA — perhaps the door to the tunnel opened for them just as it did for us. Dammit!"

"You couldn't have known," Alice said. "You're not to blame."

"That's very gracious. All the same — if we hadn't come in here, your brother — and Terry — would still be alive." Mike glanced down at Jason's body. "Now can I help you?"

Alice favored Mike with a sad smile. "We're pretty self-sufficient around here. We take care of our own — including our dead."

Mike indicated Terry's body. "We have one of our own."

"What would you care to do with him?"

"I just met him. I don't know anything about his family or what they would want."

Alice said, "We can hold him here for you. We'll treat him with respect. If you can find out his family's wishes...."

"I will. And I'll work as hard as I can to make sure no one bothers you down here."

"We appreciate that. Thanks again for helping. We wouldn't have expected that of a surface person."

"Lately," Mike said, "I've been from 'way beyond the surface. I think the people who live here and the ones I work with have a lot in common."

Mike rushed to catch up to the surviving members of his group.

RAMIRA WAS AMAZED AT HOW SIMPLE THE PROCESS WAS. THE Earth Unity had established an office in downtown

Santarem, and when she made her intentions known, she was guided to a small waiting room that already held four other people and told someone would be right with her.

Ramira sat in the dimly lit room, posture straight, hands folded in her lap. She took some surreptitious glances at the others waiting there — one middle-aged woman appeared nervous, alternately wringing her hands and rubbing an earlobe. Another woman was quite elderly — she sat quietly, hands resting on a cane, and seemed quite calm.

Two men sitting next to one another appeared to be twins. They sat quietly, although occasionally one would look at the other and give a wan smile, as if seeking reassurance.

The nervous woman was the first called into an adjoining office. Ramira could hear her muffled voice alternating with that of a man apparently asking questions of her. After a time, the woman's voice grew quieter, then she apparently fell silent for a time. After a moment, the door to the office opened and the woman shuffled out. She headed down the hall without speaking and without looking back.

I suppose she was rejected, Ramira thought. *I wish I knew what she said or didn't say, so I could avoid being eliminated.*

The elderly woman was the next into the office. Her side of the conversation seemed more confident than the other woman's, and despite her age Ramira thought she sounded much more vital. In only a few moments, the door to the office opened again. The elderly woman wasn't anywhere to be seen — presumably she'd been accepted and moved through to another destination.

The twins went into the office together. As far as Ramira could tell, they were prone to finishing each other's sentences, and demonstrated a level of enthusiasm she couldn't imagine.

After a while, the door to the office opened once again, and a tall man in a black, nondescript Earth Unity uniform called her inside. Apparently the twins had also been accepted. She'd sat across from countless bureaucrats just like this man, who didn't introduce himself, just looked down at a stack of papers — (*Papers!* Ramira thought. *How archaic!*) — and then looked up at her. *He looks bored*, Ramira thought. *How the hell could you ever become bored or jaded with a job like this? How many people has he allowed to go to their deaths?*

Never mind, of course, that I'm only the latest of those people.

The man asked, "So why are you so eager to kill yourself?"

Ramira opened her mouth to answer, then closed it. Finally, beneath the man's stare, she found words: "I...hadn't thought of it that way," she told him.

"That's exactly what you're volunteering for. And keep in mind, this technique hasn't been as effective as we'd hope."

"All the same, I want to help kill as many Jenregar as I can."

"You hate them so much?"

"Yes. I do," Ramira said, "even enough to commit the sin of suicide," and recounted the story of the death of Mr. Navarro and Mrs. Luna.

"That's it?" the man asked.

"Isn't that enough?"

"You only knew these people a short time. Although certainly you would be grieving for them, you should be able to carry on with your life as you did before."

"My life was never that great." Ramira, in a softer voice that betrayed her shame, recounted her desire for a better life which Diego had promised her, and his subsequent betrayal. Then how she'd racked up so much debt in housing and medical care with little chance of paying them off for years.

"Hmm," the Unity man said, and looked back down at his papers. Ramira leaned forward, wondering if she should say more. *I'll wait*, she decided. *At least I've been in the room longer than the nervous woman who was rejected. That may be a good sign.*

If wanting to kill yourself can be seen as a good sign.

Finally the man nodded. He stood, and Ramira quickly got to her feet, as well. The man reached out to shake her hand. "I never know whether it's appropriate, but the best I've come up with to say in this circumstance is, "Congratulations. We're accepting you."

Ramira let go the breath she'd been holding. *Soon all my troubles will be over*, she thought.

Chapter 18

Mike's much-delayed trip the rest of the way through the Chunnel hardly seemed to take any time at all. None of the tunnel's dwellers was present at the barrier in the service tunnel at the ten-kilometer mark. Neriah had been true to her word, and two of the service vehicles designed for the tight tunnel's tight passages arrived moments after they did. The woman driving the lead vehicle said, "I thought there were seven of you."

"There were — one of us died in a Jenregar attack."

The woman's eyes widened. "Are we in danger?"

"Not that I know of. But we're ready to get the hell out of here."

The vehicle was too narrow to turn around, but was designed for the driver to operate from either end. She rushed to the front of her vehicle, let Mike and the others board it as Steffen, Marie, and Raymond boarded the one now in front, and they all barreled out of there.

Mike found himself sitting next to Emily Bamford, with Alexia Fontaine behind them both. Alexia placed her hand on his shoulder. "That must've been rough for you back there."

"It was." A moment of thought, and he continued: "Terry shouldn't have tagged along with me."

"I could never have done that. I was frightened to death. I was a coward."

"No," Mike said. "You were sensible. You didn't have a weapon, or the skills to use one. Your presence would've just endangered everyone else."

"You're sweet to say that."

"I've been through enough dangerous situations to realize that an 'adventure' never turns out the way you expected. Look at what happened here — Alexia, you admit you were frightened. But you survived. Terry was foolish, but I have to admit he was brave. So was Jason, the man who spoke to me back at the cross-passage. They're both dead."

Emily said, "And the people we thought were myths...."

"Turned out to be real," Mike said. "Just as the Jenregar we thought couldn't get in — *did*."

"So where are you going next?"

"Just where I was headed when all this happened. I have someone from my past to visit."

Emily gave Mike a knowing look. "Oh — perhaps a woman?"

"No, nothing like that. Someone...well, he was as close to a father as I ever had. In fact, he *is* a father — a Catholic one, I mean."

"Yet you don't believe."

Mike smiled. "I believe in Father Edmond. That's enough for me."

"Well, all the best to you, Mike. I know this isn't what you expected when you came back to Earth. But the planet's better off for having you back — and so is everyone who was on that train."

Mike said in a low voice, "Except Terry."

"Well — without you, I think the rest of us would be lying there with him now."

"Maybe so. Thanks for the thought, anyway."

Emily said, "I've got plenty more thoughts, Mike. Maybe I can share some of them with you sometime."

That took Mike by surprise. Since Linna's death two years earlier, he'd not thought of any woman as a possible romance, or even a temporary liaison.

Perhaps my thoughts have changed, he mused. "I'd like that," he said. "I have a lot of work still ahead of me, but — "

"Don't worry about that, Mike. Things happen when they happen."

Mike could only nod and say, "If there's one thing I've learned on this trip, it's the solid truth of that statement."

<hr>

RAMIRA STOOD ABOUT A KILOMETER AND A HALF FROM THE Jenregar hive that had swallowed up much of the city of Santarem. The surrounding neighborhood had been trashed by the ground fighting between the Jenregar and Humans; windows of storefronts and homes were smashed, debris was lying all over the street and sidewalks, and a thin pall of smoke filled the air.

A technician came up to Ramira. *She looks so young*, Ramira thought, as the woman pulled out a nanotech injector. *She's as baffling as the guy back in the Unity office.*

The woman told Ramira, "I'm going to inject you with the tech that contains the scenario you asked for. It'll be the same as if you were in a virt, except it won't last as long."

"But then, it doesn't need to," Ramira said. "Because I'll be...."

The woman took a hard look at Ramira. "Any second thoughts? I'm required to ask."

Ramira took a last good deep breath. "I'm ready."

The woman took Ramira's arm, appeared to hesitate a moment, then injected her. "The scenario should take effect in just a moment. You'll believe it utterly — nothing to distract you."

That's only right, Ramira thought. *No distractions, even as my body takes me on a journey that's also pre-programmed into that nanotech. Right into the Jenregar hive to be dissected and, we hope, to disrupt the society of this mound.*

The technician nodded once to her and left her alone in the street. *No real goodbyes, then*, Ramira thought. *Perhaps that's as it should be.*

Ramira started walking toward the Jenregar mound, wondering how close she'd get before the scenario kicked in — *I can't take the chance that I'd be aware of what was happening as the Jenregar tortured and killed me*, she thought. *I'd never be able to —*

Then:

I've returned home at last, Ramira thinks. *I have only a vague remembrance of the Jenregar threat back on Earth, and it quickly fades, replaced by the overwhelming joy of being back in my new home, Minerva Habitat.*

Named after the Roman goddess of wisdom, patron of the arts, a few thousand people live here, devoting themselves to music and literature, emo-sculpting and sophisticated virts, raising children and raising crops.

All is bright, all homes are roomy and made of wood and stone, and everyone I pass on the street has a smile and a wave and a "Good morning, Ramira!"

I look straight up at the opposite side of the cylinder in which I reside, and still marvel at this inside-out world, with people two kilometers above my head going about their own lives. I'm still new here, and I wonder what their lives are like; probably not much different from mine, for after all, it's as if I could reach out and touch them, and in fact they would be less than an hour's walk away. Still, the wonder of it is far beyond anything I ever experienced back in the Amazon Confederation.

Finally I reach my destination — Mr. Navarro and Mrs. Luna's house — of course, she's Mrs. Navarro now. After so many years of denying themselves, they've brought their lives together. I can't wait to escort them back to my own home, where I've arranged a surprise party for their fifth wedding anniversary.

My husband and children and my brother Matias's wife and children, and plenty of our friends are waiting.

I've never been happier than I am at this very mom —

Chapter 19

Carrie told Kamau the next morning in the lab, "I can't imagine what you've been through emotionally. I lost my father. I've seen plenty of other people die. But you've had responsibility for an entire city, and it's led you into a responsibility for...well, perhaps every Human on the planet."

Kamau was staring at the Jenregar, who remained standing stock still in its enclosure. "I thank you for that. It's been difficult. But I've faced other emotional challenges, a major one within the past couple of years."

"Oh....do you mind me asking — ?"

"My husband died."

"I see. So that must have been — "

"He was my light. I never loved anyone more. And don't expect to love anyone else nearly as much."

A helluva part of your life to believe to be over, Carrie thought. "I wish I — "

"There's nothing for you to say, Carrie. All we need to think about now if that I've made my decision about the Jenregar, and I intend to live with it."

Thank goodness for that, Carrie thought. *If he hadn't come around, I don't know what might've happened to this effort.*

Kamau went to his main equipment table and called up a holo. Long lists of statistics appeared before them, and Carrie leaned forward and tried to extract some meaning from them. She asked, "What's this telling us?"

"I've been taking in a lot of information from the mounds all around the world — as much as we've been able to glean from them, anyway. I already knew the Jenregar is beginning to reject a lot of the suicide volunteers."

"And you've figured out why?" Carrie asked.

"It seems the Jenregar has begun to develop a complex series of scents that act as 'passwords.' So our volunteers get inside, but they're discovered and killed."

"How the hell did we even find that out?"

"Some of the suicide volunteers were entering 'in the clear,' so to speak — not living inside a virt. They saw some of the other volunteers ahead of them getting the sting and not even being allowed in. Some judicious sensor readings confirmed the rest."

Carrie said, "So it's as if they've immunized themselves against Human intruders."

"An excellent analogy."

"So what do we do now?"

"We put aside our suicide missions — distasteful concept to begin with — and infiltrate their mounds in a different way."

Carrie looked on as Kamau wiped away the stats from the holo and called up a close view of a cross-section of a Jenregar brain. The organ was smaller than a Human's, and Carrie knew it was because an individual Jenregar didn't need nearly the brainpower a Human did. Most of the decisions it made came from the hive mind, and it was furthermore unburdened with the range of emotions evoked within the Human mind.

Carrie asked, "What are we seeing here?"

Kamau pointed to a convoluted mass of material. "Right here, we have the central ganglia in the Jenregar brain that interprets light."

"But sight is such an insignificant sense for them."

"Exactly. The Jenregar don't see any better than, say, a squid or even a worm. And that gives us a doorway into an area of their brain that the hive mind rarely monitors."

"What does that mean?"

With a wave of his hand, Kamau flew in a new graphic over the image of the Jenregar brain. It showed a cartoon-like image of medical nanites descending toward the Jenregar's central ganglia. "The nanites enter here," Kamau said, "and infiltrate deeper into the Jenregar's brain."

Carrie asked, "Are we trying to destroy the brain entirely, or is there a specific target?"

"Destroying the brain outright would be beyond the abilities of our little nanite friends, here. Plus, it would tip off the hive mind too quickly that something was wrong. No, our target is the link to the hive mind itself."

"Won't that also tip it off that something's happening?"

"It will — but much more slowly. We'll have to do a coordinated attack. Certainly the hive mind loses contact with the occasional individual Jenregar at times — and in some cases it's lost contact with an entire mound like the one at Zhengzhou, China."

Carrie shook her head. "I can't imagine being that desperate — they probably killed as many of their own people as they did Jenregar."

"Some nations place their own security above all other values."

Carrie said, "I hope you don't think I've gone too far. In wanting to...you know."

"Kill all the Jenregar. Commit a form of genocide."

"I don't like calling it that."

"Then you haven't committed fully to your cause. I'm willing to help you in this, Carrie. I believe killing every Jenregar on Earth is necessary. But it doesn't mean I have to enjoy doing it. And it doesn't mean I'm going to call it anything other than what it really is. I call it a 'form' of genocide because we don't know where the Jenregar homeworld is. We can't actually wipe out the entire species."

"I'm not even sure *I'd* be in favor of that."

"It's a decision we may have to make someday."

"Kamau, with all due respect, let's concentrate on one planet at a time — and focus on saving this one."

Chapter 20

CARRIE'S RIGHT, KAMAU TOLD HIMSELF AS HE ACTIVATED THE device that would introduce the medical nanites into the atmosphere of the Jenregar's enclosure. *We'll do what we have to do to save our world. If I — we — have to do terrible things, it's because of what the Jenregar has done to us.*

Kamau, with Carrie right next to him, stared at the Jenregar's impassive features. *Listen to me,* he thought. *I sound like a murderer or an abuser justifying himself — 'they made me do it!'*

But war is different, and that's what this is — and the murderer or abuser is the one who starts the violence.

My hope is to end it.

"Look!" Carrie said, pointing at the Jenregar.

Its antenna began to move ponderously back and forth. Its tentacle-like limbs *rippled*, then it raised its hands and pressed them against the sides of its head, as if trying to block out an excruciating noise.

Kamau's first thought was, *Finally, a reaction from it*, and he was immediately ashamed. *This being is in agony*, he thought.

But then the all-too-familiar images came into his mind: the Jenregar mound toppling people's homes, soldiers being cut down by energy bolts and Jenregar stings, innocent men, women, and children falling to the ground wounded or dead, and rivulets of blood flowing down shattered streets.

And Kamau hardened his heart.

The Jenregar tilted its head, raised one hand, and repeatedly stung itself on its neck. As if from somewhere far away, Kamau heard Carrie say, "It's trying to kill itself!"

The Jenregar ran full-force against the rear wall of the enclosure, as the guards backed away, their pulse rifles at the ready. The being staggered, but turned and this time rammed his body into the transparent front wall of the enclosure. The guards aimed their weapons at the Jenregar, but the wall held.

Another turn, and this time the Jenregar's target was the rear wall again, but its run appeared half-hearted. It struck the far wall, leaned against it for a moment, then slid to the ground.

Kamau worked the sensor feverishly, feeling Carrie's eyes upon him the whole time. Finally he looked at her and said, "It's dead. It went mad when we disconnected it from the hive mind."

"Just from those nanites?" Carrie asked.

"Just so."

Carrie clasped him in an enthusiastic embrace, nearly knocking him down. "And we already have a way to deliver this, now! That's marvelous!" she said, then pulled back a step and grasped his shoulders, steadying him. "Oh, sorry!"

"It's all right," Kamau said, and he was surprised to find himself smiling. And he looked toward the Jenregar's body once again, taking in the import of what he had done and what it just might mean for Humanity. "It's all right," he told himself.

Ramira awoke.

She gasped, and opened her eyes wide, heart pounding. In the instant before she took in her surroundings, she wondered why her perfect life within Minerva Habitat had been snatched from her, then her heart leaped at the thought that she'd been taken into heaven, into a world even more joyful than the fantasy within which she'd chosen to live her last mortal moments.

But then she blinked, realized she was sitting in a hospital bed — again! — and that once more, Miyanda was sitting next to her. "I don't understand," Ramira told her.

Miyanda leaned over and embraced her. "We got you back. Just at the last moment."

Ramira pulled away from Miyanda. "*Why*? I'd *made* my decision, I wanted to...to die."

Miyanda indicated someone standing in darkness at the foot of her bed. Even in silhouette, though, she thought she recognized him. Could it be — ?

Ramira reached out both her arms toward the figure. "Matias!"

Her brother went to her and wrapped her into a prodigious hug. "Oh, Ramira, I'm so glad you're alive! If you'd managed to kill yourself, I don't know what I'd have done. To live without you knowing that I hadn't done anything, and for you to have committed the sin of suicide!"

Ramira couldn't meet Matias's eyes. "I've committed plenty enough sins as it is."

"I know," Matias said. "But I also know how Diego forced you."

"I was so certain I'd made you ashamed. How can you look at me?"

Matias took her by the shoulders and stared into her eyes. "Like this. You're my little sister. I can be sad for you, I can be angry about what happened to you, but I could never condemn you."

They embraced again, and didn't speak for a long time. Tears flowed. Then, her voice trembling, Ramira told Miyanda, "I can't thank you enough."

"The only way you can thank me is by finding a job, paying off your debts, and getting the hell out of here."

"There's two of us now," Matias said. "We can live together, both work, leave here, and head for Brazil as soon as we can."

"Which may still be a few months or years," Miyanda said. "But you can do it. Just remember what Mrs. Luna said. "Carve out that happy life for yourself. Otherwise, we might as well be Jenregar."

<hr>

When Nathan returned to the Newton Habitat's main control room, the first person he spotted was a satisfied-looking Reiko Nylund, who spotted him and rushed over for a quick embrace. "I'm so glad you're safe," she said.

"It was a close thing," he told her. He looked around the control room, which featured plenty of green lights and both flat and cube displays once again. He also saw Adam Garrick examining one of those displays in a far corner of the room. So far, the man hadn't looked toward him. Nathan said, "It looks as if you've been busy here."

"That was a lucky shot the Jenregar go in on us," Reiko said. "It not only knocked out the power, it overloaded the systems self-repair capabilities for awhile. It took awhile, but I found a way around it."

Adam came up to Nathan and offered his hand. As Nathan shook it, Adam told him, "I heard what you did down there — helping rescue people. Making sure your family was safe."

Nathan said, "I just did what I thought was best."

"I have to be honest with you. I was angry with you at first for leaving the control room. I thought your place was here while we tried to bring the power back online."

Reiko spoke up: "That's why I was here."

"She does have the technical know-how," Nathan said. "And I was concerned about my family. Plus — you were here. You were in charge."

Adam shook his head. "I don't think I was."

"What the hell does that mean?"

"It means you took charge when I failed."

Nathan said, "I wasn't trying to — "

"I know you weren't. But I didn't step up. So I've decided. I'm going to step down. You're Habitat Supervisor now." Adam started toward the doorway.

"Wait," Nathan said. "You don't have to — "

Adam paused at the doorway, but didn't look back. "Yes, I do," he said, and left.

An emergency alarm sounded. "That's a collision alert," Reiko said, and went toward the holo that lit up automatically above one console.

Nathan followed, looking over her shoulder. "What is it?"

"Looks like another one of those goddam asteroids," Reiko said. On the holo, Nathan saw the object drawing closer — it appeared to be a couple kilometers wide, with a slight tumbling movement that made it look as if it were constantly changing shape.

"Is it going to hit us?"

"Thank goodness, no," Reiko said. "It won't get any closer than about a hundred clicks."

"Still way the hell too close. Where's it headed, then?"

"Checking the trajectory — looks like Madrid, where there's a well-established Jenregar mound."

Nathan said, "The previous targets have been in China. So who launched this one?"

"Can't tell. So is Spain shooting at itself just as the Chinese did?"

"No way of knowing — at least not yet. But if China or someone else is taking potshots at mounds in other countries, that's not a good development."

"Damn. We need to stay focused on the Jenregar. The last thing we need is to fight among ourselves, even with good intentions."

Nathan watched the asteroid grow ever closer to the Earth, hopeful it would destroy the Jenregar mound in Madrid, fearful of the many other, perhaps unintended, consequences it may bring.

Thomas was trudging back into his home village not long after nightfall, Beverly at his side. His legs and back were masses of aching muscles, and he felt as if he were about to fall asleep even as his body kept walking.

But something make him look into the night sky, where he saw that a star to the west was moving. *I've become more aware of the makeup of the skies,* he thought, *since our own country began tossing asteroids to kill our cities.*

But this one doesn't seem to be coming straight down — is its target somewhere other than China?

Beverly's hand grasped his shoulder. "You see it, too?"

"Yes. I don't know where it's going."

"Thomas — I can't bear to think our country's attacking another nation."

"I can only hope...well, I don't know what to hope for that has much of a chance of coming true."

Then they were at Jiang Shun's home, and he was coming out the front doorway and across the porch and into Thomas's and Beverly's arms, and for that moment all thoughts of the asteroid wafted away.

Ramira was helping guide a little girl with a badly scraped arm to a neighborhood aid station when she looked eastward into the late morning skies. All was clear to the horizon, allowing her to catch a good look at the bright object slowly descending.

"Here you go, sweetheart," she told the girl, handing her off to one of the many aid workers who had descended upon Santarem after the latest Jenregar incursion.

Then she stood and considered that strange object in those clear skies. *I've heard the rumors,* she thought. *About nukes falling to destroy Jenregar mounds. About one country tempted to destroy mounds in another country.*

Would the Confederation send troops here to protect us, aid workers to heal us, only to drop a nuclear device to destroy the Jenregar mound? And I and Matias and everyone else in

Santarem would only be, what do they call it — "collateral damage?"

Much as she despised herself for it, Ramira made excuses at the aid station and headed toward the apartment she and Matias shared. *He'll know more about this*, she told herself. *He'll know whether that thing is headed our way. And even if he doesn't, if it's about to land here, I'd rather spend my last moments on this Earth with my brother.*

"WHY DID YOU BRING ME OUT HERE IN THE MIDDLE OF THE afternoon to look into the sky?" Kamau asked Carrie as they stood outside Kamau's research facility. *This is one of those hot, dry days that make you want to turn right around and head back inside to air conditioned comfort*, Kamau thought.

"I had to make sure to show you something," Carrie said. "Look there!"

"One of those damnable asteroids?" Kamau said.

"Not exactly," Carrie said.

CARRIE POINTED TOWARD THE ONRUSHING OBJECT TUMBLING through the sky and told Kamau, "What you're seeing is our first chance to put your discoveries into action. And — it's headed toward Madrid."

"Oh, Carrie — I know how much that city means to you. Did you pick it to be the first...target?"

"No. I didn't. But it's all right." *If it has to be, that's all the more reason to hope our experiment succeeds*, she thought. *For Damian Rivera and Luisa Torres and everyone else who was mutilated or killed there.*

Chapter 21

Mike Christopher was piloting the Unity shuttle *Chaldene* about a hundred kilometers in the wake of the *faux* asteroid, which was headed straight down toward the Earth. "Passing Low Earth Orbit," he told Neriah Fulton, who was in the co-pilot's chair. "Just a few minutes until impact. One way or another, we'll have the best seat in the house for this show."

Neriah was performing sensor readings every few seconds. She frowned and said, "We can only hope we get the ending we want. And *no* encores." A quick sensor check: "Our projectile's right on target — just at the edge of that Jenregar mound in Madrid."

Within moments the shuttle was close enough that the entire country of Spain filled most of their field of view — Mike had only a quick glimpse of the sharp peaks of the Pyrenees to the north and the wide river valley of the Andalusian Plain to the southwest before he returned his attention again to the sprawling metropolis of Madrid in the middle of the country.

Mike performed a check of his own, of the space around

their shuttle for about 10,000 K in any direction. "Looks like clear sailing, too — no Jenregar close enough to attack our projectile — or *us*."

"Starforce said they'd do what they could — but their interdiction might not hold for long."

"I think it's going to hold just long enough. That's what counts."

The shuttle was only about ten kilometers above Madrid now, and Mike could clearly see the Jenregar mound that dominated the center city. He began to level off and circle the mound's perimeter.

"Ten seconds until activation," Neriah said. "Here it comes — three, two — one!"

The projectile blasted apart about half a kilometer above the Jenregar mound. But the ensuing explosive cloud, though it covered the better part of Madrid's central city, quickly dissipated, and the city's skies cleared within seconds. *It's not really an explosion, in a sense*, Mike thought. *More of a percussive delivery.*

Although he couldn't perceive them, Mike knew nanites meant to disconnect individual Jenregar from the hive mind were descending upon the mound. Many of them would simply skitter on microscopic legs through any number of entrances around its perimeter, others would use tiny wings to avoid being stepped upon, while still more would dive into lakes and streams that provided entrance into the mound.

Mike leveled off the *Chaldene* and set its autopilot to circle a couple of kilometers above the mound. He said, "I'm not even sure what the hell we're going to see from up here."

"Maybe not a lot," Neriah said, working the shuttle's sensors. "Maybe everything. I'm reading a lot of activity down there."

"What kind of activity?"

"Lots of movement among the Jenregar. All of them scurrying about, but to no purpose that I can figure out. It's all chaotic, unorganized."

Mike brought the shuttle around and hovered over one of the mound's larger entrances. "Look at that!"

Dozens of Jenregar poured out of the mound, some of them with their hands pressed against their heads as if trying to block out an agonizing sound. Others were attacking one another, pounding each other's heads and bodies as if they blamed one another for whatever was torturing them.

Neriah leaned forward to take in the sight. "I can't believe it," she said. "Thank goodness for Kamau Kimathi!"

As Mike watched Jenregar bodies begin to pile up outside the mound, he asked, "What kind of casualties are they taking?"

A quick sensor check, and Neriah said, "There's about ten thousand Jenregar inside there, and a little under three thousand — no, wait, that just became a little *over* three thousand — are dead. And the number keeps going up."

"Sounds like we need to give the word — launch all the projectiles we can."

"I agree," Neriah said as she opened the shuttle's main comm channel. "This is Neriah Fulton to all Unity forces. The word is given."

Within only moments, Nathan found himself looking at long-range sensor readings that revealed a frightening sight. "It's more of those damn asteroids," he told Reiko Nylund. "What the hell is going on?"

"Hard to tell," Reiko said. "As far as I can tell, the one that was aimed at Madrid didn't have any effect, at least not on the mound itself. I'm trying to get more refined readings, but Madrid's just about over the horizon from us."

"These new asteroids are coming toward Earth from every direction — each of them targeting a Jenregar mound. So that has to be a good sign — doesn't it?"

THOMAS, HIS BELLY FULL OF HIS FATHER'S USUAL RICE AND soup dishes, stepped out onto the front porch. Beverly was already there, arms folded, staring into the sky. He was about to place his hand on her shoulder as a preliminary to a fuller embrace and perhaps a kiss, but when he caught a glimpse of her face silhouetted against the starry sky, he lowered his hand.

He came up next to her and asked, "What's wrong?"

Beverly pointed to the west. "Look there. Another of those stars."

"It looks like it's headed about where that last one was."

Now Beverly indicated a patch of sky to the east. "But look there."

"Another one." And Thomas looked toward the north. "And another!"

"Where are they coming from?"

"The real question," Thomas said, "is where are they going?"

KAMAU, BACK IN HIS LAB, STOOD WITH CARRIE MOLINA AND watched the live feeds coming in from several angles above

Madrid. He watched with a mixture of joy and disgust as multiple images showed effects of his weapon on the Jenregar. *What have I become*? he wondered. *I witness the deaths of hundreds, thousands of beings — deaths I'm caused, and I feel I've done a good thing.*

He realized Carrie was sobbing quietly, wiping tears away as she watched the same scene. She told Kamau, "Thank you. Thank you for saving my city." She turned to him and took him into a warm embrace.

Kamau had no words.

Carrie pulled back from Kamau and said, "You can never know how much I appreciate what you've done — how much I *love* what you've done."

Kamau said, "I may be able one day to accept my actions — but I could never bring myself to love them."

"It had to be done. And if I ever found myself starting to grieve for a single Jenregar, I'd just think back to what happened to my father — just as I imagine you must be looking back at all the people you saw here in Nairobi as the Jenregar swept them down."

"All the same, I have to resign myself to the idea that the only way to save my own people was to resort to mass slaughter."

Carrie thought, *I've wondered what I'd do with myself after we defeated the Jenregar. I thought of myself as being free — free to grieve for my father, to try to find a new life for myself.*

But I fear Kamau might never be free.

RAMIRA LEANED OUT THE LIVING ROOM WINDOW OF THE apartment in Santarem she shared with her brother Matias.

"I told you!" she said, waving for him to come to the window. "There's more of those things coming!"

"We don't know *what* they could be," Matias said as he joined her at the window. "The news nets aren't saying anything."

"Oh, sure, like the ones here would know anything — or tell us if they did. Look, they're all over the sky, going in all different directions."

"You're right. Wait a minute." Matias leaned farther out the window than Ramira dared.

She grabbed her brother's arm. "Be careful," she told him.

"I see another one — almost straight up."

"Which way's it going?"

"Ramira?"

"What is it? Where's it going?"

"I believe it's getting bigger."

"You don't mean — "

"It's headed right for us."

Ramira pulled her brother away from the window and started toward the closet. "We've got to get packed and get out of here!"

Matias said, "No time for packing. We've got the clothes on our backs — let's go!"

Chapter 22

After the better part of an hour, everything had grown still around the Jenregar mound in Madrid. Mike told Neriah, "Looks like it's all over."

Neriah said, "Sensor readings show just a few Jenregar still alive. Most of them deep inside the mound."

The Jenregar mound loomed beneath them, rising from a height of just a couple of meters around its entrances to about sixty meters at its distant center. It stretched across many kilometers in the center of the city, and until the nanite weapon had been deployed, had been expanding at the rate of several meters per minute in all directions, consuming all materials before it, whether natural or man-made, to enhance its growth.

Hundreds of Jenregar bodies were lying outside the mound, most of them unmoving.

Mike said, "I want a closer look."

Neriah looked at him in disbelief. "You want to *land*?"

"Don't you? Aren't you curious?"

"Curious, yes, but not crazy!"

Mike smiled. "This is what I do, you know. I explore."

"You don't explore on Earth! And you don't explore where tens of thousands of beings want to kill you."

"You can stay in the shuttle if you want. But I'm going."

"No," Neriah said. "I'm the Unity representative here. If you're going, I should be with you."

"Here we go, then." Mike landed the *Chaldene* about two hundred meters from the mound. As he powered down the shuttle, he asked Neriah, "You've got a disruptor, right?"

She patted her hip. "Right here."

"Good, because I just have a stunner. It works against Jenregar, but some bigger firepower is always a good idea. Ever shot anyone before?"

"I'm not sure a Jenregar qualifies as 'anyone' as much as 'anything.'"

"Which doesn't answer the question."

"Well, no. I haven't."

"All I've ever shot is Jenregar. I haven't regretted it. But it's tough, the first time you take aim at a living being."

"I...think I can manage it."

"All the same," Mike said, "I'll be first out. You might not want to shoot at something unless I do."

Neriah only nodded. Mike pulled his stunner, led the way through the inner and outer airlock doors, and stepped onto the barren ground. He shielded his eyes against the sun and looked up at the Jenregar mound. It had stopped growing, and the entire area was strangely silent. *No Jenregar chittering*, he thought, *and no other sounds, either. No birds chirping or insects buzzing — nothing.*

The area had once been a lovely park, he knew, filled with carefully tended rose gardens and lovingly sculpted water fountains. Now each step kicked up small dust clouds where the Jenregar had scoured the land of anything living.

The bodies of the Jenregar themselves became more and

more plentiful the closer Mike and Neriah came to the mound. Here, one had collapsed against an outcropping of rock, having bashed in its own brains as it tried to escape whatever agonies the Human nanites had invoked within it. There, two more Jenregar had fought one another, and now they were sprawled in the dust, one missing an arm, the other with its head snapped back.

As Mike and Neriah drew even closer, the sight of the bodies of individual Jenregar gave way to groups of them lying together, which in turn became piles of bodies, an indication of just how desperate each of these Jenregar had become in their futile attempts to escape their torment.

"I'd almost feel sorry for them," Mike said, "but I've seen too much of what they can do." Neriah didn't respond, and he looked back at her. She was supposedly staring directly at one of the piles of Jenregar bodies, but Mike could tell her gaze was actually falling past them, unfocused.

They used to call it the thousand-yard stare, Mike thought. "Neriah," he said. No response. He touched her arm, gently. "Neriah."

Neriah gasped as if awakened from a deep sleep. "Yes — oh, sorry."

"Time to focus. I know it's tough."

"I shouldn't have come here."

"No, this is exactly where you needed to be. You saw a fear within yourself, and you're facing it. I've been in enough dangerous situations to know how brave that makes you."

Neriah considered that for a moment, and said, "Let's keep going, then."

The closer they got to the nearest entrance to the mound, the more densely packed the bodies were. Mike said, "It's hard to find a place to walk without stepping on Jenregar corpses."

Neriah was leaning forward, her disruptor at the ready. She asked, "So are we going in, or not?"

"Don't be quite *that* eager," Mike said. "We don't want to do something foolish. Let me take a couple of steps in, and we'll decide how far we want to go." He peered into the entrance, which was about three meters wide and two tall, and in which dozens of Jenregar bodies were lying. *Got to do it sometime*, Mike thought, and stepped onto several of those bodies as he started into the mound, his head barely clearing the low ceiling. Jenregar bodies cracked and crunched beneath his feet, and a smell began wafting upward that disgusted him. It made for rough walking as the bodies gave way beneath his stride. *Maybe this isn't such a good idea after all*, Mike thought, but kept going all the same.

The corridor glowed with a luminescence that came directly from the walls of the mound. The farther back he looked, the deeper the layers of Jenregar bodies became.

Neriah, from behind him: "What do you see?"

"Just what you'd expect. A lot of dead Jenregar. And it looks like this corridor gets wider — maybe opens up into a large room of some kind."

"I'm coming in."

"Watch how you step. Don't turn an ankle."

"Mike, Humanity may have just defeated the first attack on Earth by an alien race. I'm not worried about my ankle."

"Don't say 'alien,' not even about the Jenregar."

"We're not so sensitive about such things down here, Mike."

"I can go back to talking about your ankle."

"Just — give me a hand getting over a couple of these bodies."

Mike turned and grabbed Neriah's left hand as she stepped over a couple of Jenregar bodies that threatened to crumble beneath her. Once she was standing next to him, he told her, "Be ready to back off if we see any live Jenregar."

Mike led the way deeper into the mound. As he'd already noticed, the corridor opened up into a much larger area, a couple of hundred meters across and fifty meters high.

Jenregar bodies covered the entire floor.

Mike thought he could hear a faint chittering in the distance, as if some of the Jenregar might still be alive. As quickly as he noticed the sound, however, it faded. Only the musty smell remained.

"I'm pretty much a fool," Mike said as he raised his left hand, palm up, and checked his wrist sensor. "I just now thought of this."

As Mike checked the lifeform readings, Neriah told him, "Not a fool. Just overwhelmed at the sight."

Mike said, "They're pretty much all dead. Just a few still holding on, and they're fading. Goddam. It really worked."

Neriah said, "We can only hope it's working all around the world."

"For now," Mike said, "let's get the hell out of here." He turned back toward the entrance, Neriah following. "This place is creeping me out."

Nathan Carlsson stood with his wife Tana in an observation area next to Newton Habitat's main control room. They looked down upon the damage the stray energy bolt had inflicted upon their home. It had entered on the "tech" side, destroying two research buildings and exiting through one of the vineyards on the "ag" side, and, more importantly, punching two holes in the habitat's skin, which led to a potentially massive — and fatal — loss of air.

As Nathan put his arm around Tana's shoulders, hers went around his waist. He leaned toward her for a brief kiss. "I was so afraid for you," he told her.

"You were afraid for *me*?" Tana said. "I was nice and cosy in the hospital."

"If you consider having patients backed up into the lobby and out into the street 'nice and cosy,' I guess you were."

Tana said, "*You* were the one digging through rubble and getting dirty and cut up and having to drag poor Frank halfway across the habitat."

"At least he lived. We lost about a hundred people. I've still got shuttles out recovering bodies that got pulled into space."

"You helped save the habitat."

"*Reiko* saved the habitat. I was worried more about you and Randi."

"Well, I certainly understand that — as concerned as I was about my patients, I was more worried about you."

Nathan said, "We'll be better prepared next time." With Adam Garrick having resigned as Habitat Supervisor, the Habitat Council had unanimously appointed Nathan to the post on an interim basis. Everyone told him he was a lock to win the special election set for a couple months later, after repairs were expected to be complete.

Tana said, "I wonder what 'next time' will bring."

"No way of knowing," Nathan said as he pulled Tana closer.

"It's just -- our habitat seems so fragile, compared to the Earth."

"Don't look toward Earth as being so secure. Down there, it's not a hundred dead, it's millions."

"Maybe we should help them. I know Randi said something about it."

"She wants to go down to *Earth*?"

"She's just fifteen. She has romantic notions."

"I remember those days," Nathan said. "This habitat will be cleaned up and completely repaired in a few weeks. If Randi wants to help, they've got years of recovery ahead of them down there. We've got time. It may be the only thing we have that they lack."

***

"I FEEL AS IF WE HAVE ALL THE TIME IN THE WORLD," RAMIRA Espinosa said as she stood on the balcony of the apartment she shared with Matias that overlooked Sao Paulo, Brazil. A flash of lightning at the horizon thrust away the night for an instant and illuminated the tall buildings of the former business district, where once fortunes (and sometimes fates) rose and fell. Thunder, only a low rumble, followed sluggishly.

Ramira took in a deep, cool breath. "I can smell the rain," she told Matias. "I love it."

"And I am perfectly happy enjoying my drink," Matias said. He was sitting on a plush couch in their living room, drinking a cachaça, said to be the national drink of their adopted country. Ramira found it too sugary for her taste, but enjoyed its lime flavor. *So wonderful*, she thought, *to have something like that to consider after the past week or so.*

They'd made a desperate 2,000 K retreat southward from Santarem. They now knew what they'd seen was not an asteroid, but a nanotech weapon that killed all the Jenregar in Santarem even as Ramira and Matias were running out of the city.

They decided to keep going. In the confusion following the downfall of the Jenregar, they'd hitched rides with people also headed away from town, made it across the border into northern Brazil, then gotten onto a series of buses and finally an actual maglev train headed from the city of Itaituba to Sao Paulo.

Here, a replicator economy meant they could have decent housing and food simply for being accepted as residents. They could perform whatever work they wished that they were qualified for — if they wanted to work at all.

Ramira turned from the window. "We have to go back sometime, you know."

Matias placed his drink on a table. "To Santarem, you mean? The place where...such things happened to you?"

"Such things" was as close as Matias ever came to referring to Ramira's former life in forced prostitution. "Yes. That was Diego's doing. Not the city's. Remember Santarem was also where I met Mr. Navarro and Mrs. Luna."

"You want to do this for them."

"Yes."

"We'll have to speak to the authorities here — see if Brazil is sending any aid to the Amazon Confederation."

"That would be good," Ramira said.

"We could still see difficult times there. And Mr. Navarro and Mrs. Luna only wanted you to find your own happiness."

Ramira thought back to the night she and Diego and his brother Julian were running from the Jenregar — how both men had died, and specifically, of how she had smiled as she blocked the attic door to ensure the Jenregar would catch up to Diego and slaughter him.

It's taken me this long to realize, Ramira thought, *that I might never forgive myself for that smile. Not for making sure Diego died — my heart and my soul tell me that was justified. But I should never have taken pleasure in it. I'll never tell Matias, but helping the people of Santarem will be my penance for that moment. There will be time enough for us to enjoy our new life here in Sao Paolo.*

Ramira told Matias, "I think the way for me to find my own happiness is to provide what little I can to others."

She turned back toward the window, and watched as the cleansing rains began to fall.

***

"WE BELIEVE IT'S THE BEST THING WE CAN DO FOR ourselves," Thomas Jiang told his father. They stood with Beverly outside Jiang Shun's home, suitcases packed, waiting for the bus that would take Thomas and Beverly to Zhengzhou.

Thomas embraced Jiang Shun, a rare event that brought tears welling up in his eyes. As he released his father, he fought to keep his eyes open — a single blink would've brought those tears flowing down his cheeks, and that would've been unacceptable.

Beverly embraced Jiang Shun, as well, which provided Thomas the distraction he needed to pinch those tears away unseen. A stray one became a salt taste on his lips.

"I wish you weren't leaving," Jiang Shun said.

Thomas said, "You know it's what we have to do, Baba."

"You want a modern life for yourself."

Beverly spoke up: "It's *our* life. Just as yours is here."

"I suppose," Jiang Shun said, "they do need you in Zhengzhou, now that the Jenregar threat is gone. Just as their arrival was the reason you first came here, Thomas."

Thomas tried not to show his exasperation. "Not the only reason, Baba. I was glad I...got to know you better."

"You *do* call me Baba, now."

"Just as you call me Thomas. Yes, this is for the best. Though we may live in different worlds, we still share our lives when we can. Now that I know you have a datalink, I can talk to you whenever I want."

Jiang Shun waved that concern away, then indicated Beverly. "You need to spend all your time with your new bride."

Beverly said, "That's one thing we're certain of. We'll return here for the ceremony."

"By then, perhaps much of my farm will be restored."

Thomas said, "Soon you'll have your former life back."

"No," Jiang Shun said. "That, I will never have. My former life felt secure. It never admitted the possibility that strange beings could attack my country — or that our own soldiers could take over our village!"

Thomas saw movement out of the corner of his eye. The bus had just topped a hill and was approaching the village. Thomas told Jiang Shun, "You can visit us anytime."

"I haven't been to Zhengzhou in years. I don't know if I wish to go there, especially after the Jenregar destroyed so much of it."

"They could use your skills, too, Baba. They have large community gardens. And buildings that need to be rebuilt."

Jiang Shun said, "I suppose things will keep changing, whether we like it or not."

The bus pulled up in front of Jiang Shun's home. A final handshake as the driver loaded their suitcases aboard, and Thomas and Beverly boarded.

As the bus pulled away, and Jiang Shun waved goodbye, Beverly said, "He'll be fine."

"I just wonder if he'll ever be happy. So many things have changed, and he doesn't like change."

"It's not the change itself, Thomas. It's the type of change. Sometimes it's for the better."

"Perhaps. But Humanity was supposed to go outward and explore new and strange worlds. Those worlds were not supposed to come here — they especially weren't supposed to try to take the Earth for themselves."

Beverly leaned toward him, and Thomas put his arm around his shoulders. He made himself think only of her as kept his gaze upon the road ahead.

As Kamau Kimathi stood on the rear deck of his cabin just outside Amboseli National Park and looked out at the looming presence of Mount Kilimanjaro, he couldn't help but smile as a single elephant lumbered past the edge of his property. Tourists could view similar images in dozens of guides to the area — it embodied the stereotypical view of the region in many people's minds.

But there's so much more here, Kamau thought. He squinted to see if he could make out any movement of the clouds that ringed the middle of the mountain this morning, but he could not. Apparently the skies were still at nearly 6,000 meters up, as it was down here at the cabin.

He took a deep breath of fresh, natural air and all the

competing scents it embodied, from flowery fragrances to the tang of animal dung. He loved them all. *I had to get away from these unnatural environments*, he thought. *As much as I love Nairobi, and the work I've done there, it was time to leave awhile — get away from glass and metal. Away from prying reporters. Even away from colleagues and friends who only wanted to honor me.*

And, truth be told, away from the Jenregar and what I had to do to them.

In the excitement and confusion immediately following the defeat of the Jenregar, Kamau had said a quick goodbye in person to Carrie Molina, and by cube to his colleagues in Nairobi, and rushed to this cherished retreat.

Looking out across the landscape before him, Kamau saw that the elephant was long gone, but now a small flight of Madagascar pond-herons flew past, easily identified due to their white plumage and blue beaks. Over a century ago there were considered endangered — now they thrived here.

I wish I could be one of them, Kamau thought. *Taking flight away from all my problems, soaring above the land, the lakes, the trees.*

I could, in a way. Masika suggested it — a vacation on the Moon, perhaps, or on one of the orbital habitats.

But I couldn't. It was unthinkable — inevitably I'd find myself looking down upon the Earth and knowing how much work remained to be done here. As it is, I'm allowing myself only a few days of rest and reflection before I return to Nairobi.

Kamau's back felt as if it might betray him, and he went to a corner of the deck where a wooden lounge chair stood next to a small table. He eased his old bones into the chair, then reached for a glass of cool tea that was on the table. A couple of sips, and Kamau closed his eyes for a moment. He enjoyed the feel of a warm breeze that was just starting up. He could hear the cawing of a bird nearby, but didn't recognize its species. *I've been too long away from here*, he thought.

Maybe I shouldn't return to Nairobi after all. Maybe I've done enough. Certainly there were enough people who told me I'd earned a good long respite.

Without warning, emotion overwhelmed Kamau and he put a hand over his face and shut his eyes tightly so the tears wouldn't flow.

In the next moment, he decided that was ridiculous, and let the tears fall. His chest heaved with sobs, his anger at the Jenregar for the actions he'd brought upon himself mingled with his ongoing grief for Nyaga.

Though no one was around to hear, he said aloud, "What else could I have done?" The Jenregar, after all, contained no mercy within them — no sympathy. No one could reason with their hive mind.

Would I rather be sitting here grieving for Humanity? he wondered. *Not that I'd be here at all. I'd most likely be somewhere within the ruins of Nairobi.*

Kamau wiped his eyes, took a deep breath. *Carrie was right all along*, he thought. *She hated the Jenregar from the beginning, wanted to kill them all. What I embraced reluctantly, she was adamant to do from the start.*

He ignored the pain in his back and made himself get up. He went to the edge of the deck again. Several giraffes were sauntering along in the opposite direction from the earlier elephant. Beyond them, the clouds ringing Kilimanjaro moved sluggishly now, as if reluctant to leave.

Another great tourist photo, Kamau thought. *I'm lucky, if not blessed, to be able to live among such wonder, which is far beyond anything travel to the stars might hold for me.*

Especially since I know the dangers that can come from out there.

He said his next thought aloud, as if to imprint it within his consciousness: "I won't be returning to Nairobi. At least, not for now."

At that, he chuckled: *Look at me, a 92-year-old man standing on a deck talking to himself.*

But my colleagues were right — I deserve a respite — from the Jenregar, and, to be truthful, from Humanity itself.

The decision made, Kamau shuffled back to his chair. Sat. Had another sip of tea. And the tension began to flow away, both from his body and his mind, and he couldn't imagine wanting to be anywhere else but right here on his beloved Earth, enjoying the touristy view and finding the courage within himself to think only of the good times he'd had with Nyaga — always his light.

I'M SO GRATEFUL TO BE GETTING AWAY FROM THE EARTH, CARRIE Molina thought as she made her way through the terminal at the Brussels starport. Already, she could feel the tension easing in her neck and shoulder muscles, and what had been the beginning of a magnificent ache behind each temple was beginning to fade.

She was awaiting the arrival of the shuttle that would take her up to the Earth Unity light cruiser *Admiral Susan Kojima*. Just as the Jenregar attacks had begun, the starcraft had been diverted from its usual patrol duties to return the famed explorer Mike Christopher to Earth — he'd fought the Jenregar before, and his experience, Carrie knew, had proven invaluable to their defeat. *I'd love to meet him sometime*, she thought. *We'd have lots of stories to swap.*

Carrie's return to Brussels had been much easier and faster than her journey to Nairobi to assist Kamau. Neriah Fulton had helped her arrange the lift aboard the shuttle, a testament to the role she'd played in the demise of the Jenregar.

I had to come home to help, she thought, *and I was proud to work with Kamau, but I couldn't stay. With any glimpse of what's left of the beauty of Madrid, of any of the parks and gardens that remain, I would only be able to think of my papa.*

I can't help but think about all the times he saw me off from some starport or another, each time trying to hide just how worried he was that his little girl was headed out into the unknown.

"Isn't the Earth enough for you?" he'd plead, and I'd have to tell him it wasn't, that I was looking for adventure and a way to do good for people — and that being a Unity "fixer" was the best way I knew to go about it.

He worried so much that I'd be killed out there somewhere. Turned out he's the one who died, and right here on Earth.

As she walked through the terminal, she heard parts of all the little dramas that were common in any port, but which made it clear to her that many other people had it even worse than she did. Most air lanes and maglev routes were back open, but hopelessly overcrowded, adding to people's desperation.

"But I have to find my son!" one woman told a Unity representative. "I have to get on a plane, a shuttle, *anything* to get to Australia."

The Unity representative was a tall, thin man whose face seemed carved from marble — the result, perhaps of having to hear so many such stories, of having to hand out one disappointment after another. "I'm sorry, Ma'am," he said, "but there's just nothing headed that way for another day or so."

Carrie heard, "But I've *got* to," as the woman's voice faded behind her. For an instant, the temptation came: *Could I ask the Kojima shuttle's pilot to make a side trip to Australia? The delay wouldn't be over an hour.*

But then, to her right, Carrie heard a man's desperate voice, as he buttonholed any stranger who passed him: "How can I get to America? They say there's no flights, no trains, but I can't believe that. I have to get to Chicago. My...my brother and sister-in-law died there."

Carrie pushed onward, hoping she wouldn't draw the man's attention. *No*, she thought. *I can't help them all.*

They're living in a new world. I saw some of this in Kamau's reactions. Trying to cope with the idea of an attack from space, of cities covered with Jenregar mounds, of Human governments destroying their own cities in order to "save" them — they don't know where to turn.

Another Unity rep guided Carrie through hidden passageways in the terminal, and she came out onto the tarmac just as the shuttle from the *Kojima* was landing.

Carrie gave only perfunctory greetings to the shuttle's pilot and co-pilot as she boarded, and went right to a seat behind them. She was its only passenger, and Carrie gave silent thanks to Neriah, only now realizing just how big a favor she'd done for her.

The craft lifted within moments, and Carrie watched the landscape dominated by the remnants of the Jenregar mound covering much of Madrid recede, watched as the shuttle broke cloud cover into clear blue skies that quickly faded into the blackness of space. Her own concerns began what she knew would be a slow process of receding, yet never quite to fade away.

One night as I fall asleep, Carrie thought, *I'll realize I haven't thought of Papa all day, and on that day I'll be both relieved and sad. Relieved that I've started to "move on," as people say, and sad for the very same reason.*

I'll come back to Earth again someday, but I don't think it'll be soon, and I have no idea what would convince me to return.

Chapter 23

Mike stood outside Madrid's Jenregar mound, which still dominated the view, but at least wasn't growing anymore. The musty smell of dead Jenregar bodies permeated the air. Beside him, Neriah was consulting her wrist comm, looking for evidence of the extent of the Jenregar defeat.

Mike heard the sounds of gravitic drives directly overhead, and looked up to see an Earth Unity gunship and a couple of shuttles flying over the city. "The skies must be ours again," he said, as he watched the craft circle the city.

Neriah looked up from her comm. "They are. All the Jenregar ships are leaving — breaking orbit. A couple have already tried to go into stardrive a little too close to the planet, and they've broken up. We're picking off some of the others."

"So the Jenregar knows the planet's still ours — and will stay that way."

Neriah held her wrist out to Mike. Its comm displayed a holo of another Jenregar mound. "This is Santiago." The scene there was much the same as it was in Madrid —

Jenregar bodies scattered all around, Unity craft flying overhead. Neriah touched her wrist and the scene changed. "It's the same at all the other mounds. This is Nairobi — Zhengzhou — Arlington Heights." Neriah looked at Mike. Tears flowed down her face and she didn't bother wiping them away. "We actually did it!"

"It's so hard to believe," Mike said. "I never even dreamed I'd be back on Earth one day. To come here and...." His voice broke. He found no more words.

Neriah embraced him so tightly he could barely take in his next breath. After a moment she stepped back from him and said, "I don't think you have to worry about people's reactions to you anymore."

"Oh, I think there'll still be some people who'll find good reasons to hate me."

"So what are you going to do now?"

"People are always asking me that. Like I have some kind of plan to my life. I'm just making it up as I go along. The two biggest decisions I ever made were to leave Earth to become a spacer — and then to come back to face the truth about how I was conceived. Twenty-five years separated those two decisions."

Neriah said, "It seems like decision number three is coming a bit faster."

Mike took Neriah's hand. "I don't have to make the big decision just yet. Maybe we can celebrate. There's plenty of places here in Madrid the Jenregar didn't touch. A little dinner, a little champagne, maybe...?"

Neriah eased her hand away from Mike's. "I'm flattered, really I am. But I'm married. Jim's waiting back in Brussels. And I promised him that if this was successful, I'd get back to him as soon as I could. I've only seen him a couple of times in the last few weeks."

Mike worried that he was only managing a wan smile as he told Neriah, "I can only wish the two of you every happiness."

Neriah indicated the Unity shuttle *Chaldene*. "I can drop you off anywhere on the planet you want to go, Mike, or take you up anywhere in Earth orbit. Just say the word, whatever trip you want to make."

Mike considered the offer. *I'm feeling the urge to become an explorer again*, he thought. He looked into the blue, cloudless skies beyond the Jenregar dome. *Everything I've ever wanted to learn about is out there. From Splendor to Moruteb to the Station of the Lost — from trying to decipher the intentions of alien intelligences to watching two star systems collide — what does the Earth have to offer that can rival that?*

Maybe it's time to find out.

"Mike?" Neriah asked.

"You're right. I think it's time for another trip."

"Then let's get into the shuttle and — "

"No. Not the shuttle." At Neriah's questioning look, Mike continued: "Where I'm going, I'm going to walk. At least to start out."

Mike strode away from Neriah, away from the Jenregar mound, and past the shuttle *Chaldene*, on his way to explore the alien world called Earth.

A REQUEST FROM THE AUTHOR

If you enjoyed ALL HUMAN THINGS, please consider giving it an honest review on Amazon. It's the best thing you can do to help out an author whose work you like!

ABOUT THE AUTHOR

Dave Creek is the author of the novels CHANDA'S AWAKENING and SOME DISTANT SHORE, novellas TRANQUILITY and THE SILENT SENTINELS, and short story collections A GLIMPSE OF SPLENDOR and THE HUMAN EQUATIONS.

He's also published the Great Human War trilogy, including A CROWD OF STARS (2016 Imadjinn Award winner), THE FALLEN SUN, and THE UNMOVING STARS (2018 Imadjinn Award winner).

Dave also edited TRAJECTORIES, an anthology of stories about space exploration and its many challenges, and is the author of MARS ABIDES: RAY BRADBURY'S JOURNEYS TO THE RED PLANET, a non-fiction look at Bradbury's Martian stories.

His short stories have appeared in ANALOG SCIENCE FICTION AND FACT, AMAZING STORIES, and APEX magazines, and the anthologies FAR ORBIT APOGEE, TOUCHING THE FACE OF THE COSMOS, and DYSTOPIAN EXPRESS. He's also been published in the Russian SF magazine ESLI and China's SCIENCE FICTION WORLD.

In the "real world," Dave is a retired television news producer.

Dave lives in Louisville with his wife Dana, son Andy, Corgi/Jack Russell Terrier mix Ziggy Stardawg, and polydactyl cat Hemmie.

Stay in touch with Dave:
	E-mail
	dave@davecreek.com

Website:
	http://www.davecreek.com

Facebook: https://www.facebook.com/davecreek

Twitter:
	@DaveCreek